The King's Beekeeper

The King's Beekeeper

A Beeswood Chronicle

By Elena Timms

Title: The King's Beekeeper

Author: Timms, Elena

ISBNs: 978-1-7637499-0-0 (print)

Subjects: YOUNG ADULT FICTION / Fantasy / Folklore

Edited by Mitchell Timms.

Interior book design by Eilidh Direen.

Cover illustration by Elena Timms. Cover design created in Canva by Elena Timms.

Dedicated to Thea Jane Timms,
whose love of bees inspired me to write Myrtle Beeswood's story

Contents

Prologue

Long shadows were cast by the flickering candle, the wax dripped, forming milky pearls as the girl held it tightly, waiting. Before her was the fragile shape of her mother. Moonlight kissed her glistening skin through an open window. A breeze puffed at the curtains, gently pushing and pulling. The figure suddenly crumpled on the bed and succumbed to a fit of coughing. The girl watched, paralyzed, helpless.

"Here." The woman beckoned the child, gaunt face lifting, her hollow eyes meeting her wide-eyed daughter's.

The girl - for first the time - remembered the bowl clenched in her white knuckled fingers and stepped forward toward her mother.

"Have you the lemon juice?" She rasped, "The Chamomile?"

"Yes." The girl answered.

"Mix them together." The woman motioned.

The child stood beside the bed, bowl in hand, the acidity of the lemon and sweetness of the honey mingled in the air. The spoon trembled in her hand and the contents of the bowl sloshed, threatening to spill. Her mother heaved again, the crackle in her chest was like that of a roaring fire, then she was still. Too still. The girl stopped, eyes wildly darting to see the rise and fall of her mother's chest.

"M-Mother?" The child croaked.

"I'm alright." The answer came as a whisper, the thin reminder of life between her cracked lips.

"It is time for the words."

"Yes, Mother."

"Do you remember them?"

Myrtle nodded, while her mother had laid in bed, a week without improvement, her assignment had been to learn the words of healing. The candlelight caught a shimmering object, moving through the air outside the window. It hummed at her, its tiny wings beating. Its stripes became visible as it moved closer. A bee. They always appeared for her mother when it was the time for healing, and it was a comfort that they had appeared for her also. The girl turned back to the bowl, the fire light caught the syrup and turned it into molten gold. It was time for the words, she could delay no longer.

"O Wild King." She murmured her voice growing in confidence as she continued, "We come before you, though unworthy. We ask for you to make blameless the Beekeeper before you, and to bring any transgressions forth into the light. Speak now Beekeeper, of any transgressions."

"There have been none. None that I have known of, except the ones of my human flesh." The girl's mother answered.

"Then we ask, O Wild King, to judge your Beekeeper as righteous." Myrtle nervously wavered for a moment, waiting for a sign that she shouldn't continue. Nothing came, so she went on.

"Then we ask, O Wild King, if you are willing, please heal your servant. Restore this Beekeeper to health with your life. We ask for your strength, let it be given through the honey of bees."

"Good," Her mother's voice came again, "Now let me take the medicine."

She offered the bowl and spoon to her mother.

"If you are willing, Wild King." The woman dipped her head, for she was too weak to bow. Then she took a spoonful of syrup to her lips and drank. The child waited, heart fluttering. As moments passed, the candlelight was reduced to a dull red, leaving the room in darkness before, suddenly, sparking back to life. Words bubbled inside, but Myrtle held them down letting the silence reign.

Finally, her mother heaved a sigh.

"Not yet." She whispered, "He is not yet willing."

Something stirred within the young child. It was a yearning to heal the unhealable.

"You did well," The woman coughed, "Now, hop along into bed."

It was a hope uncrushed by the fear which now stopped her feet from moving away from the bedside. *If only,* it said.

"Your father will help me now." The voice of her mother came again, "No need to worry."

A large hand was on her shoulder, she turned to see her father, his kind, dark gaze was on her mother.

If only I could heal her.

A Beekeeper's Duties

A flustered girl appeared over the rise of a wind-swept hill. She clutched a pot of honey firmly to her chest as she ran, stumbling. Pausing only for a moment to catch her breath before she continued down the stone path which was now visible as a thin snail's trail of haphazard stone down the hillside. The wind huffed at her, as if frustrated. Her two braids caught in the air, the sky-blue ribbons unfurling in the gust. The girl didn't stop to fix her hair, but continued down the path until she reached a house.

"Myrtle Beeswood." She stuck out a hand that had been holding the precious pot of honey.

The woman at the door looked down at Myrtle with a creased brow. Crying from inside the house broke the silence. The woman closed the door slightly as if to muffle the interruption but did not accept the offered handshake. Myrtle frowned and glanced down at her fingers, now noticing that they were sticky with honey. She felt her cheeks burn.

"I'm the Beekeeper. I heard there was a sick child?"

"Oh! This way." The woman had barely finished before Myrtle had slipped through the door and was on the other side, looking around trying to find the source of the plaintive cry.

It echoed down the narrow hallway, and so she followed it until she came to the nursery. The child, barely past its first year, was swaddled in a cot. As she neared the cot, the baby cried out again.

"Please could I have some hot water and a towel?" She asked as the woman appeared in the doorway.

Myrtle set the pot down on the wooden floor and brought the less-sticky back of her hand to the child's brow. It was hot with fever. The woman entered the nursery again with a clean towel and a pitcher filled with warm water. First, Myrtle washed her sticky hands and dried them on the towel. Then she unwrapped the child and checked for any obvious cuts or wounds, but she could find nothing that would warrant the infection.

"Has she been playing near the pigs lately?" Myrtle asked as she checked the child's breathing.

"Well, now…" The woman drew in a breath, "I…. I am not sure, her sister watched her a few days back when I had to work the fields."

"The pigs in the village have contracted a disease. One of the farmers recently imported pigs from Winspern, I believe that to be the source. I saw one of the farmer's children had the same symptoms just three days ago."

The child's breathing was laboured, and a rattling filled her chest. The woman scratched her brow.

"John." She began, "He bought a new sow from the village market… last Sunday."

"And how long has the child been sick?" Myrtle was starting to grow anxious, the last child she had treated barely survived.

"Two days now." The woman whispered.

"Get me another jug with a little hot water."

The woman left and Myrtle got to work. She knew she did not have much time. Undoing her belt, she unrolled the leather bag attached. The lining of the leather bag was lambskin. The soft fur held glass bottles of dried herbs gently, ideal for occasions like today, when she needed to run and... because she was prone to tripping.

There were many herbs: chamomile, mint, feverfew, ginger, clove to name a few. She popped the corks off a dozen bottles, letting the scents seep out. Lavender's tender, but strong fragrance stuck out among the others and Myrtle took hold of it, recalling what she had used to treat the other child. She grasped the stem and removed the flowers but left the leaves. She placed the lavender in a small wooden bowl also carried on her belt. Adding chamomile and ginger, she crushed them with a smooth stone and added a sprinkling of feverfew for good measure. As she worked, a sleepy bee drifted out from her ribbonless hair. Hovering without purpose, it seemed to watch Myrtle work.

The woman appeared again and handed her the hot water and spoon. With the spoon she scooped up the main ingredient of all her remedies, honey. Not just any honey, but honey from the Beeswood hive. A swarm of bees that had been with her family for generations. She dripped the golden honey into the bowl with the hot water. The sweet smell stained the air around them and enticed the sleepy bee. It landed on her hand.

After the honey had dissolved into the water and was cooled, she crushed half a seed pod of clove into the mixture. The concoction though a mismatch of flavours always smelled sweet, overpowered by the honey. She supposed it tasted sweet too but couldn't be sure. Only once had she tasted the medicine, it had been when she was very young and she could only remember it being hot, like fire, but it did not burn.

She handed the bowl to the mother. The mother in turn, took the child, propped her exhausted head up with a shoulder and carefully spooned the contents of the bowl into her tiny mouth. At first the child yelped, but then, as she realised that the medicine tasted good, she grasped the bowl with tiny fingers. Once finished, the child fell asleep almost instantly, and when Myrtle checked her breath, she could no longer hear congestion.

"She will still take a few days to recover." Myrtle explained, "And if I were you, I would keep everyone away from the pigs."

The mother gave a sigh of relief, "Yes, of course. Thank you. Can we do anything to repay you? We have a few gold pieces?"

"Spreading the word is enough payment." Myrtle smiled, but then added "and…. perhaps a little bread, if you can spare it."

"Come along this way, we have some fresh out of the oven."

The woman led the way to the kitchen and wrapped a loaf of bread in cloth, along with a wedge of cheese and some strips of jerky. As Myrtle was leaving the woman stood to wave her off, and she saw another figure in the shadows of the doorway. It must have been the woman's eldest daughter. The mother turned to speak to her daughter, and Myrtle caught the words on the breeze.

"That girl… her work is beyond that of even the most seasoned healers."

* * *
*

"Walk on Podge." Myrtle climbed on top of her little rickety wagon. The Beeswood hives buzzed harmoniously behind her, their hive sat in the shelter of a small awning which was draped with a translucent cloth. The cloth had once been her and her sister's summer nighties, lace still peeked from its edges hinting at its past life. Hodgepodge, her pony, stood scratching his knee with his mouth. He often had a mind of his own.

"Come on Podgy! Giddy up!" Myrtle flicked the reins.

Hodgepodge lifted his face, took in a sharp breath and snorted loudly. The wind on the hilltop made it splatter back into Myrtle's face.

"Hey! Mind yourself!" Myrtle wiped the snot off with a sleeve, "Come on, Get a move on!"

Hodgepodge sighed, and then finally moved, picking up a brisk trot. Myrtle knew that she should chastise him but was just happy to be moving and so let the pony have his way. Hodgepodge Eveningswood - or Podge as Myrtle often called him, was a gypsy cob. At first glance, he looked exactly like the giant work horses; Clydesdales and Shires, only he was miniature. While he could easily pull a wagon, there was no way Podge could pull a large log to the mill, or even plough the field. He was of a noble line of gypsy cobs called the Eveningswoods. Her parents had owned Podge's mother, who was also an Eveningswood and Podge's father, Dally Eveningswood had come from the farmer down the road. Both dam and sire were stout little cobs often used in work around the farms. Dally Eveningswood was such a gentle stallion that even the kids were allowed to take a ride on him, while Podge's dam was often used in cart by Myrtle's parents before she was born. Myrtle was told she was the more mischievous of the two and had apparently passed on this trait to Hodgepodge. She had never met her parents's mare, but her parent's memory gave a vivid image of the strawberry roan with shaggy mane and fluffy feet. Dally was still just down the road, occasionally offering rides, he was black and white and rippling with powerful muscles. So fearless was Dally, that in his youth he had led hunts in the forest for the elusive drop bear. They came back with 5 of the large cats one year, and they were all as big as lions! There was a legend of the Eveningswood ponies, that spoke of a knight gifting the first one to a girl in the village. Given Dally's bravery Myrtle considered the tale as proven fact.

True to his name Hodgepodge was a patchwork of colours. His coat had stark white splotches all over, they covered his left eye and ear, and ran like a splash over his stomach. His two back legs were shaggy white to the knees and then suddenly midnight black, but only for a few inches before fading to bay. The splashes of colour over his stomach blended to light speckled red. The colour on his head was also bay that became fainter, bleeding into the strange speckled red colour. He looked almost pink in some seasons. His mane and tail were crisp white, interspersed with deep black, although…. More often than not his fluffy tail was brown rather than white. Myrtle thought the colour looked like someone had dumped a bucket of rust over a white horse.

They trotted down the windy mountain path, passing farmers returning home. Some waved, some didn't. Most looked tired but seemed content after a day's work. As they reached the bottom foothills of the mountain they passed the village school, a small, repurposed barn, which for now was abandoned as Wendermere could only afford a tutor for a small portion of the year in the cooler months. The sun had set by the time they made it back to the forest clearing where Myrtle had pitched her tent. The forest was in the valley below the mountains and grew cold quickly when the sun's warmth had left. She took Podge's harness off and allowed him to graze on the knee-high patches of grass that were dotted around the campsite. It was late spring, and Wendermere got much of its rain in spring, so she was told. The lush grass was a tell-tale sign of the heavy rain. Then she set out to make a fire, and soon had a pile of glowing logs within the rock ring she'd built a few days before. A yawn rolled out of her mouth as she lay down on the mat in her tent, leaning her head on her elbows. It hadn't been a busy day, but rather a long one. Over the other side of the fire Podge chewed grass lazily. Myrtle observed him - pausing often, mid mouthful, not because he was startled or heard some noise, but because he could barely be bothered to chew. Legend may have spoken of the Eveningswood ponies being a worthy gift from some knight …. but Myrtle was sure that whatever 'gallant' steed Podge's ancestors may have once been, Hodgepodge was a much more watered-down product.

She reached into the tent taking out the bread and cheese she'd been given and cut a slice of each. It was a pleasant meal, much better than she'd had on the road. She was just about to fall asleep, with the crackle of the fire dying and the buzz of bees fading as they retreated into the hive, when a distant crack awoke her. She would've ignored it if she hadn't caught a glimpse of Hodgepodge on the other side of the glowing embers. His neck stretched around, and ears pricked to the sound. He turned on his haunches to face the noise.

Myrtle leapt up and grabbed at a stick, its tip was hot from the fire. Her heart was pounding and she tensed herself ready to strike if some beast came through the trees. But, the panic slowly faded as she remembered that large predators had not been seen in Wendermere for centuries. Hodgepodge went back to his grass, agitatedly ripping at the stalks, as if frustrated that something would interrupt him, and Myrtle went back to her mat, falling asleep until morning.

*   *   *
*

The sun beams filtered through the tall trees and fell dancing on Myrtle's tent. Myrtle stretched out her hands and brushed the grass outside; her fingertips came back wet. She poked her head out and saw the grass sparkling with dew. Her bees were already awake and buzzed lazily beneath their awning. Hodgepodge had wandered off, she hoped not far. Pulling on her butter-yellow smock and boots, she got up and pushed back the sheen curtain that held most of the bees inside her cart. They flew out, eager to find the dainty bright-yellow and purple flowers that dotted the clearing.

"Podge! Podgy!" She called as she walked to the edge of the clearing and peered out into the forest.

She listened but there was no reply. As she passed the first line of trees a strange cold breeze met her that she was sure had not been there before. Like sea spray, except when she felt her face, it was dry. It seemed to get thicker and thicker as she continued into the forest and the trees grew closer and closer together.

"Hodgepodge!" she yelled, "Where are you?!"

Through the trees she saw a dark shape rear its head toward her. The figure was huge. She almost ran but stopped herself as she saw the equine ears flick, it was Hodgepodge. She sighed with relief and then immediately grew angry.

"Hodgepodge Eveningswood, come right here! You naughty pony!"

Hodgepodge nickered in reply and trotted over to her.

"Why are you out here anyway? There was more than enough grass in the clearing." Myrtle patted Podge's forehead and swept a length of his forelock out of his face. The pony had an honest look in his eyes, as if he hadn't heard her before or perhaps was too engrossed in whatever snack he had found. She walked through the undergrowth towards where she first spotted him. Behind the thicket there was nothing. Not even a blade of grass. She turned to Hodgepodge and frowned, hands on her hips.

"I think maybe you have some explaining to do."

The pony turned an eye to her in reply.

"Sorry whatever you're trying to sell with that look I'm not buying it."

She turned and walked back to the clearing, making sure that Hodgepodge was following behind her. When she passed the forest's edge she was met with a new surprise. Sitting on the ring of stones around the fireplace was a boy. He had his back turned to her, but as she stepped into the clearing Hodgepodge stepped on a branch and it snapped under his weight. The boy flinched, scrambling around to face them.

"A-Are you Myrtle Beeswood." The boy stuttered.

"Yes, I am."

"I have a letter for you Miss Beeswood."

"Oh?" Myrtle was handed the letter and turned it over, in dark blue ink was written, *'Blessings from your father, 42 Banksia Road, Wattleshire.'*

"Well, have a good day Miss." The boy bowed and turned to walk off.

"Wait!" Myrtle called and the boy stopped, rigid. "Have there been any accidents this morning? Or any illnesses to report?"

"U-Um" The boy hesitated, "N-no, not that I've heard of. Sorry Miss Beeswood."

"Alright then have a good day. Thank you for bringing the letter all this way."

Myrtle turned to pack her things in the wagon, but she did not hear the boy step away. When she got to the wagon she turned again, the boy was looking even more nervous if that was possible. She waited for him to speak, but after a few awkward moments she had to say something.

"Well?"

"U-Um."

"Well?" She raised her voice a little.

"Is it true that they follow you?" He motioned to a group of bees busily pollinating wildflowers.

"Sometimes."

"Can you really heal people with honey?" He shuffled, but he looked less nervous.

"Of course, otherwise, why would I be here?"

"C-Can you heal *anything*?"

"No." She frowned, "No I can certainly not heal *everything*."

The boy grew visibly more comfortable, "So you're just like a normal doctor then."

It didn't sound like a question, and Myrtle wasn't so sure how to answer it.

"It's a bit different." She answered after a moment.

"Is it magic?"

"I'm not a witch if that's what you're asking."

"O-oh no… T-that's not what I meant." The boy grew anxious again, "Y-you're definitely not one of them Miss. Witches are greedy, they only want money or power, or something like that. I-It's true, isn't it? That you only ask for bread?"

"Sometimes." Now she too grew uncomfortable.

"But you don't ask for money, do you?"

"No, of course not, that would be blasphemy. But it's not *only* bread. Sometimes it's milk, cheese, or carrots."

"Do you have a home?"

"Sort of…"

"B-Because…Well this clearing sometimes floods. It rains heavy on the mountains in late spring and when it does, this valley's stream becomes a river for a few days."

"Oh."

"My Pa said to offer you a room if you want one. There's a stable for your handsome pony too." He paused, "Well, I better be going now."

"What's your name?" Myrtle asked

"Finn, Finn Strawby."

"Well, thank you Finn Strawby, but we should be fine where we are." Myrtle said with confidence. She was yet to understand that 'confidence' can sometimes just be a mask for pride.

"Okay then Miss, have a good day." He touched the rim of his hat and walked off into the north side of the forest, where the trees were thinner, and thinner until they met the road.

Myrtle turned back to the letter, she hopped into the driver's seat on the wagon and began to read.

My dear daughter, Myrtle,

Your mother and I hope you are doing well in Wendermere. Gwendolyn insisted that I tell you to make sure to eat more than just bread and honey and bathe at least once a week. Your mother is also concerned for your wellbeing, but trusts that you are looking after yourself. Make sure Hodgepodge doesn't get too fat and remember to be back by late autumn, the bees become slow and weak, they may need a permanent hive.

Unfortunately, I wish that this letter could be only an exchange of good wishes, however your mother has taken a turn again. She has been unable to leave her bed for a few weeks now. Gwendolyn is taking good care of her. Your mother wishes for you not to worry about her health. She believes she will be feeling better soon, and even as I write this, she was able to sit in the rocking chair for a little while today. As for the rest of us, Tara is still busy teaching in the orphanage and Penny is enjoying the spring break. She has been a great help in the kitchen. We've been making stews together while your mother rests.

Remember also that this time in Wendermere is important; both for your training as the next Beeswood Beekeeper and to secure a good reputation. Persevere and you will find yourself a far greater Beekeeper than when you started. You will always have a place here in Wattleshire, but we believe your want for adventure and purpose will not be satisfied if you return before autumn.

> *A Beekeeper's Duties are to never be forgotten.*
> *Help others, above and before yourself.*
> *Never ask for money, but only what the poor*
> *can give - a little bread, a little butter, a pillow to lay*
> *Your head. Remember that your duties are sacred*
> *and what you lack will be given to you. Your*
> *power does not come from within you, do not flatter*
> *yourself with such thoughts lest they be your end.*
> *Your power is lent and borrowed from the Wild King*
> *and when you come to the end of yourself you will*
> *Find him there.*

With love and blessings, your family.

Beeswoods

Pride's Flood

It was a clear, bright Sunday morning. The sun shone from the sky unhindered by clouds, which only edged the far horizon. A wind blew, the kind that wasn't cold, but had the slightest edge to it. It brought with it the promise of a perfect day, warm but not hot. The gentle clip-clop of Hodgepodge's hooves accompanied Myrtle as she drove the cart up the mountain road. Today, she would visit the Cottonflowers, who were an elderly couple. The grass rippled along the hillside, like a wave and Hodgepodge's neck bowed as the incline became steeper.

"Steady on Podgy." Myrtle encouraged, "We are almost there."

In reply, Hodgepodge huffed. Soon they met the path which was cut flat across the side of the mountain, and then they pulled up at the Cottonflowers' house. It was a peculiar house, a mismatch of stone and wood, like fabric patches sewed together. The door was answered by a grey-haired woman who introduced herself as Mrs Cottonflower, she took Myrtle to the living room, where her husband sat.

She could hear the elderly man's cough before she saw him. He had been sick for some time now and Myrtle was unsure that he would ever fully recover. She didn't need to put her ear to his chest to hear the rattle. It was unmistakable and incessant. She carefully picked up one of the man's white hands and checked his pulse. It was weak. The man wore a heavy woollen jumper, but still looked cold. Wrinkles and smile lines ran along his face like well-travelled roads. This was a man who had lived a full life. She unrolled the lambskin to reveal her herbs. The small glass bottles glinted in the light that strayed through the window and the herb's scents eagerly filled the room, like a blossoming garden. Feverfew was not among them, and she knew that she would need it most of all.

"Mrs Cottonflower, do you happen to have any feverfew in the garden?" She looked up to the man's wife.

"Ah… I don't believe so, but I'll ask Mrs Merryweather, I'm sure she'll have some in her garden." Mrs Cottonflower hurried from the room to ask her neighbour.

"So, Beekeeper-" The man, Mr Cottonflower, had to pause to cough, "What's the verdict?"

"Well, I have heard that you've had this cough for some time now, haven't you?"

"Mmm." Mr Cottonflower nodded, "Nigh on six months, it was worse before though."

"With an illness lasting this long, the best thing is consistent care." Myrtle scooped a little honey into the wooden bowl, "I'll leave your wife with two pots of honey and show her how to make the medicine. You'll need to have it every day until you feel better- No skipping!"

"Hahaha…" Mr Cottonflower's laughter quickly diverged into a fit of coughing, "Well if you're bringing my wife into this, there's no way she'll let me skip. No, I'd be sleeping with the goats that's for sure!"

Myrtle smiled, and mixed in warm water with clove, chamomile and thyme. Once Mrs Cottonflower had returned, she mixed in the feverfew. She then gave the bowl to the man. He drank it all in one draught.

"They all taste different." He said after a moment, "Daffy's honey was nuttier, but yours is more… floral."

After a moment of confusion Myrtle realised, he must be talking of another Beekeeper. She nodded slowly.

"All swarms are different, and the honey's taste can change from season to season, or even different areas depending on the flowers around. My bees have been feeding on the wildflowers down in the valley the past few weeks. But, this honey was gathered from them before I left Wattleshire."

Mr Cottonflower looked thoughtful, "Daffy lived in the walnut orchards on Barefield Lane."

Something sparked inside her, the intrigue of a former Beekeeper… but she chose to ignore it, moving to write down the recipe for Mrs Cottonflower. However, curiosity got the better of her before she could even put the pen to paper, and when she looked up into Mr Cottonflower's eyes she found him expectant, he had been waiting for her to give in.

"Well?" She said

"Well?" He echoed

"What happened to Daffy?"

"Oh…" Mr Cottonflower cast his gaze down for a moment as if pretending that he had hoped Myrtle wouldn't ask, "She was a good healer, older than you. She was in her early twenties."

"Hm?" Myrtle prodded after he paused.

"She had her whole family in this village, well not here on the mountain but across the valley. First Beekeeper in the family too, she got her bees from Mrs Cloverfoot who was the Beekeeper from Pinesdale. Cloverfoot brought her through the apprenticeship."

Myrtle's mother had not mentioned any former Beekeepers who lived in Wendermere, all she knew is that the area had been without a Beekeeper for quite some time. Coming to know that there was not only a former Beekeeper who had resided in Wendermere not so long ago, but also that there was another Beekeeper, who trained her, in a neighbouring village, was quite a surprise.

"And where are they now?" Myrtle asked

"Daffy served here for four years, two years as an apprentice and two on her own, travelling to Winspern, Pinesdale, and Irisgrove whenever she was needed. Towards the end, her family went a bit odd… The Clivesfields were well known, in Wendermere. They used to trade their cheeses as far as Winspern and Pinesdale, it was famous all throughout this region."

"Towards the end of what?" The pen and paper now lay on the little table, for the moment, forgotten.

"Well…. to be honest none of us can be sure exactly what happened. You see…. She just... disappeared one day. The rest of her family stopped answering the knocks at their door after she disappeared, and they stopped trading cheese. Within six months they had moved on somewhere, but no one knows where. Folks reckon they were scared someone must be out to get them after their daughter vanished."

"Did she take anything with her? Surely, she didn't just vanish. What was her house like when she left?"

"I've heard when they searched the house, the washing was still on the line and a cake had been cooling on a rack, everything was normal, she just wasn't there. No struggle or signs of hurried packing, just vanished."

"And her bees?"

"Oh-" he looked taken aback for a moment, "I'm not sure, didn't hear anything about her bees."

"Hmm." Myrtle looked down to the unwritten recipe, she picked up the pen but hesitated again, "And what of Mrs Cloverfoot her teacher?"

"Well, she was seen around here often in those first two years, a little less in the last two, but she would occasionally check up on Daffy."

What a short apprenticeship, Myrtle thought. *Especially for one starting out Beekeeping later in life.*

"And where is she now?"

"Not sure, she wasn't seen much after Daffy disappeared…" He paused as if for the first time considering that this could be a piece of the mystery.

"And no one tried to track her down or talk to her?" Myrtle asked.

"I'm not sure to be honest. I believe Mr Farthington, Mr Jackson and Mr Merryweather were the ones who headed the search of her house and the forests surrounding. Perhaps they would have talked to Mrs Cloverfoot?"

"Your neighbour Mr Merryweather?"

"Yes, indeed."

Myrtle wrote down the recipe hastily and handed it to Mrs Cottonflower along with the two pots of honey. They walked to the doorway.

"Here dear, will two silver and two copper pieces suffice? We don't have much this season." Mrs Cottonflower held the coins in her wrinkled palms.

Myrtle frowned, "Oh no, please I don't need money. If you have any spare bread though, I would be a happy partaker!"

"Are you sure?" Mrs Cottonflower looked almost startled

"Absolutely positive!"

"Well, aren't you a dear thing. Here you go, a nice big loaf of seed bread, It has sunflower seeds in it!"

"Looks delicious, thank you." The soft, yet hardy scent of the warm bread wafted from the paper bag that Mrs Cottonflower handed her.

Mr Cottonflower stood in the doorway with his wife, the colour was returning to his hands, and he looked much better already. She smiled at the couple, bidding them goodbye, but as she took a step from the doorway, the thought of Miss Clivesfield's mystery became even more tantalising.

"Oh- one more thing." She added, "How long ago did Daffy disappear?"

"Three years ago," Mrs Cottonflower answered the question, "Did Jack tell you of Daffy? She was such a nice girl. So sad what became of her…"

"Yes, very strange." Myrtle murmured thoughtfully

"Strange? Maybe the fact that she forgot the valley floods in late spring, but there's nothing to it. The poor girl must've drowned."

"Now there, Lindy, No one saw her along the road to the village." Mr Cottonflower retorted.

"Yes, but the Smiths were expecting a visit from her, Timothy's father was due to be checked on account of his bad back." Mrs Cottonflower argued.

"Well, how do you explain why she'd left both her horses at home?" Mr Cottonflower responded, crossing his arms.

"She was a smart girl, maybe she remembered the water, but thought she could swim it." Mrs Cottonflower in return placed her hands on her hips.

"Or maybe she didn't go at all because she was kidnapped. It would've taken her at least two hours to get to the village on foot and it was already late."

Mrs Cottonflower huffed at this, "How ridiculous, nobody has ever been kidnapped in Wendermere."

"Well, I better be off, thank you for the bread." Myrtle waved.

While the conversation was interesting, she wished to excuse herself from the couple's argument, and she wanted to pay the Merryweathers a visit before going back to the valley clearing.

* * *
*

A cup of steaming tea sat before her. The sun's afternoon rays reached through the curtain casting shadows across Myrtle's face. Mrs Merryweather was buttering corn fritters. She had told the older woman that there was no need to feed her, but Mrs Merryweather had insisted.

"Now dear," Mrs Merryweather said as she set the platter of corn fritters on the table, "We are all well, so I suppose you haven't come here to heal anyone. Is there anything I might be able to do for you?"

Myrtle found herself embarrassed, perhaps it was a little rude for her to visit the Merryweathers just to ask about Miss Clivesfield. She took hold of the warm tea, letting the steam swirl over her face, she hoped it might mask her burning cheeks.

"I was just with the Cottonflowers and they told me about the former Beekeeper in Wendermere."

"Yes Daffy made quite an impression." Mrs Merryweather smiled, "Such a sweet girl…. bless her soul."

"Cottonflower mentioned that Mr Merryweather was involved in the search for her after she went missing."

"Yes, he was." Mrs Merryweather met Myrtle's gaze, her hazel eyes darkened by the sun behind her, "What did you want to know?"

"I was hoping you might be able to tell me about what state her house was left in when she disappeared?"

She held Myrtle's gaze for a few moments before sighing, "There was no trace of where she could have gone. No signs of struggle. Everything was left as it was. The oven was still warm from baking, a cake lay on a rack and documents from her work were left strewn across the table. There were a few strange things. Her horse Dusty was tied to a post, the saddle and bridle slung over the fence." Mrs Merrweather paused, "But, the Fodderhills can confirm that Dusty was being untacked, not tacked up, as Daffy had just arrived back from a short visit. Dusty also had the telltale signs of saddle sweat that had dried on his back."

"Did the Fodderhills live far up the mountain?"

"Only a brief trot up the road. The Smiths were expecting her that afternoon, but she never arrived."

"Did she leave even her bees?"

"Yes, her whole swarm was there, not a single hive out of place. They were quite a trouble to move…. My husband got stung twenty-two times!"

"Where is her swarm now?"

"Oh, just here in our garden. We took them on when she disappeared in the hopes she might come back. We aren't really very good beekeepers though and they haven't produced any honey for us. The best they do is pollinate our garden."

Merryweather gestured through the window behind her, and Myrtle was surprised she hadn't seen the bees. There weren't many, but a few buzzed quietly around a lavender bush.

"And what of Mrs Clivesfield's mentor? Mrs Cloverfoot?"

Mrs Merryweather looked taken aback, as though she hadn't been expecting that question, "Oh, Mrs Cloverfoot. Well, she lived in Pinesdale." She answered after a moment.

"Yes, I've been told Pinesdale is close, did she not expand her area of practice after Mrs Clivesfield disappeared?"

"We certainly didn't see her around here after Daffy vanished. I heard from those in Pinesdale that she came to visit less and less. By summer of that same year she had completely stopped coming. Rumours have it that she moved up North." Mrs Merryweather frowned.

"Did anyone talk to her about the disappearance?"

"N-Not that I know of." Her frown deepened, she drew in a sharp breath, "The woman was a little hard to track down when you needed her most. Before Daffodil started Beekeeping Mrs Cloverfoot would come to Wendermere to treat us on occasion but was often too late for the sickest of us, I supposed she was so busy with those in Pinesdale. She was also getting on in years, so I can imagine travel would have been harder for her."

Myrtle frowned at this too, why would an elderly widow Beekeeper upend her life to move further North in the first place then? She held her tongue. It seemed she'd exhausted that avenue of questions.

"May I see the bees?" She asked instead.

"Of course dear, here, come follow me to the back door." Mrs Merryweather led the way to the little wooden door. The door opened onto one of the most beautiful gardens Myrtle had ever seen. Creeping vines covered the house walls, hiding it from view. Bright irises stood tall in the wind. Roses crowded the vine covered corners and daffodils flooded at their feet. Poppies and forget-me-nots dotted the lush grass on either side of a stone path. The grass was knee-high and going to seed. Chamomile sprung out of a wooden flower bed, its white flowers lay like snow around the box. At the far end of the garden stood a sullen oak tree and under the oak tree there were three beehives. Bees hummed near Myrtle, and she bent to inspect one who had landed on an iris near her. She noted that these bees were redder than her own, while they still had yellow stripes, the yellow blended into orange and red. She could hear their hum, but it was far fainter than her own bees, even with the three hives.

She hopped down the stone path, careful not to disturb the bees pollinating flowers. Once she neared the hives, she knew something was wrong. There were a handful of bees buzzing about two of the hives, but the third looked empty from the outside. She needed to have a look inside to see what the real problem was. The prospect of opening up one of the hives led to a new potential hazard, one could not tell how the bees would react to an unknown Beekeeper.

She had been stung a handful of times by her family's bees when she was a child, but not since she became their keeper, and she wasn't fond of the idea of being stung again. She wrapped the long sleeve of her dress around her hand and then lifted the lid. It was empty. Using uncovered fingertips, she touched the sides and wooden framed panels, they felt slippery as the residual wax slowly melted at her finger's warm touch. Even the beeswax had been chewed away by hungry worker bees.

She replaced the lid and made her way to the more active hives. Mrs Merryweather had now made her way over to Myrtle, carrying some gloves.

"Here," She handed the gloves to Myrtle who hastily put them on.

"Thanks," Myrtle whispered.

She gently lifted the second hive's lid, disturbing the few bees that had been flying around it. Some landed on her, crawling up her sleeves, she tried to ignore them. This second hive was still active, and dozens of bees crawled through the beeswax.

Suddenly, their amber backs filled the air like a cloud. The swarm flew from the hive rushing out. Her ears filled with the flapping of tiny wings beating like drums all around her and she brought her hands up to cover her eyes, bracing to receive the stings. But no sting came. Strands of her hair lifted as the air was disturbed by the bees' wings. Myrtle uncovered her eyes to see the swarm just hovering about her head, some were hidden beneath her blond curls. She cupped her hands in front of her, and the tiny insects landed.

"And how do you do little bees?"

Myrtle stilled her shaking hands, she had never been swarmed by bees before, wild or otherwise. Her anxiety started to melt, and she smiled at the creatures. They sat patiently on her palms, big eyes reflecting the sun like mirrors, back legs heavy with pollen. She peered past them into the almost empty hive. Now that it was uncovered, she could see that while there were rows of beeswax, the wax was mostly unfilled. Honey only oozed from a few hollows in the corner where the queen bee lay. Myrtle stooped to see the queen more closely. Her large stripes appeared dull, grey and weathered. She was old. Too old, this queen should have passed quite some time ago. She moved her hands to pick up the queen, and the swarm lifted into the air again. Gently, she scooped up the small pulsing body.

"Your kingdom is safe." She whispered to the queen, "I'll take good care of it. You are free."

And with that the queen gave up her life. Her body stilled and grew cold. She thanked the Wild King, as was the custom whenever a queen died. Then laid her to rest inside the hive, where the bees flocked to mourn their ruler. Mrs Merryweather had stood out of the way watching this all, and no doubt was wondering a great deal of things. She hadn't spoken until now.

"Will they be alright?" She asked.

"Yes, they'll make a new queen, they'll rebuild. That queen had been sick for quite some time, I am not sure what prevented her from passing."

Mrs Merryweather nodded, "I don't think that the last hive has a queen at all." She pointed to the last wooden box.

Myrtle lifted the lid on this last one, and saw that Merryweather was indeed right, this hive, although not entirely dead, had fewer bees than the last, and all the bees were workers. There was no queen, and no honey. The beeswax was patchy, tiny bite marks had begun to tear at the rows of white hexagon. She did not know why these bees had not chosen a new queen. Perhaps they had forgotten how? She did not know that a bee could forget how to do what bees do.

Mrs Merryweather helped her to carry the hives to her wagon. She then thanked the elderly lady for the tea, promising to come again and set off on her way. Podgy was sick of waiting by the time she finally climbed into the rickety cart, and so he took off, trotting all the way down the hill. He stumbled along, almost tripping and Myrtle was sure the cart would fall sideways, but he did not heed her when she pulled on the reins. All Myrtle could do was hold on.

Hodgepodge only slowed to a bouncy walk as they neared the little forest clearing. Breathing a sigh of relief, Myrtle slumped in the seat, but not a moment had passed when the pony's ears pricked at sounds of laughter. They were approaching a group of children along the road. Two girls and three boys. She recognised Master Strawby among them. He took off his soot-coloured cap as Hodgepodge passed them. She nodded to him in reply.

"Miss Beeswood."

"Master Strawby."

A snigger came from within the group, and one boy whispered rather loudly to his friend.

"Oi, that's the one who thinks she's *magical* right?"

"I'm a Beekeeper, if that's what you're asking." Myrtle replied, turning to look behind her, narrowing her eyes at the boy, as she passed.

The boy regarded her with his flecked green eyes. A smug look on his face. He hadn't cared that she had heard.

"Oh, yeah. A *Beekeeper.*" He rolled his eyes and chuckled, elbowing Finn in the ribs.

"Have a good afternoon, Miss Beeswood!" One girl called after her, blond ringlet's swaying as she struggled to keep up with the cart.

*   *   *
*

Bright light trickled out around the clearing, casting shadows on Hodgepodge and the wagon. Myrtle found herself jumping when she saw the dark shadows shift, but the fear quickly turned to laughter after realising that the shadows were Podge of course. The strange shadows were cast as he picked up his head, with bottom lip wobbling and heavy with grass. Her laughter faded. The people of Wendermere had been generous givers and for dinner, she was roasting a sweet potato with some cheese and a hunk of lamb. She turned the potato in the fire, with a long stick and took a bite of a cheese wedge, but she couldn't shift the lingering prickle of fear against her skin. She took a glance over her shoulder, when she thought she heard a creak, but it was just the pattering of rain beginning. First it fell in small sizzling droplets upon the fire, and then a sudden downpour.

"Aggg!" Myrtle cried out as she scrambled to pick up her hot meal and retreat into the tent. She burnt her fingers in the process. Soon the fire was little more than a retreating glow in the night. She could dimly see Hodgepodge seeking shelter behind the wagon.

The rain fell in sheets, tumbling down the slanting tent walls and seeping into the tufts of grass. Her bees were all safe in their hives under the cover of the cart. The rain came in torrents. Soon water was spilling from the wooden awning and was sucked up by the eager ground below. Quiet worry fogged the back of Myrtle's mind. She could tell that her bees, though safe, were also restless. They should have been asleep, but even as the last light from the fire faded, she could still hear a hum of wings, and see the faint amber outline of a few solitary insects. The worry didn't fade as the light did, but soon her eyes grew heavy, and she allowed herself to give into an uncomfortable sleep.

*   *   *
*

Pounding.

It resounded and echoed and grew in momentum with each passing moment.

Breathless.

Myrtle was fighting for breath as she woke, forcing her eyes open, trying to make sense of the pounding; was it her heart? Or of the rushing… the rushing air… or was it.

Water.

Shock cascaded through her, and she was made suddenly aware of her surroundings. She was wet and water had leaked in through the sides of the tent. The ground had drunk its fill and puddles were forming. She shook her sleeve and droplets fell, she shivered. Her heart was still pounding, and the rain still thrummed on. It was now that she began to think of the boy. *Strawby. Finn, Finn Strawby. Drat this awful, awful rain!* The thoughts came with the realisation of how cold it was. She was soaked through to her skin. She decided to abandon the tent and hop into the back of her wagon, while she wouldn't have enough space to lie down, she would at least be able to sit in the shelter. Anxiety lingered in the back of her mind as she fumbled with her bag. Soggy blankets were hastily stuffed into the wet sack, as well as a pair of socks and hair ribbons. She tried her best to wring the water out of the blankets, a scowl framing her face as she worked.

A sharp whinny split the pitter patter of rain. She stopped, frown deepening. The sound of the rain came back, this time louder, thundering. She scrambled to tuck the last of the blankets into the bag. The whinny came again, this time sharper. Louder. Anxious. The pounding shook Myrtle, her heart leapt into her throat. She wrenched the tent door open, it was still dark, only the faint outline of things remained. Something told her that she needed to hitch Hodgepodge to the wagon. She questioned the thought as she threw the bag into the wagon. *Now why should I hitch the wagon at this hour? It is only a little rain. I can't go to the Strawby's now.* But her bees were up, the two hives were busy, including Daffodil's hive. Her eyes began to adjust to the dark, she could see their tiny bulbous shapes lifting through the air.

"Rain disturbed you too?" She sighed to them.

Hodgepodge was nuzzling her, his warm breath in her palms, his velvet nose dripping. He drew his head up quickly, and swung wildly, lungs heaving. He whinnied again, it was ear splitting.

"I'm here... I'm here. It's alright Podgy." She took hold of his cheeks and stroked his forehead, but it did not ease him. He walked toward the cart and pushed his head into it. The bees buzzing filled her ears, louder now than the rain.

C R A C K

Myrtle and Hodgepodge whipped around to see a tree branch slipping and tumbling, rushing…. It filled the air and seemed to lift every leaf from the forest floor.

Hitch Hodgepodge to the wagon.

She needed to, she didn't know why, maybe because the wind was picking up. She grabbed the collar and pulled it around Podge's neck. The rushing grew louder. She buckled Hodgepodge's collar and girth to the wagon and began fumbling for the bridle, the fiddlier of the three parts especially in this dark. Hodgepodge was having none of it, he tossed his head and began walking off. Myrtle grunted.

"Oi come back here! I am not done with you!"

The pony didn't listen but took off in a trot, Myrtle only just caught the back of the wagon and pulled her sodden body up into the cart flinging the bridle along with her.

CRUNCH

It was a soggy crunch. Like the slurping of mud, followed by a series of loud cracks. She turned to look up, the moon pierced through the clouds. Water filled her view as it came plunging down the silhouetted mountain side. A roar filled the air. She could see the outline of trees quivering as the water plummeted. A river poured out as though it were poured from a pitcher. Branches groaned under the sudden assault, trembling, then cracking, and falling. Catapulted by the raging current.

Hodgepodge launched into a gallop.

A Flattering of Bees

She was a soaking mess by the time they arrived in Wendermere's Town Square, and she sat shivering beside her hives in the back of the cart. The town was barely visible through the haze of water and night, but the clear clip-clop of hooves on stone, and vague shapes of large town houses told her where they were. The few bees that had stirred with the thunderous downfall, had flocked to her head and shoulders, their wings fluttering softly at her ear. She feared that her clothes were so wet that even landing on her might drown the small insects. What a sorry sight she must have been.

Hodgepodge hadn't needed any prompting as to which direction the town was, and what was even more extraordinary was that the bridge across the river into town had not flooded yet. The river's roar had been so loud that Myrtle had held her breath as they crossed the bridge, heart pounding, fearing that the bridge would be washed away by the force at any moment. Perhaps she had almost met the same fate as the town's previous Beekeeper.

She reached through the wet curtain, and took hold of Hodgepodge's tail, attempting to ask him to stop. Unfortunately, without the reins, he completely ignored her and continued trotting through the empty town square. The rain had eased a little for a moment.

"Woah, woah boy." Myrtle called softly to the pony.

And Hodgepodge did stop for a moment, raising his head, snorting, turning it this way and that as they came to a crossroad leading out of the square.

"That's it, good boy Podgy." Myrtle stroked the pony's sodden rump, his fur was slick and her hand slid like soap.

Something spooked Hodgepodge and he lurched to the side breaking into a canter. The wind whipped her face dry in seconds, but then it grew wet again as another downpour started. The pony flew past several village houses, until they started to thin out as the town turned into countryside, it was only then that he turned to a brisk trot. Myrtle had no idea where they were, nor where they were going, and she doubted Hodgepodge did either. But her steed would not listen to her.

The bees hummed quietly within their clay kingdoms from the back of the cart. Their sounds comforted her however, it would do nothing to stave off the cold as her wet clothes drooped from her body. Her teeth began to chatter, her lips went numb. Her feet had lost all feeling and were like dead weights. She drew herself nearer to the hives hoping that the clay might bring her warmth. The life that beat beneath, was tepid, but it did little to relieve her cold body. Tired, she felt so tired. The moon glared down on the world through the veil of clouds and showed no signs of retreat. Myrtle closed her eyes against the dark world, wishing her bees could be warmer.

* * *
*

44

"I'll get some blankets." A woman's voice, and then a man's: "No, don't worry, I'll get them Martha, you go make some tea for when she wakes."

The voices were distant, down a hallway perhaps. Myrtle felt that she was being carried and strong arms surrounded her. She tried to open her eyes, but all she could do was open them for a moment before they became too heavy to lift. A steady numbness had crept through her whole body. She tried to speak, but the words came out wrong, they were slurred, her jaw felt stiff.

"You're going to be alright Miss Beeswood, you just hold on."

She felt the man's warm breath momentarily breathe life into her icy face. First, she was placed on the hard floor, and could feel it even through numb skin. There was a fire, and warmth prickled back into her body, like hot needles.

"Let's fix up that nightgown." The woman's voice whispered.

A gentle hand took off her drenched nighty and replaced it with a soft blanket. She managed to force her eyes to open, as she felt her body being lifted again. This time, she blinked the fogginess away and found a black bearded man, the woman at his heels.

She looked surprised to see Myrtle awake, "Don't worry dear, you're in safe hands now. We're just about to get you into a nice warm bed."

"Would you like me to help you out of your undergarments?" Her voice came again.

Myrtle blinked in reply, she knew that she didn't have the strength to take off her soaked undergarments, but as miserable as she was, the thought of being even more humiliated made her almost cry. She was sat down in a new room in a wooden chair and the man left the room briskly.

"I'm sorry, dear but you'll still be cold with these on. Here, I'll only take the under dress."

The thin fabric clung to her like clothes on a marbled statue. But the woman still managed to remove it without tarnishing Myrtle's pride, and the sodden nightdress was replaced by a new dry one. The man then returned to carry her again to a bed.

Fluffy quilts engulfed Myrtle as she was tucked into the warm bed. She wiggled her toes as the pins and needles subsided into feeling. Her foot brushed a hot water bottle. She sniffled and sighed.

"Here's a cup of tea." The woman placed the mug on the side table, "If you're feeling alright now, we might go and get your pony sorted."

"Yes, thank you so much." Myrtle mumbled, "I will be quite fine now."

Myrtle saw a boy appear in the doorway, it was Finn. Of course, Hodgepodge would *miraculously* know the way to Finn Strawby's house, a house they had never been near.... Myrtle frowned. He caught sight of her looking at him and retreated into the shadows of the hallway. Perhaps her bees had known where he lived, they did sometimes fly a long way in search of pollen.

"Try to get some sleep, there'll be hot porridge waiting for you in the morning." The woman, Myrtle presumed now must be Mrs Strawby, patted the quilts down once more and left the room, closing the door behind her.

*   *   *

*

Myrtle opened her eyes to steamy porridge. Light streamed through the curtains, in brilliant orange and then quickly faded to a bleak white as the veil of clouds shifted. She could tell it was about noon from the sun's position. While the warmth had returned to her body, embarassment's coy sting had not. Why had she decided to stay in the clearing after such a downpour had started? The decision had left her half-drowned and the Strawby's now burdened with her care.

Finn's mother must have known that she would sleep late because the porridge was still hot. She felt guilt's heat on her cheeks. Pushing feelings aside, she sipped at the warm tea. The porridge reminded her of Wattleshire, where the village was filled with the scent of fresh oats every morning, often closely followed by honey's sharp fragrance. She held the bowl and let the steam tickle her nose.

It was well past noon before Myrtle had regained her strength enough to think about leaving the room. It would've been much easier to lay in bed the rest of the day, but she owed Hodgepodge a visit. In fact, she probably owed him a whole cart full of carrots as well, but couldn't bring herself to ask the Strawbys for even just one.

Myrtle slunk out the door, careful to tiptoe and hoping to not meet any of the Strawbys on her way. As she slipped through the door, she was struck by the thought that she could just leave. In fact, she could leave all of Wendermere behind her and with it, forget last night.

She stroked Podge's forehead. He had been given a cosy stall. It was filled to the brim with all the hay he could ever hope to eat and so he stood there pensively chewing.

"Thank you." She told him, "You saved me back there."

The pony snuffled at the hay on the ground and then lifted his head to look back at Myrtle, his deep, dark eyes blinking. She swirled his forelock and tucked it behind his ears. Her cart with the bees stood in the shelter of the barn a few paces away. One bee flew past, stopping for a moment to hover before her face. Someone must've drawn back the makeshift curtains to let them gather pollen. One landed on Hodgepodge's velvet muzzle and then crawled down her arms.

"What a night we've been through." She whispered to the bee, "I hope you were all safe in there."

Before she had put rational thought behind the decision Hodgepodge was strapped up to the wagon again. She had dried off some soggy paper in one of her boxes and written a quick note to the Strawbys. It was a letter of thanks, explaining that she needed to go off to a neighbouring town as she had caught wind of sickness. She didn't write the name of the neighbouring town nor any indication of what sickness, because she wasn't so sure which village herself yet. Hodgepodge pawed the ground as she gathered the reins, he was reluctant to leave his golden hay, but Myrtle managed to coax him out of the barn. She was happy to see no signs of any of the Strawby's in the stables, and she brought Hodgepodge into a trot down the road.

"Wait! Miss Beeswood!"

She jumped and was so startled that she accidently pulled harshly on the reins bringing Hodgepodge to a sudden halt.

"No, no no…." She muttered under her breath. She waved a whip frantically. The pony in turn kicked out and flicked his ears back angrily, so she poked his bum with the whip and Hodgepodge leaped into a canter.

"M-Miss Beeswood! Wait!"

To Myrtle's dismay Finn's voice seemed to be closer not further away. She took up the reins urging Hodgepodge to go faster. The pony slowed to a trot, swishing his tail and jerking his head around to give Myrtle a dark look.

"Come on! Come on!!" Myrtle groaned at him

"M-Miss Beeswood."

Myrtle came face to face with Finn Strawby atop a stocky white gelding.

"Oh! Finn." She let surprise place a smile upon her face, but really it was just to hide the embarrassed blush from her cheeks, "I was just going out."

"I hope you aren't leaving." The boy for once wasn't stuttering, "You're not going back to that clearing, are you? It'll be all washed away."

"No." Myrtle grimaced, "I am on my way to a village nearby,"

His silence was pointed, and Myrtle knew that she hadn't given enough.

"Ah-." Myrtle knew the hesitation was too long, "Winspern." She dug the name out from recent conversations, "I'm on my way there."

"You won't get there before dark."

"I *was* going to stop over." The words came out too fast and Finn recoiled, the look on his freckled face changing from worried to perplexed. There was silence between them, except the cartwheels slowly grinding and the horse's hooves against the stone.

"You should stay here."

Myrtle was taken aback by his forwardness, her frown deepened in frustration, "I'll be fine thank you very much."

"Y-you were almost gone when we found you."

He was exaggerating obviously. She hadn't been in good health, but she also hadn't been on death's door.

"I appreciate the concern," Myrtle tried in vain to keep her voice in check, "But I've been on my own for quite some time now and I'll be fine on my own for quite some time more!"

The boy pulled his horse up at this, and to Myrtle's dismay her pony stopped also.

"You don't have to be on your own."

"Is the shyness and stuttering an act? Because clearly, you're not shy when you don't want to be! Maybe I just want to be alone!"

Finn rubbed the reins in his hands and looked at his toes pointed up in the stirrups.

"Y-you don't really mean that do you?"

The moments past and Myrtle's frown dissolved. She could see now that the sky was already dotted with pink clouds and that she had been unfathomably rude.

"We're having pumpkin soup tonight… a-and my father said you can stay… a-as long as you would like."

With the searing anger subsiding, pride's twisting thorn was able to be felt. Myrtle knew Finn was right, it would be silly to leave at this hour.

"Fine, I guess I can stay another night." She swung Hodgepodge back around and gritted her teeth.

Relief flooded Finn's face, but Myrtle groaned inwardly, *oh to endure another night in the debt of the Strawbys*. She would just need to find a way to repay them. Perhaps a few pots of honey would do.

*   *   *

*

Myrtle made sure to be extra polite over dinner, thanking the Strawbys at every opportunity, and it wasn't difficult because the pumpkin soup was *very* good. Over dinner, Mr Strawby made it clear that they wanted Myrtle to stay as long as she was in Wendermere. When she had crawled into bed at the end of the day, she found herself feeling a confusing mix of comfort and fear. Fear not because she didn't feel safe, but because she couldn't accept such kindness, she could feel it gnawing at her. What could she do in return? Surely, she was in great debt to the Strawbys. Myrtle had nothing but her bees and her pony and she couldn't bear to part with either of them. Nor was she sure of what use would come from her parting with them. She contemplated the previous night's feelings as she gathered her things for the day.

"Miss Beeswood," Finn's voice chimed.

Myrtle spun as she heard his voice, blond braids bouncing. Finn's eyes widened and he shuffled his feet as she caught his eyes.

"I-I was just going to tell you that I'm headed to the back fields."

"I'll be headed off soon myself."

She was met with a bleak stare, Finn scuffed his shoe in the dirt.

"Don't worry," She sighed, "I'll be back before nightfall."

Finn nodded, and began to walk away, but before he walked more than a few paces he stopped to look back at her, and the sun hit his freckled cheeks.

"I like your hair today."

Myrtle felt her cheeks go hot, she raised a hand to shield her eyes from the sun. He wasn't waiting for her reply, he was already turning to run to the back fields. She tried to search for something to say, before he left.

A new day was beginning, and with it fresh possibilities. Today was a warmer, brighter day, the sun was peeking through the ashy clouds. Like fire through smoke. Myrtle was outside buckling Podgy to the cart. Finn had returned home from running letters yesterday evening and given her news of a man who had injured himself while cutting down a tree. Apparently, the man had been injured for days, but was too far out for a doctor to call on him. Finn had said he was halfway between Wendermere and Winspern. She was about to climb upon the little wagon, when she realised that her leather pouch was missing. It wasn't in the back of her wagon either. Her bees hummed bumping into the transparent curtain that separated them from the Strawbys' garden. Had she been wearing it when she fell asleep the night of the flood? She didn't often fall asleep with it on, but she had occasionally forgotten to take it off.

"Wait here Podgy!" She eyed the pony, he pawed at the cobblestone of the courtyard in reply. Knowing her pony all too well, she knew he would not wait, and so she slung the reins around a trough's hitching post.

"Don't you dare break them." She glared at him. Hodgepodge had a habit of breaking through the leather bridle when tied and charging off on whatever errand he supposedly thought that 'they' were going on.

Racing back towards the door she tried to bring together the few useful memories from that night. It felt like trying to untangle a knotted ball of wool. She could pull the string, but she didn't know where the ends were. She finished searching the guest's room that she was staying in with no success. The Strawbys were all working out in the back fields, which were a lengthy walk from the house, and she didn't want to bother them. So, she strolled to the kitchen and dining areas, riffling through the room, but her search quickly drew to halt as there weren't many places her belt could be hiding. Perhaps Mr Strawby, or Finn's elder brother had accidentally taken the leather belt, thinking it was meant for tools?

She slunk down the hallway. Careful not to let the floorboards creak, though she knew that no one was in the house. She came to the wooden door that led into Mr and Mrs Strawby's bedroom. For a moment, she paused on the edge of committing such an outrageous action. It felt like such a violation, but the herbs she could use to heal the sick man were more important. Quietly, Myrtle grasped the door's knob and pushed.

The room was neat. The bed had been made and turned down, sheets white and the doona a patchwork of colours. In the corner stood a stool beside the window and a great oak wardrobe sat facing the wall. With a quick glance over her shoulder back into the shadowy hallway, she made her way into the room. Bending to look under the bed and open the wardrobe. She didn't find what she was looking for, but only a sense of deep shame.

Frustration and stubbornness spurred her on. She left the room, closing the door behind her and continued down the hallway to another room. This one was Finn's. It was also tidy, but clearly a more rushed job, as the duvet was slightly askew. She opened the wardrobe, only to find a few coats and his big leather mailbag. There was no sign of her belt. The next door at the end of the hallway was Michael's, Finn's older brother. She had come to the conclusion that Finn had five brothers in total, but two were married and one lived as an apprentice to the blacksmith. She had only come to gather this knowledge through the dinner conversation the night before. It was however possible that the Strawby's had more children who did not get mentioned.

The door swung and squeaked on its hinges as she pushed it open. Michael's room was much more disorganised compared to the other members of his family. Papers littered the dresser, and days' worth of dirtied trousers lay slung across a chair. His bed wasn't made either. Myrtle entered the room with caution. Crunching alerted her to a crumpled page beneath her foot. She groaned inwardly, picking up the paper to try and flatten it out again. Or had it already been crumpled?

Too late… Myrtle had straightened the paper and by doing so found myself staring at someone's private words.

A flower
You were scented like buttercup
Flowing hair like honey
Fragile as an orchard
And I wasn't the gardener to your heart

She tried to forget the words, but curiosity kept them turning in her mind.

"Focus." She muttered to herself, *you're here for the belt.*

Her eyes swiftly took in the desk, she placed the page next to the many others like it. Before she drew her attention to other areas of the room a necklace caught her eye. It was slung over the poems, as if it were being used like a paperweight. The shining silver was caught by a dappled ray of sunlight as it strayed from the window. The reflected sunlight glowed bright red, as if the necklace had copper inlay, except that it was entirely silver. More interestingly, the necklace was in fact a locket. As Myrtle peered closer, she could see the engraved initials, D.C. There was no time to wonder, she needed to find the belt. Her gaze darted around the room until it rested on the lambskin belt, slung over the chair by the desk. She hurriedly snatched it and left.

Winds From the South

The man was dying.

He lay on his side in a sweat, face pale and contorted, chest heaving. The wound on his arm smelling of sweet vinegar, it was the stench of rotting flesh. Myrtle was not accustomed to healing such an injury, the sight made her gag. The man had broken his arm a full week ago after he had slipped and fallen from a tree that he was cutting down. The fracture was compound, meaning the bone had pierced straight through the skin. She forced herself to focus.

"Will he be alright?" The man's wife clasped a clammy hand around Myrtle's arm, her eyes were bright with panic.

Myrtle could barely hear the woman's voice, for the pounding of her own heart filled her senses until she no longer felt the coarseness of the floorboards beneath her bare feet.

"Dear? D-Dear?!" The woman's pleading voice brought Myrtle back into reality.

Breathe. She told herself. She had helped the gravely sick and injured before, but none had been quite so close to facing their own mortality. Hot water. She needed hot water.

"Fetch me some hot water."

The woman was wide eyed, hand gripping at Myrtle's dress sleeve, her fingers white knuckled.

"I need it now." This time Myrtle made her voice low, almost a growl.

This spurred the woman into action, and she flew out of the room, leaving Myrtle alone with her dying husband. She hurriedly unfolded her belt, hand shaking as she picked up the herbs. Feverfew? Ginger? Clove? Garlic, definitely garlic.

She hurriedly minced the garlic in the wooden bowl. The pungent smell made her eyes water. She wiped the tears with an elbow before they could fall down her cheek. A bee hummed near her ear, and she gave it a finger to land on. It alighted on her, wings quivering, antennae bobbing, tiny, swirled tongue poking out between its big eyes.

"Which herbs should I use with your honey?" She whispered anxiously to the bee.

The bee buzzed in return, lifting into the air and flying out of sight. Perhaps she would just have to do this alone.

She hastily picked out a few more herbs; Rosemary and ginger which she crushed vigorously. The woman returned looking calmer and handed Myrtle the hot water. Myrtle in turn took hold of the warm pitcher and sprinkled it in the bowl until the crushed herbs became a paste. The man lay still now, and for a moment Myrtle thought that she might be too late. She brought a shaky hand next to his mouth and felt a little breath stir the hairs on the back of her hand. Another bee was crawling up the man's sheet white face, its yellowed back shining in the sunlight which streamed through an open window. She sprinkled some warm water from the pitcher into her wooden bowl. Carefully, she spooned the honeyed medicine through the man's pale lips and watched him as he attempted to swallow.

But something was wrong. The man howled and drew back from Myrtle, choking. The shriek filled the room and echoed down the hallway. Floorboards creaked suddenly, as the man's wife came running.

"Tim? Tim!" Her shrill voice added to his shrieks.

Myrtle froze, and out of her fingers slipped the spoon, clinking onto the floor. And the man writhed in front of her. What should she do? *What should I do?* Was there something she was missing from her training?

Could she save this man?

The thought was immobilising. Bees slowly filled the room, sifting through the open window and landing on the man she was realising that she had not healed. That she *could* not heal.

The harsh reality came over her like burning ashes, prickling at her skin leaving her raw. She could not save him.

The man was dying and all she could do was watch. A bee crawled up her cheek, wings buzzing as it slipped. She absent mindedly let it creep onto a finger, as the man's wife bent down crying beside her husband.

The man drew his last breath, and died.

His wife held his hand, weeping. It burned in Myrtle's chest. Pressing against her throat.

"Oh, Wild King… I couldn't save him." Myrtle choked, "I'm so sorry I couldn't save him."

She knew that this day would come again, the day that she would find herself unable to save someone, yet still she was unprepared for the waves of searing pain that radiated through her chest. It threatened to crack her open, to crumple her, and open the floodgates. Her vision filled with tears. She wouldn't bow to its whims.

Her hands crumpled into fists as she knelt beside the man and his wife. Eyes filled with the blurring of tears, she could barely hold them back. *Surely, he couldn't be dead? Surely? I could've saved him, if only I'd been a better Beekeeper. Her mother could have saved him.* For a moment she could feel herself slipping back in time, beside her mother's bed. Powerless. But she felt a still small voice answering her.

It is I who lets you save them. For your power does not come from yourself.

"Could you not save him then?" Myrtle gritted her teeth, "Does he have to die?"

Through the haze of her tears, she saw the bee who was still on her knuckles. Antennae waving. Behind the bee was the silver spoon, honey still dripping on the floor as the bees flocked its side. But as she watched something changed. The bees lifted from the honey, hovering for a moment and then flew over to her belt. Swirling, they floated slowly until they reached one single herb. She leant over to see which herb. Rosehip. They were clustering around the rosehip, its shiny red seed protruding beneath their black and amber stripes.

You only need to ask, child.

She grasped the bulbous seed, and taking the stone and the wooden bowl, she crushed it, the air filled with its crisp and fragrant scent. The woman heard the noise and turned her tear stained face to Myrtle.

"What are you doing? He's already dead." She cried.

"He can still be saved." Myrtle took the honey and emptied the rest of the jar into the bowl, mixing it until it became a milky yellow paste, "Open his mouth."

The woman carefully took her lifeless husband's head and lifted it onto her lap. Myrtle took hold of the spoon from the floor and scooped up the Rosehip-honey. The sweet syrup left the spoon, drizzling into the man's mouth. Moments passed, Myrtle waited, poised. The woman in turn sat in silence.

Then suddenly there came the sound of breath being sucked into every inch of the man's body. It was a low roar. Coughing, spluttering, gasping and the man's eyes flicked open.

* * *
*

Over the next few days Myrtle's reputation grew. There was not a person in the whole of Wendermere who did not know that Myrtle had raised a man from the dead. She couldn't help the feeling that they had gotten it all wrong. She hadn't raised the man from the dead. Instead, she had watched him die, helpless.

Myrtle had returned to the Strawby's farm as she said she would. The last few days she had treated a boy with a broken wrist, a woman with a sore back and a baby with a cough. Today was her day of rest. Unless an emergency arose, she would have the day to write a letter to her family, among other things.

A gentle breeze rolled through the Strawby's garden as she sat outside on a wooden bench. It ruffled the lush bushes, ladened with a heavy floral bounty. Lavender swayed, its tiny flowers enticing the Beeswood Bees. Their backs shone in the light as they buzzed happily. The daffodils were preferred by the Clivesfield Bees. They were like tiny, winged tigers flying through the air, their stripes far redder than her own bees. The large heads of the daffodils bounced, waltzing in the tender wind. She noticed a new colour of bee emerging from her flock as it flew past her, it was headed towards the soft pink chrysanthemums. The bee was a blend of both the Beeswood and Clivesfield Bees. It had a brighter, warmer tone to its stripes. Like a sunset. A smile crept up her face as she saw it, this would mean that the Clivesfield Bees had a new queen. And a queen would need a coronation. She twisted the quill idly in her hand as she took in the scene, the garden, her bees and a perfect spring morning.

Dear Family,

I think I have finally begun to grow into the skin of a real Beekeeper. There has been much that has happened since I left Wattleshire. I feel as though I have been here in Wendermere for such a long time, even though it has been only a month. I am beginning to realise that there is a great deal more to Beekeeping than healing the sick and injured.

Indeed, she felt that so much had happened and she wasn't sure that she could write it all down in one letter. Perhaps it was also that she didn't want to tell her family everything. Especially, that she was now staying with the Strawbys and the unfortunate situation which had brought her there. She thought briefly about telling them of the previous Beekeeper, perhaps they had ideas of where Beekeepers might disappear to, but for some reason she found herself feeling silly at the idea of recounting the story to her parents. However, the changing colours of the Clivesfield bees was sure to interest her mother, so she decided to add a brief report of how she came to acquire the Clivesfield bees. She wondered too whether her mother might have met Miss Clivesfield's mentor Cloverfoot.

"Miss Beeswood."

Myrtle picked her head up from the paper to see the dark hazel eyes of Finn Strawby. He touched the brim of his flat cap.

"Master Strawby." Myrtle nodded in return. There was silence between them, as Myrtle waited for the boy to reply, a few moments ticked past with the boy looking down to the lush grass at his feet and then up again at Myrtle.

"Did you really raise Mr Jefferson from the dead?"

Myrtle knew that it was only a matter of time before the news returned to the Strawbys. She still wasn't quite sure of how to respond to such a question.

"Yes." The reply came out of her mouth almost before she had time to think and realise that, while it was the easier answer it also wasn't entirely the truth.

Finn's eyes grew wide, and he gave Myrtle a freckled smile.

"That's miraculous." It was almost a whisper, and then he drew his gaze to the ground again.

Myrtle's cheeks grew scarlet. She could feel the embarrassment burn all the way to her ears.

"C-Can other Beekeepers raise people from the dead?" Finn asked.

"I'm sure others have."

"What about animals?" Finn's cheeks were singed red as he met Myrtle's gaze again, all the awe and wonder had fled. He took a step back from the table.

"I don't think that Beekeepers can heal animals."

"Can you raise anyone from the dead?"

"What do you mean?" Myrtle's eyes narrowed, he was incessant.

"H-How long can the person be dead for?"

"Umm…" Myrtle paused, she supposed it had to be almost immediate, but she wasn't sure, "I don't know. That was the first time I've done anything like that."

Finn nodded slowly, "Well, these letters won't mail themselves. Good day Miss Beeswood." and with that he was off again, a heavy leather mail bag swinging as he walked away.

A bee, one of her golden ones landed on her nose as he walked away. Its transparent wings like stain-glass windows, antennae like flower stamen twirling in the breeze.

"Yes. I know I didn't *exactly* raise the man from the dead." Myrtle mumbled, "But the truth sounds…Well people would think I'm crazy if I started mentioning that I can hear voices."

Had it really been the voice of the Wild King? The King from her old nursery books? Had it been a whisper from the bees themselves? The thoughts left her feeling anxious. Whether she was imagining it or not, she wasn't entirely sure, but she could've sworn the bee tipped its head to the side.

"I guess people already think I'm crazy, but I'd prefer to preserve any dignity I have left."

The bee fluttered its wings in return and flew into the sky, trailing on the breeze as it went back to the business of pollinating.

*　*　*
*

The woodcutter's house was squat and fat. The large logs it was made up of looked as though they were bulging. Pine trees and lush grass shaded its rotund edges, but the foliage

63

made an abrupt end as the ground disappeared. The lodge was perched precariously on the edge of a cliff.

She had travelled south of Wendermere to get to Windy Ridge. Even further south than the Jeffersons lived, she was in fact almost in Winspern. She tapped on the hard oak door and a large man answered it.

"You must be Miss Beeswood?" The man smiled, the lines of his face were soft, and often used, Myrtle instantly wondered whether he was a father.

"Yes! And you must be Mr Woodswell?"

"That's me alright. We've heard lots about you Miss Beeswood. No need to worry, they've all been good things!" Mr Woodswell motioned for Myrtle to join him inside.

It was comfortable, and well lit, light spilled through two large windows overlooking a magnificent view across the deep valley where the lake known as Giant's Eye glittered. The lake had gotten its name from its almond shaped appearance and a green island which floated in its centre. Up from the lake, directly opposite them was a view of the ragged mountains, which enclosed the valley all the way around. The mountain range was named Cloud's Tears, as a river tumbled from their north peaks. The stream became a waterfall for the last hundred metres and plummeted into Giant's Eye. There was also a waterfall from Windy Ridge, but you couldn't see it from the Woodcutter's dwelling.

"Now, what can I do for you?" Myrtle asked as she set her things down.

Mr Woodswell sat down, with a loud grunt, in a plush green chair, beside the fireplace. He gestured towards a seat opposite himself for Myrtle to sit in. There was a steaming pot of tea on the table as well, the smell of mint leaves wafting from its spout. Mr Woodswell's wife appeared from the kitchen, a plate of scones in her hands. She smiled at Myrtle before being called away by a small child who was playing in one of the other rooms. She whispered a thank you to Myrtle, and then left.

"Two weeks ago, a branch fell on me while I was cutting a tree down with my son." Mr Woodswell grimaced, "Unfortunately, since then it's been so stiff I haven't been able to do a great deal. I was willing to give it another few weeks, but the wife is…. you see, a bit worried."

"Oh, alright then…" Myrtle trailed off in thought. The man was clearly in pain, she could tell from his ever-present grimace, the awkward crooked way he sat and the tensed knuckles clutching the chair.

"Well, let's be honest here, it was probably something to do with her being sick of my complaining, as it's been awfully sore."

"Have you noticed any swelling?" Myrtle murmured, as she lay her belt out over her lap, revealing the herbs. She didn't feel that any particular one was speaking to her, but she'd noticed this feeling more and more lately. She felt less sure of herself than she used to. Perhaps it was because she no longer had the guidance of her mother.

"Ahhh…" Mr Woodswell scratched his head.

"Yes, of course there's been swelling Gilbert!" Mrs Woodswell's voice could be heard from the adjacent room. A moment passed and she popped her head through the doorway.

"I believe, Miss Beeswood, that he may have possibly shattered something. He couldn't move his back at all the first week and he's barely been out of bed since the incident."

"I was afraid that's what it sounded like." Myrtle nodded.

She came back to the herbs, lavender, rosemary, and thyme. She'd picked a lemon, its acidic smell tickled her nose. Still, none of the herbs seemed right to her, and no bees flew in to help. Perhaps, she would have to ask, as she had for the dying man, still she felt silly doing it.

O Wild King, if you are truly there, please show me how to heal this man.

Instantly, she felt as if a fog had been lifted from her vision. The scents of herbs that she hadn't noticed before became pungent. She picked the evening primrose and oregano. She wasn't sure how she knew that these were the herbs that would heal him, but she knew that they would.

She crushed them into a thick paste and then dribbled the honey into the bowl. This time she had chosen to bring the new bee's honey, it had a slightly orange hue to it and little air bubbles floated through its syrup, like tiny pearls. The bees had been quick to make it, but there were only a few teaspoons of the new honey. She handed the mixture to Mr Woodswell. He in turn drank it in one mouthful, though it took a few moments for the thick medicine to run from the bowl to his mouth. He licked his lips afterwards.

"It's warm."

Myrtle nodded in return, "Yes, Beekeeper's medicine always feels warm."

And then the man sighed a deep sigh and slouched further into his chair, his bushy hands resting on the arms of the chair.

"Golly." He exclaimed, "It really does work! My back feels better than it has in years! Jane?"

Mrs Woodswell trotted into the room grinning, having heard her husband's exclamation. The child ran at her feet, black ringlets bouncing. Myrtle felt herself beaming, she couldn't help it, her cheeks burned with embarrassment, but she ignored it. Had the King really answered her? It felt so silly, and yet she felt joy as she watched the couple, enraptured with excitement, they shared a teary embrace.

The Woodswells offered her money, three shiny gold coins, stared back at her from the palm of Mrs Woodswell's hand, so shiny that she could see her face staring back. It looked worried, for some reason. She shook her head after a moment, explaining that some goat's milk might suffice. That she, as a Beekeeper, could not accept money as payment. The couple seemed perplexed but agreed to give her some milk. After loading three jugfuls of goat's milk onto the back of her rickety wagon, they begged her to stay for tea and biscuits, and she promptly accepted the invitation.

*   *   *

*

Ferns poked through the knee-high grass that lined the cliff top. Mottled light shifted through the thick brush and down the open cliffside, illuminating the dainty honesty, a purple flower that shone freckled orange in the half-light. The purple flowers dotted the undergrowth and foxgloves reared their bountiful heads proudly, wavering in the wind as yellow butterflies danced around them. She found the flat, dimpled edge of a curled tree trunk. It was the perfect size for two or three people to sit and watch the waterfall cascading down the dense mountain side. It emerged ten metres away from her between sloping trunks and quivering leaves, its mist throwing a rainbow against the soft green backdrop of the bent mountain. The waterfall then threw itself with vigour down the steep cliff, falling hundreds of metres before it tumbled into the Giant's Eye.

Across the valley behind Cloud's Tears the sun was setting. Its light streamed out against the mountain casting the cliff top in its fiery gaze. It reflected off the wet leaves surrounding the waterfall, brandishing them until they were dripping with gold.

Hodgepodge's snort came above the roar of the water, he nudged Myrtle as she sat and returned to nibbling the grass. One of her bees had come to join the butterflies and eagerly crawled into the bell-like shape of a foxglove disappearing from view.

She crossed her legs and leant back on Podge's strong neck behind her, laughing as he brought his nose to her ear and blew a long breath out, pushing her curled hair forward. She drew a hand up to sweep the hair back behind her ear and as she did, she caught sight of an odd indentation in the trunk. Shuffling over to get a better look, she realised that someone had carved several initials into the tree, curling along its underside. There was an M.G. and T.K. written next to each other, a S.C. and C.L., and a P.M. and H.H. The last hollows, which were written on a more prominent part of the branch, formed the Initials D.C. and M.S. They must all be lovers she assumed, and peered closer, letting her finger rub over the letters. The D.C. reminded her of the necklace in Michael's room. Myrtle's eyes lit up. Could it just be a coincidence that the initials were the same?

Could it be a coincidence that the locket in Michael's room had a D.C. engraved on it as well, or that Michael's initials were indeed M.S? She couldn't think of anyone else with the same initials, but last names starting with 's' and 'c' were very common. For the other initials carved into the tree she could already think of a few people whose names would fit, and she hadn't even yet met the entire population of Wendermere, let alone all of the people who lived from Wendermere to Winspern.

Still, she couldn't help thinking that perhaps Daffodil Clivesfield and Michael Strawby were an item? Windy Ridge was a long trot in the wagon, but it would've made a spectacular romantic outing. Especially if one was hoping to propose.

*   *   *

*

"Word has been going around town of what a fine job you're doing Miss Beeswood." It was Mrs Strawby who spoke at the dinner table, as she served Myrtle a large bowl of lamb stew.

"Yes, I've never heard of a Beekeeper who could heal a man after death." Mr Strawby scratched his beard, "You must be very talented."

Myrtle took a spoon full of the stew, the smell of garlic, rosemary and tender lamb filling her senses.

"I'm just glad that I can be of help, and that Mr Jefferson is alive" Myrtle murmured.

"Yes, aren't we all dear!" Mrs Strawby exclaimed, "What a miracle! And now I've heard that all of Winspern are hoping you'll visit? How wonderful! There'll be plenty for you to do now, for miles around."

"Yes, I'm sure there won't be an end to my work, especially over the next few months." Myrtle couldn't hide the smile that was creeping onto her face, "Could you please pass the bread Mr Strawby." She gestured to Michael, who in turn handed her a roll with the calloused hands of a farmer.

"I was wondering why my belt was in your room?" Myrtle didn't dare meet his gaze, and in fact as soon as the question had slipped from her mouth, she wished she could retract it. Especially since it had been a whole week since the incident.

"Oh." Michael sounded startled, "Yes, I'm sorry I must have misplaced it as my own tool belt… I didn't even notice. I trust you found it then?"

"Yes, it's alright I found it."

Michael nodded, and returned to his dinner although it was clear he was still flustered. Myrtle couldn't help herself but prod, though she knew that she shouldn't.

"Do you know of a Daffodil Clivesfield?"

Michael almost choked on his dinner. He gave a cough, swallowed and then met Myrtle's gaze wide eyed.

"How do you know of Daffodil?"

"Well, Miss Clivesfield was the last Beekeeper in Wendermere, wasn't she? Why shouldn't I know of her?"

"Yes, that's right Daffy was a bright young lady, not unlike yourself. Ah, but older." Mrs Strawby answered.

"I was told that she disappeared?" Myrtle continued, trying to stave off the burning from her cheeks, she pushed further.

"Yes, that's also right… It's quite a tragic story. They've never been able to find her."

Michael now was looking far more than just wide eyed, he had stopped eating and was frowning at the floor.

Abruptly, he shoved his chair from the table, clattering the silverware.

"If I may be excused, I've had quite enough." and with that he left.

Myrtle felt as though she'd been struck. The burning sensation flooded back to her cheeks, and she found herself trying to hide behind her water cup.

"S-sorry, I didn't realise what a sensitive topic it might be." but she knew that she was lying, because while she didn't *know* that it was a sensitive topic, she could've made an educated guess, in fact she had made an educated guess which was exactly why she had prodded.

"It's quite alright Miss Beeswood." Mrs Strawby sighed, "It's a bit of a sore spot for Michael as he was quite taken by Daffodil. She was a very pretty little thing, beautiful black raven hair, striking green-blue eyes. Well, a fair few boys were taken by her... but her and Michael were the closest."

"It's because of them you know ma." It was Finn who spoke, though he had been silent until now, "They didn't agree with the match."

"What on earth are you talking about?" Mrs Strawby gave Finn a fierce glare.

"The Clivesfields, they didn't agree with the match. Michael knew it. They disapproved of him. So, Daffy's family sent her far away, that way she'd never be able to marry him, not even in secret."

"Oh Finn, what an exaggerated imagination you have." Mrs Strawby said the words carefully, but sternly.

"Well, then explain why the Clivesfield's were acting so strange before she vanished? It was as if they knew that it was going to happen."

"Finn, that's quite enough, you can go and help wash the dishes."

Finn complied, and hastily finished his stew, dishes clinking as he hurriedly picked them up, which was enough to make all parties know he was not happy with how the conversation had been left. Although Myrtle was ashamed by the way in which the details had come out, she found herself feeling the satisfaction of her suspicions being found true. Finn's ideas seemed to hold some weight, it tied the mystery up neatly. The Clivefields acted oddly because they knew Daffodil and Michael's future intentions. Michael was a farm boy, and so had not been seen as a worthy match for the Daffodil who was the talk of the town. Because of all this, the Clivesfield's planned to have Daffodil sent away, likely before the proposal, or before word of the proposal came out. Daffy would, of course, not have been expecting this, which was why everything was left the way it was, including her bees.

The Horse and Its Rider

It had taken the better part of the morning to travel to the Taskin mansion, and Myrtle now stood before the house, dwarfed by its enormous sandstone walls and sloping rooftops. At first, she had been resistant in answering the summons from Mr Taskin, because by all accounts from the people of Wendermere, he was a cruel man. Swindling the poor out of money, lending money with doubled interest, and taking what little possessions that the poor had if they were unable to pay him back. Romero Taskin had once been a gentleman of average wealth before marrying and receiving a profound dowry from his bride and then subsequently her inheritance after her death. And here was his home, built like a fortress to shut out the rest of the world. She knocked loudly and a maid came to answer the door. She was guided through a long hallway before being seated and asked to wait for Mr Taskin. He finally appeared through the doorway of an adjacent room.

His mouth was crooked, there were gaping holes in his smile, but the remaining teeth were pearl-white. He was a fat man, belly protruding as he wobbled to the chaise lounge. Myrtle couldn't keep her hands from turning bone white as she gripped her jar of honey. Myrtle had never treated the rich before, she was not accustomed to seeing lives of luxury and the ornate gold inlay of the couch she sat on made her feel very uncomfortable. She wondered why, out of all the places that you could choose to live when receiving such fortune, would you choose to live here... on the outskirts of Wendermere; a poor country town. She supposed that perhaps his wife had been related to the lord that used to rule over Wendermere. But the days of Lordship in the cluster of country towns around Wendermere had long since been forgotten. Why then stay now that she had passed away? The answer seemed clear after a few moments, poor people were easier to extort.

She tried to set her mind on the task at hand, the quicker she could treat Mr Taskin the quicker she would be able to leave. Unfortunately, she had to admit that the crystal candelabra and delicate silver pitcher, everything down to even the shiny gold doorknob; it was all so distracting.

"And what can I do for you Mr Taskin?"

"I've always had this problem with my legs, one is longer than the other." Romero spoke in a half-drawl, which sounded somehow both guttural and posh at the same time.

Myrtle replied with narrowed eyes, "What do you propose that I do? Birth defects are among the hardest to heal."

The man took hold of the couch's arms, his hairy knuckles clenching the red velvet.

"Hard to heal doesn't mean impossible to heal."

"Let me see." she masked a disappointed sigh, but part of her hoped that he may have heard it.

Romero straightened his legs out in front of himself and rested them on a short footstool. His right leg was a good five centimetres or so shorter than his left. Myrtle's frown deepened, but she started unfurling her belt. The Wild King surely would not heal this man. Many lived with birth defects, many poor people whose lives were deeply affected by such defects, while this man lived a comfortable life of luxury and yet still wanted more.

She poured the honey out first, and then waited, staring at the herbs until she had a feeling of certainty on which ones to add. After moments though, it never came. She hesitated, perhaps she should try asking, but she quickly dismissed the thought. She would not beg for this man. A little half-smile escaped her lips, the Wild King had made his choice, there would be no healing for this man. She handed the bowl, with only the honey, to the portly gentleman.

"That's the best I can do, I'm afraid."

Romero in turn took the bowl, grasping it shakily.

"Thank you." He murmured almost sounding sincere, and then lifted the bowl to his lips.

Myrtle caught sight of a painting at the far end of the room. It was of a knight riding a stallion. The snorting horse was rearing on the edge of a precipice, a wild look in its eyes. The knight looked so much smaller than his mount, almost cowardly. The stallion looked ready for battle. Except... Now that she had looked more closely, she realised that the knight was not any smaller than was ordinary, his vague shadow was in good shape. But that was just it, the knight was nothing more than a brief impression in the painting, while the stallion was swathed in complex strokes and details. Beneath the stallion lay a bed of brambles at the bottom of a precipice, and the stallion looked as though it had every intention of charging right through them. A yelp from Romero brought her back to reality.

"My leg! My leg!" The man yelled

Myrtle frowned at the big man in front of her, he had now sprung up from the couch and was motioning fanatically at his right leg with childish excitement.

"My leg! By King's riches!! My leg! I-It's IT'S!" He was almost screaming now and bouncing up and down, the commotion bringing servants who hurried with concern into the room.

"I'm *healed*!"

Myrtle couldn't stop the gasp from leaving her mouth, it was quickly replaced by a frown, surely Romero was sorely mistaken. Seeing the doubt upon everyone's faces Romero hopped back onto the couch and hurriedly began taking his shoes off.

"No really!! It is! I could feel it!" And with that Romero produced his pale, hairy feet and straightened them again on the velvet footstool for everyone to see.

The sight was daunting. The sight of the two perfectly straight, perfectly symmetrical legs. It was in fact as if they had never been defective, there was no scar, not even a scratch. Myrtle found the fury rising in her. The servants turned to one another, shock upon their faces, whispers circulating. Until the surprise was replaced with joy and they joined in with their master's wild glee.

"Oh Miss Beeswood!" Romero exclaimed, turning to her with hands clasped, "What will I ever be able to do to repay you? I will forever be in your debt for this great miracle."

"A-ah." Myrtle wasn't sure how to reply in such a situation, she could see even the servants shuffling back in awe of her. She saw a few even bow their heads staring at the ground in reverence.

It suddenly dawned on her that she had the power to ask for anything, and this man would give it to her. For a moment she could see it all, the mansion, the carriage, the sparkling candelabra, the magnificent spread on the banquet table, a life where she would truly want for nothing. Never be too tired, or too hungry or craving something sweet.

She felt the lights glitter and fade with the small hum of a striped bee. It glided gently to her side and found a perch on the tip of her nose, tiny wings fluttering as it hovered and then stilled.

Was it you who healed Romero?

Was it you who cared for him?

Was it you who saw something broken and in need of mending?

The voice stirred around her, a whisper and then a roar. N-no… She felt her reply lodged in her throat. She felt it so powerfully that it threatened to escape with tears. She recovered after a few moments and for the first time she truly looked into Romero's eyes. They were deep and overflowing *literally* with joy, tears ran down his face freely and he did not bother to wipe them away, no he could not wipe them away because he was so caught up in it all. The *joy*.

But, more than the joy, his eyes were soft and pleading. These were not the eyes of a tyrant. These were the eyes of a broken man finally beginning to mend, the walls breaking and tumbling bringing him to the ground in awe. In *humility*.

And now Myrtle found herself caught up in it all. The joy of the mending that she had been a part of her own heart softening. She pursed her lips- considering.

"There's no need for payment. Consider the debt nullified" and then as if her voice were not her own, she went on, though she had thought she would stop, "Your debt to me and all others. Let the healing change your life."

The man now had a twinkle in his eyes, and they became wide like small moons, he stood a little straighter in the chair as if in thought.

"I will!" He announced triumphantly, "I will give to the poor and let them into my home! My servants will never go hungry, and I'll plan a feast for the whole of Wendermere!"

*   *   *

*

The soft light paper crumpled easily in Myrtle's eager hands. It tore and was cast aside, unveiling the crisp buttercup yellow dress beneath. The material was satin. It had lavender and blue bells embroidered on its belt in brilliant purple and blue, and a sparkling gold inlay. Lace peaked behind the skirts and sleeves also glinting with gold thread at the edges. Even the collar had delicate floral lace on its border. It was more precious than any dress she had ever laid eyes on. A note on the box read, *for changing my life indescribably, and I hope you would wear it at the village feast! -Romero Taskin.*

What a spectacular gift, she stared at the dress, taking in every inch of detail for what seemed like hours before carefully taking a hanger and placing it in the wardrobe. As the glint of the dress faded behind the closing door, she found herself feeling suddenly anxious. *But I didn't change this man's life… I didn't even want it to change. I didn't even ask for the healing.* She tried to shrug off the feeling, whether she *had* or *hadn't* changed Mr Taskin's life. He was now a much better person and for the first time Myrtle would be going to a *real* ball. One with oysters and lobster and whole pigs, stuffed and roasted. There would be foods of which she had never tasted or dreamed or even imagined.

She skipped outside, for she could not walk carefully while in such glee, and none of the Strawbys were around to catch her in the uncharacteristic act. Except that as she rounded the corner of the pastel pink rose bush, her eyes met with Finn Strawby's and she stopped.

"What are you doing here?"

"I-I" Finn blushed, his freckled cheeks turning a bright red, "S-Sorry Miss Beeswood, I was only meaning to give you t-these." He held out a woven, wicker basket brimming with soft, juicy strawberries. They were so ripe she could smell them from where she stood.

"I-I… picked them especially for you." He shuffled forward and handed her the basket.

"Oh." Myrtle felt embarrassment now creep upon your face, "Well… Thank you Master Strawby."

She stood motionless as the boy walked away. Strawberries shining bright red in the almost summer sunlight. She sighed, feeling the embarrassment fade as the clouds glided across the sun, leaving the air feeling cool for a moment.

It was time for the coronation of the new queen bee. She turned to her cart and drew back the sheer curtain to reveal the buzzing hives beneath. She had transferred

Daffodil's wooden hive colony into one of her clay hives. She couldn't remember her mother's practice on different hive mediums… so perhaps there had been no reason to disturb the colony, except now she felt as though they were truly her own bees. She removed the top segment of the hive and bees swarmed out around her. They flittered into her hair, tickling her nose and eyelashes. The humming filled her ears. She chuckled at their excitement.

The bees finally calmed, some landing on her shoulders and head, others flying off to other duties. Myrtle could again see the inside of the honeycomb hive. It glistened with newly made honey and many bees crawled over the wax hexagons within, busy bringing the whole kingdom to life.

"Now… where are you," She whispered as she began sifting through the bees carefully, letting them crawl over her cupped hands. After searching this first segment thoroughly, she could not find her and moved down to the next segment. It was then that she located the large, amber-coloured queen, around her larger body was clustered many of her royal subjects. Gently, she scooped the queen up, taking with her a few of her guards by accident.

Myrtle glanced at a book that she had laid on the ground, writing was scrawled across the page, it had been jotted down hastily as her mother dictated. She remembered her mother's teaching, on that stormy autumn day, as the queen bee of one of the eldest colonies lay dying in her mother's creased palms. The soft murmur of a melody came to her lips. It was the queen's tune, a tune that any Beekeeper could use to locate the queen of her flock. Each tune was a little different for each queen and was bestowed upon them at coronation. Myrtle began to hum, and the other bees abruptly lifted into flight until only the queen remained on her palm. A queen's melody always came within the coronation and was never composed with forethought. It surprised her how the melody bubbled up from within, as though she always knew it, familiar and yet somehow entirely new. It shared similarities to the tunes of her other queens, but not in ways she could have planned. The queen quivered in her palm, antennae waving with the whispers of the music, tiger-stripe body pulsing. Its large black eyes reflecting the sun in the small ways that it could. She was captured for the moment by her Beekeeper, listening to her song. And once the last note left Myrtle's throat, the memory was seared into both keeper and queen's hearts.

Myrtle glanced at the book again before moving on.

"O Young Bee, born into Queenhood. I bestow unto you the blessing of the almighty, the Wild King, who is King over all wilds, nature, sky and sea. And with the power of the King, I proclaim you Queen over this Beeswood hive, alongside your sisters, Lavender and Petunia." She gazed long and hard into the new Queen's eyes, it crouched almost as if in awe before her, waiting silently, waiting for Myrtle to say her name, *"You shall be known as, Rose. Queen Rose."*

* * *
*

After the coronation of her new queen, she ducked over to where Hodgepodge was stabled, bees greeted her as she slung her arms over the gate. They buzzed in a song of welcome. Podgy slunk over to Myrtle, nuzzling her arms looking for treats, and scratches. She brought a hand to the corn-ear spiral on his forehead. His dark eyes looked content, his coat was sleek, all of the raggedness of winter

81

had worn away to now reveal his shiny summer coat. Sure, his white patches were still brown with dirt, but his red patches were a perfect ombre from black to deep red on his legs, and deep red fading to the freckled, almost pink hue of his stomach.

She held some of the bright strawberries out for him, on her palm and he snuffed them up. A few bees were crawling up her arms and one flew onto Podge's muzzle. He snorted, a great big sneeze and the bee retreated to her hair, a safer place than the great steed.

She stayed with Hodgepodge until almost nightfall, laying against him as he slept. She flicked through a book on herbalism and shared the juicy strawberries with him when he awoke. The bees buzzed happily around them.

As nightfall approached it was time to prepare for the feast. Pulling on the crisp new dress was a feeling like no other. Slipping into its satin sides, the sleeves gliding up her arms, lace resting delicately at her wrists and ankles. The fabric puffed lightly at her shoulders. Next was her hair, which she had tied neatly into coils after her bath. Now she undid the fabric ties to let the ringlets bounce. She pulled back most of her hair into a bun, letting the front curls free. Myrtle didn't have any jewellery, but with the dress, she didn't feel as though there was any need for rubies or sapphires. *Though, they would be nice.* She thought, fixing herself in the mirror. The Strawbys had offered to take her in their wagon, but she had declined the offer.

Taking the saddle from the back of her cart she slung it over Hodgepodge's back, he looked around at her curiously. She didn't often use the saddle, but such an occasion as this called for it. She had oiled the tanned leather a few days prior, so it shone in the light of the lanterns. Carefully, she pulled the brown bridle over his ears, offering the bit first which he chewed idly. Earlier, after he awoke from his nap, she had taken his long fluffy mane and bobbled it, plaiting each little segment and pinning them into balls along the top of his neck. Now, she tucked roses into his mane's crest. Although, Podge did have something to say about the roses. He stretched around back to his shoulders and pulled out the only one he could reach, the pale flower quickly disappearing between his smacking lips. *Oh well, good enough,* Myrtle smiled. It was time to leave for the feast.

*   *   *
*

Myrtle pulled Hodgepodge to a halt at the steps to the huge mansion. They were lit along the sides with glowing lanterns. A fountain behind her splashed. Many were arriving in the best of whatever they owned. Some, she could tell, had even given their wagons a few extra coats of paint, like Mr and Mrs Merryweather, whose little two-seater coach glinted in the dim-light. The families from the mountain would have a very long trek back to their homes tonight, they were unlikely to get back before the sun began to rise, but with such a grand event everyone was coming no matter how far. A manservant appeared, jolting Myrtle from the splendid scene.

"May I take your steed to the stables Miss Beeswood?" The man bowed.

"Oh! Of course, thank you." Myrtle dismounted, giving Hodgepodge one last pat. He pawed at the earth as she handed the reins to the manservant, it was a protest for being handed over to someone he didn't recognise.

83

"Don't mind him, he won't bite. Probably." She laughed.

The manservant nodded in return and led Hodgepodge to the stables. He gave her a last nicker before disappearing from view. She turned and set her eyes upon the steps of the great Taskin manor. The townspeople stood marvelling before they climbed the sandstone steps, trailing their fingers over the curved railing, stopping to stare at the carved roaring lions. Stars in their eyes. Women had their best dresses on, and though they were not high society, all had done their best to dress as if riches were not a problem, for this one night. They all looked elegant, even the poorest villager in her brown smock, for she had washed that brown smock with excitement and wore that ancient silver broach passed down from generation to generation with pride.

Myrtle began to climb the stairs, she wanted to skip and run! But instead, she contained herself and stepped with dignity, soaking in every detail. People noticed and stopped to stare as she made her way. The Merryweathers, who were a little further up the stairs to the side nodded to her as she stepped past them. The Strawbys were about to enter through the large oak doors, which were open and inviting. Warm light spilled from within like a golden carpet. Guests already inside laughed and chatted eagerly. Mrs Strawby's eyes met Myrtle's, and she embraced Myrtle, kissing her on the cheek. Mr Strawby took one of his strong arms and wrapped it around her shoulder tightly, grinning.

Myrtle dipped her head and curtseyed to them. As she looked up again, her eyes locked with Finn Strawby's glistening and dark. They were surprised, in fact his mouth was ajar, had he not expected her to be here?

"Master Strawby." She bowed her head to him.

"M-Miss Beeswood." He stammered.

There before her stood those great oak doors, swung wide open. Oak leaves were etched into its sides, spiralling around its edges. She walked forward until she stood within the pooling light. Inside, the beaming faces of the guests could be seen mingling around the tables. Some spotted her as she walked into the light and they dipped their heads to her. Among the faces who were already inside were the Cottonflowers who waved to her. It was then that she caught sight of Mr. Taskin. He was no longer hobbling but walking with the grace and balance of his now very ordinary legs. When he reached her, a giant smile framed his round face.

"Our most honoured guest has arrived!" He shouted.

Clapping erupted from the guests in the hall, and the ones who had made it up the steps were peering in at the party.

He turned to Myrtle again, "I am most honoured to be able to hold this party, for the town of Wendermere, I've already talked to so many interesting people who I would've never so much as laid eyes on. And it is all due to you Miss Beeswood. An extraordinary, young lady, who healed my leg. Dare I say who even changed my life."

Myrtle couldn't stop herself from grimacing, "I am just so glad that you've thrown such a wonderful party for the people of Wendermere."

"Yes, but it is all only because you gave me such a gift as these new legs. A gift like no other."

Myrtle held her eyes downcast. *But it wasn't me who healed you.* She looked up at Romero again, his eyes generous, features soft and overflowing with joy.

"Well, I am just glad I could be of service."

"If only Emilia were alive to see such an occasion." he sighed, surveying the hall that many more guests were now trickling into.

"Is Emilia your wife?"

"Emilia *was* my wife, yes. She loved parties, not sure she would have approved of the guests…" He clasped his hands together, "She passed away at sea. Sadly, I'm not sure even you could've saved her."

Myrtle nodded.

"Please, enjoy yourself, there will be feasting and dancing shortly!" Romero left her to go and ask a maid to help him with something.

The hall was decorated in white and golden drapes, crystal candelabras hung from the ceiling like rain drops caught in the air. They refracted the light into rainbows, across the white drapes at the side of the hall. The floor was polished so that you could see a distorted face staring back at you. The tables were already laden with food, not the true feast, but refreshments.

She took a bite of a pastry and was surprised by the smooth feta and spinach inside. It was delicious. While she was eating, Mrs Cottonflower found her and drew near.

"Miss Beeswood, how do you do?" She asked, her greying hair was braided and swept into a neat bun. She wore a beautiful floral blue dress with lace edgings.

"Very well thank you, Mrs Cottonflower." Myrtle finished the pastry, "How has Mr Cottonflower been?"

"Oh, very well dear, that honey you gave us has been working its wonders. I haven't heard him cough for a few weeks now." Mrs Cottonflower took a step back in wonder, "What a gorgeous dress you have!"

At this Mr Cottonflower, who was in a conversation behind them, came to join his wife. He wore a smart navy coat with silver cufflinks.

"Miss Beeswood, you are looking bright and beautiful tonight." He nodded, smiling.

"Yes, and so she should be, as she is the reason for such celebration as this!" Mrs Cottonflower beamed.

Myrtle shied away at the thought that she was the reason for the celebration, but a smile concealed those thoughts. Mr and Mrs Cottonflower were soon wrapped up into another conversation, and Myrtle found herself alone again. She fingered another pastry, but it was a waste as she knew she would not eat it, because she was leaving room for the dinner feast. Many people had come to greet her, but none had stayed long. Finn was lingering at a table beside her with other girls and boys, some looked close to her age. She recognised some of their faces but had not met any of them. One face in particular, she noted, was the sister of the baby boy she had treated who had fallen ill due to a swine disease.

"Myr-Miss Beeswood."

She had been absent mindedly staring at the girl and hadn't noticed Finn lurk nearer. She came face to face with the boy in surprise.

"Yes." She frowned.

"I-I was just wondering-."

"What?" Myrtle's frown deepened as she became frustrated by the stammering boy.

"Would you like to meet my friends?"

Myrtle hesitated, she could see them behind the boy, a gathering of laughter, eyes alight with wonder, sparkling. Were they playing games? She had once played games with her sisters, but that felt like so long ago. Suddenly, she found herself feeling tired. Could she politely decline to meet these children? Surely, he would tell them she had refused, and then her reputation would be sullied.

Myrtle nodded to Finn, and he stuck out his arm for her. She slipped her elbow around his arm, and let him take her to the gathering. When they grew near to the circle, the chattering abruptly ended. One boy sniggered, and a girl lightly punched him in the arm, blue eyes furious for a moment.

"This is Miss Beeswood." Finn gestured politely.

"Hello, Miss Beeswood, I'm Miss Pineswood." The blue-eyed girl gave her a curtsey, blond ringlets swaying.

"And I'm Miss Jensen." This girl was definitely younger, Myrtle found her hazel eyes warm, although they only briefly left the floor. Her hair was in a tight bun, and she wore a light blue dress. It was plain, but not ugly.

"Master Fodderhill." The boy wore a buttoned shirt with suspenders, he had mousy hair, a round face and a welcoming smile. He struck out a hand for her, and she briefly took it, dipping her head.

"Miss Cobblinghill." This was the girl whom she had seen before in the shadow of her mother. She wore a pink-almost purple dress with puffed sleeves and was taller than Myrtle. Her brown hair was curled in tiny ringlets at the front, over her forehead, and heavier ringlets towards the back.

"Master Farthington." This boy stood a good foot taller than her, and his voice was a little croaky. He wore a more reserved expression on his face, his skin was a deeper tanned coloured and his hair was black.

"Derek." The green-eyed boy stuck out a hand enthusiastically, *too* enthusiastically.

He wore a sneer on his face, this was the boy who she had met on the road. She gave him a pointed stare and did not give him her hand. Miss Pineswood scowled at him.

"What?" He asked incredulously, eyebrows raising.

"There's no need to be rude, *Master Pineswood*." Miss Pineswood glowered.

"Come on! We don't need to pretend we're some pompous idiots just because we're at *Mr Taskin's* party." He mocked, "We showed up, and that's more than *he* or *she* deserved."

Miss Pineswood's scowl deepened, and she folded her arms at the boy.

"My parents only came because they were scared of what Mr Taskin might be provoked to do if they didn't." The comment came from Master Fodderhill.

The whole group seemed to fumble at this uncomfortably.

"Well, we have the witch to thank for that, don't we." Derek jeered.

"My family has been looking forward to Mr Taskin's feast ever since they received an invitation." It was Finn who spoke, his soft voice was unwavering.

Master Pineswood gave Finn an exasperated look, screwing his nose up as if he'd caught a whiff of something rotten.

"Of course *you'd* say that."

"What's that supposed to mean?" Finn took a step forward, Myrtle saw some of that strange confidence that she had seen weeks earlier at the dinner table, when talking of Michael and Daffy. It sparked life in his now piercing gaze. Myrtle found her skin prickling.

"What do you think it's supposed to mean, *Strawby.*"

Finn stepped a little closer to Derek, his breath swirling the boy's fringe. Derek didn't seem threatened, in fact, one corner of his mouth was pulling back into the half-smile he seemed fond of. But his tough exterior waned a little after a moment, perhaps just because he lacked perseverance and so he replied with less anger.

"It means, for one, I'm not gonna act any more differently for Taskin or for your guest." Derek flicked his eyes to Myrtle when he said guest.

"He'll grow up one day." Miss Pineswood sighed, "I'm so sorry for my brother's uncouth manners Miss Beeswood."

"It's quite alright." Myrtle gave Master Pineswood one more wary glance up and down.

The conversation turned to idle chatter. Master Fodderhill talked about how his father was helping the Jensens break in some fillies. Apparently, there was a lovely, dappled grey in the mix who according to Miss Jensen would make a fine pony, she hoped for herself. Master Farthington was sure that he had tasted the strange cheese filled pastries somewhere before. Miss Pineswood then told everyone the name of the pastry and where it had come from before Master Farthington could hazard a guess. Finn whispered to Myrtle that the Pineswoods were merchants and Mr Pineswood travelled afar often, which is why she had known of the pastry. Miss Cobblinghill rarely spoke, Myrtle wasn't sure whether it was shyness or the presence of Myrtle herself that made the girl mute. Derek was subdued, he didn't add much to the conversation, but often grunted, or made little comments that were obsolete or downright inappropriate. No one took much heed of him, on occasion Miss Pineswood gave him a nudge.

Finally, the musicians arrived, their curved instruments gleaming, black shoes shining. There was a violin, a viola, a cello, flute and drum. Soon the room was filled with the glorious tones of music, weaving in and out, flowing like water; it begged feet to move and hair to bounce, and hands to find hands.

A Dance of Wildflowers

"May I have this first dance?"

Myrtle was surprised to find Finn, freckled face confident as he spoke. She hesitated, eyes wide. Why she hadn't even considered… that Finn or anyone close to her age would ask her to dance.

"Miss Beeswood?"

"Ah-Yes." The answer slipped out before she had time to decide whether a dance with the farm boy would be sensible. *Oh well, it would be impolite if I said no.* She consoled herself.

Soon the dance floor was filled with couples, trickling at first like the nervous scurrying of mice and then flooding. The musicians stopped to tune their instruments in preparation of the next song. She took Finn's arm, and he led her to the set. The set included the Merryweathers and she was thankful for their familiar faces. Michael Strawby was also with a girl who she didn't recognise and all the way at the very top of the set was Miss Pineswood and Master Farthington. The dance master announced the dance, The Rye on The Mountains, and gave a brief explanation as to the figures of the dance. It seemed simple enough.

Then the music began again, a sweeping melody held by the violin and embellished by the flute, while the drum kept a steady beat. And Finn was bowing, taking his flat cap in one hand and his other behind his back, face serious. She barely remembered to curtsey, taking the folds of satin between her fingers. He held his hand out to her, and she let her hand find his, fingers fumbling, bumping and then grasping. She glanced at his face, to see him beaming at her, the serious expression had faded as he was swept up in the moment, or perhaps he was laughing at her. Bright red peeked from her cheeks. Then suddenly she was swept up in it all and they were turning, Myrtle's dress puffing in the motion, its golden-yellow peeling out like a daffodil. Feet scuffling on the ground, hearts pounding.

Melody and memory guided her feet. Though the dance master had given an explanation of the dance, the steps had almost evaded her, it was only the memory of late summer parties in Wattleshire that allowed her to be somewhat graceful. Her shoe briefly collided with his. She hastily looked up, but Finn was still smiling, as if he hadn't even noticed the mistake. And suddenly, she was smiling too, as she cast off, weaving in between the other couples, and finally coming to the very bottom of the set where she took hold of Finn's hand once more. It was pale-freckled, like little flecks of mud that couldn't be washed off from a life on the farm, from a life in a quaint sandstone house with cows and a wonderfully lush garden. She could be happy there. She was in fact happy there. The thought struck her.

The tones of music wafted around them, the flute interweaving its flowing sounds with the low earthy cello. Her curls bounced as they stepped, drum beating. They twirled so fast Finn's cap almost fell off, and he had to bring a hand to his head. A laugh escaped her, but she immediately stopped the outburst, how silly it made her seem. But Finn was laughing too, a silly grin on his face, and so she let herself join in. As she spun, and skipped and twirled she felt the embarrassment fade. Finn's brown eyes shone like melted amber honey in the candlelight, his smile as wide as a dinner plate.

They spun, hands on elbows now, as the music moved to its crescendo. Feet almost slipping on the floorboards, giggling. She could see the room spinning before her, couples also turning, some faster, like Michael who was practically lifting his partner into the air, and some slower like the Cottonflowers, but all were beaming, faces shining in the light of the candelabra. Eyes glittering like molten gold, like syrup honey. The colours blurred and faded, flickering as they spun, and Finn's face became crystal clear, his springy dark brown hair curling in their wake, his cap now falling off, bouncing onto the floor. His kind almond shaped eyes.

D-

D a r k.

Behind him.

Something dark.

The shadows blended and bent.

But the room became filled with laughter and drowned in the shimmering candlelight. Finn slowed a little seeing an anxious expression on her face.

"I'm fine." She nodded to Finn.

The shadows wavered again, darkening every figure. Black bled from couples' shifting feet, pooling. Vines. Tendrils of red thorns and dark green leaves with flowers of wilting purple wrapped around arms and legs and slipped up the cream-gold walls of the hall.

Clapping erupted. The clatter of the party filled her ears once more. The dance had in fact come to an end. She was standing motionless. The room returned to its bright warm glow, shadows retreated, vines had slithered away.

"T-Thank you Miss Beeswood." Finn spoke, and then seeing her blank expression added, "Ah- for the dance."

"Oh, It's quite alright Master Strawby."

Couples were chattering all around her, slowly disintegrating into new groups as they found a different partner. She made her way back to the edges of the room, and found another pastry to nibble on, as she tried to make sense of what she had just seen. From the edges, the now mostly uncovered dance floor was polished red-oak boards so glossy that you could faintly make out reflections. The shadows of the new couples drifted slowly across the floor as new partners gathered. These shadows didn't bubble or bleed, they stayed attached to their persons. The hairs still stood up on the back of her neck.

"*Miss. Beeswood.*" Master Pineswood gave a bow, twisting his hand mockingly, "Would you be so kind as to let me have this next dance?"

It took all of Myrtle's control to not let a scowl cross over her face. She knew that she shouldn't refuse him, for it would surely make a scene. She did not want that kind of attention. Instead, she gave him a curt nod and let him take her arm. They came to a set and found themselves the bottom most couple. The dance master began his explanation of the dance which was going to be a slower paced slip-step called Polly's Locket. The dance was famously inspired by a story of a poor slum girl, called Polly, who while digging for potatoes in the forest found a golden locket. Instead of selling the locket, which could've gotten her out of poverty, she kept it thinking that the locket was too precious to sell.

And then the dance began, it was tedious, though Myrtle tried to enjoy it she wished it could've been over a whole lot faster than it was. Derek was a lazy partner, she was constantly trying to keep them in rhythm with the music, but no matter how hard she tried, she felt the drum beat pulse wonkily through her chest, like clocks striking out of sync.

She hurriedly snatched Master Pineswood's hand to turn him as the next couple was already beginning their turn. He wobbled, scowling at her. But she was just thankful that they were out of the way. Moments passed before it was their turn again, Pineswood attempted to catch her gaze, but Myrtle politely kept her gaze on the sparkling floorboards. Tracing each knotted swirl and striped line, until she was sure she had almost committed the boards to memory.

When it was their turn again, she held his gaze for a brief moment, but only so that he knew it was indeed their turn. She was sure that she saw contempt in his deep flint eyes. Just a flicker passed his features, but it was enough to drive her further into sourness.

At least the shadows stayed pinned to each person. They turned and cast down to the bottom of the set again, the slow swish of her dress followed her. She slipped down past the rows of couples. For a moment she caught a glimpse of Finn's flat cap, and then his warm eyes, like roasted walnuts in autumn. Recognition lighted in his eyes as he too saw her, but then they were wrapped up in the dance. He with Miss Pineswood and she with... Master Pineswood. Finally, the dance drew to its final closing chords. She curtseyed and was about to part ways with Master Pineswood. When he snatched her arm and leaned in.

"I know who you are. And I don't care whether others like you." He hissed. "I see right through your act."

All Myrtle could hear was her heart as Master Pineswood turned away. She could barely control her feet as she stepped to the outside of the hall.

Doors loomed before her, and she found herself heading towards them. They yawned wide, showing the starry sky as a blanket, the damp cool air a sea by which they hung, floating. Blinking. She let her hand find the gold gilded sides of the doors and leant out. The breeze stung her nose and ears. After a deep breath, she found herself gasping as the chilled air reached her lungs, like prickling tendrils. The courtyard outside was glowing with lanterns, their little fires held steady by the glass surrounding them. A large fountain sloshed and bubbled at its centre.

He's just a stupid boy. She told herself. *He doesn't know me.* She willed herself to forget the encounter, to continue enjoying the evening. After all, no one had heard what Master Pineswood had said and she hadn't run from the room. Had she? Had she exited too fast?

Myrtle turned and strolled into the frigid courtyard. The floral scents of roses, gardenia and chrysanthemums wafted on the breeze, they were pungent even with the cold breeze dulling their sweet tones. Carved marble benches stood around the edges of the courtyard and then beyond was the abundant garden. Oh! How her bees would have loved to feast upon the nectar laden flowers that were spread out before her. She walked to the fountain and peered over its stone basin, watching the water tumble and flow as it cascaded down the statues at its centre. The statues were of a knight on a rearing stallion. The stallion was depicted as powerful, muscles rippling on its shoulders and hind end, his strong neck bowed. Waves sprung from the horse's hooves and water spurt from its open mouth. It seemed little detail was given to the knight in comparison, he wore armour although from some angles it looked more like interweaving slabs cut into each other. It reminded her of the painting she had seen in Romero's sitting room.

She made her way around the fountain, fingertips trailing on the stone rim. The far side revealed a white gravel path leading deeper into the garden. It was lit by lanterns every four or five metres. The light showed thick undergrowth, twisted trunks and vines. Lilacs, their heavy heads drooping with little flowers, framed the trail and gardenia's soft white bounty gleamed in the lantern's glow.

Leaving the fountain's edge, she began to step down the path. The shine of the party between the great oak doors faded with each step. Soon she was utterly alone. The faintly flickering candles casting their feeble light before her illuminating more plants, varieties she had not seen from the fountain. Jasmine, its small-star flowers spilling, fell from tree trunks, lantern posts and crept along the path. Clematis was draped over a lattice arch way in front of her. Its bright purple flowers like pinwheels swirling lazily in the breeze.

S n a p.

She froze at the sound of the breaking stick, swinging around wildly, eyes darting back through the archway and up the white path. There was a willow tree swaying, its leafy curtains clapping quietly against each other. But there was something else. A vine. It was snaking along an outstretched branch, weaving and curling around a string of leaves. Scarlet thorns glinting in the gleam of a lantern. Myrtle shuddered. She made a step, as if to turn back, but the firelight behind her was too tantalising. Big green and orange moths fluttered around the flickering glass.

She sighed, perhaps she had been imagining it all, the vines, the shadows, they couldn't be real. Besides, she had been unusually jumpy at times and the encounter with Master Pineswood hadn't helped. Continuing down the gravel path, she came to another paved section, this section of the garden ended in a circle, like the first courtyard, but smaller. Lanterns poked between leafy oak trees. The sweet smell of roses filled the air with a certain warmth that the evening breeze couldn't shake. Myrtle found herself lost, for a moment, so caught up in the wonder. She paused, eyes closed and standing on the tips of her toes breathing in the scents of the wild garden.

When she opened her eyes the splendour of the evening sky fell before her. A charcoal palace for the winking stars and moon. In that moment, she wished for nothing more than to have her dear pony beside her. Of course, Hodgepodge wouldn't care for the glittering stars and moon nor for the fragrant garden, except of course, for flowers to munch on. But she deeply wanted her friend. Her companion. His velvet muzzle on her palms and warm breath.

After a few moments, she decided to head back to the party because the thought of the feast she could be missing made her stomach rumble. Master Pineswood certainly wasn't worth going hungry for. As she turned swiftly on her heels something caught her eyes. Something just beyond the rose bushes, between the gnarled oak tree trunks. Something that the light from the lanterns barely touched, that was wreathed in shadows. She moved closer, leaning over one of the shorter rose bushes, careful not to injure its delicate flowers. A figure. She frowned. Perhaps a statue? She drew a branch of the rose bush back, cautious, so as to not prick herself, and pushed herself through the bushes. On the other side now, she could see the figure better, as her eyes adjusted. It was a statue, a statue wrapped tightly in vines. The same vines she had seen on the willow tree. Thick, green vines, with bright scarlet thorns. The statue was frozen in a kneeling position, its hands covering its face, large grey-purple flowers poked from beneath. They were trumpet shaped. A stench wafted to her, it was sickly-sweet. Far less delicate than the roses behind her. It was an overpowering odour. So sweet, that she could almost taste the scent on her tongue, sweeter than honey. Not even sugar, boiled and refined would taste this sweet. She felt sick. Darting back through the rose bushes, she found an acrid taste in her mouth. It was metallic, like blood. She touched fingers to her lips, but when she searched her hand, it was clean. Perhaps she had bitten her tongue?

The beauty of the garden faded, as she hurried back to the glowing courtyard. Fear gripped her once again. Through the thick undergrowth she swore she could see the ground shivering with vines, red tips dripping with poison. She walked faster, and faster, as trees became thick like serpent's heads rearing and ready to strike. Now she was running. Lungs heaving, feet slipping on the gravel. Each lantern she passed drew her closer to the bubbling fountain, to safety. Though the dancing had not loosened her hair, the trees she ducked under, tore at her, and curls became loose. Something scratched at her cheek. Something grazed her leg. Something gripped her, she was sure.

Finally, ahead of her appeared the golden doors, wide open. Blurred figures nestled safely inside. She stopped, huffing as she reached the gurgling fountain, her hands on her knees as she tried to catch her breath. Once her heart had begun to ease its thrumming, she shot a glance behind her. There was now a stillness to the garden, the willow trees stood sullenly, draping leaves motionless. The great oaks were quiet. The smaller bushes and flowers along the edges of the quaint path once again looked inviting and welcome. She must have imagined it all, the vines and the bright thorns, the stench of the purple-grey flowers. In the darkness she had become anxious, once again. She stepped over to the fountain and perched there, smoothing her dress and making sure that her hair had not fallen out of its bun.

buzzz...zzz

A bee drifted slowly through the air, its back shining in the lantern light. It shouldn't have been up at this late hour, it should have been asleep, snuggled in its hive surrounded by thousands of other tiny warm bodies. She brought a hand up, and it landed on her finger. Its wings fluttered against the breeze that abruptly started again. It was one of her own bees, the stripes a blend of orange and yellow, making a warm-bright tone. The strange product of her own bees and Daffy's. One from the new Queen Rose's colony. The bee didn't stay long, it clearly had important business to attend. It launched off into the air, flying away down the white gravel path.

The bee faded into the shadows and then reappeared as the next lantern light hit its back making it glow. Soon the bee disappeared altogether. Myrtle turned back to Romero's mansion. She could smell a myriad of scents, sweet, sticky and hot. The tender smell of roasted lamb and the savoury taste of gravy. Apple sauce stung the air with its tang and many other scents too of which she hadn't the faintest idea what they might be.

She left the fountain and walked swiftly across the courtyard into the light of the doors. Sure, enough the banquet table was set, all the guests were waiting patiently around the edges of the room as Romero made the final toast. He was rambling about how life could be changed in an instant, and that this party was one of the best he had ever had the pleasure of hosting. He thanked everyone for coming, especially due to his previous grievances. Then he asked five families to come to the stage, the Pineswoods, the Smiths, the Walters, the Charles and the Meadowbrooks. Unfortunately, only the Pineswoods and the Smiths had attended the party but nonetheless both families rather hesitantly came to the stage.

Romero publicly apologised to them for the particularly heinous ways he had treated them and gave both families a lady's small chest with articles of jewellery and precious silver and gold coins. The families stood dumbfounded.

"I know that I must've mistreated others as well, please, if you feel that I have done you wrong, let me know so that we can settle this, and so that I can repay you."

The guests were hushed by this and unsettled by such a display. Myrtle too, felt herself grow very quiet, Romero had truly changed, what could've made such a rich calloused man so generous? Surely it was not merely his legs being made symmetrical. It was as if fixing his leg had in turn fixed his heart.

"I've also paid tutor Mary Smith her wages for the next five years so that even the poorest among the village may have an education, and the school will be open an additional two months per year."

There were many gasps and whispers, and then finally someone began to clap, it was Finn's father, Mr Strawby and then the whole assembly erupted with cheering, whistling and clapping.

"And now to the feast my guests!"

With a raised glass Romero's speech was finished and the banquet table was uncovered. The table was practically spilling over with scrumptious food fit for royalty. Stews, fruits, roasted vegetables, glazed lamb, chicken with a spiced aroma that Myrtle had never smelled before. The green of the asparagus next to roasted eggplant and the bright red of a steaming pot of beef. The colours of the foods seemed to blend and mix with each other in a rainbow. Dotting the rainbow were plates full of breads and thin pastries that looked as though they would crackle with one crunch. A whole pig stood at the table's centre, its round body a crisp tan and a strange spiky fruit protruding from its mouth.

Myrtle found herself piling her plate high, with many foods that she didn't know the names of. The guests were assigned to places on long tables around the edge of the hall. She found her place next to the Merryweathers and eagerly sat down. It took all of her control to make sure she had cut the food into polite chunks before biting into them. And it was delightful. Every dish had a unique taste. She was told that the spiced chicken was something called a curry, which was an everyday meal in the far east. The glazed lamb was so tender it seemed to melt on the tongue. The pig was succulent and lightly smoked. The roasted vegetables were served with gravy seasoned with rosemary, the pumpkin was sweet, the potatoes were soft but crunchy on the outside. These were surely the best dishes she had ever tasted.

"Miss Beeswood, how have you been?"

It was Mrs Merryweather who spoke as she took a chair beside her. Myrtle quickly finished her mouthful before replying, for a moment she worried that perhaps she looked a little messy from her garden stroll, but she pushed the thought away.

"Yes, I have been quite well. Have you been well?"

"Yes, I've been very much at ease since you came and collected Daffy's bees. It was awful seeing them become more and more poorly and feeling so… helpless." Mrs Merryweather picked at her food.

"You can rest assured knowing they are doing very well with me. They've recovered fully and have even been producing a little honey." Myrtle smiled.

"How wonderful, I am glad that you are taking care of them," Mrs Merryweather returned the smile, then she went on, "Your mother was also a Beekeeper, yes?"

"Yes, that's right, and my grandmother, and great grandmother -and so on. I am the eleventh generation in a long line of Beekeepers." Myrtle answered.

"No wonder you are such a skilled Beekeeper then!" Mrs Merryweather's eyes gleamed, "What kind of family does your father come from? Is he also from a long line of Beekeepers?"

"My father is a potter, and his father also was a potter. His family name was Smithfield before he married. There haven't been any Beekeepers in his family, at least not that I know of."

"Pottery is a very fine profession." Mrs Merryweather nodded, "My uncle was a potter."

"Yes, it works out very well for mother and father, because my father makes all of the clay pots and hives." Myrtle agreed, "My mother still uses clay pots for the honey. Since coming to Wendermere, I've started using glass jars. I shattered a few too many of my father's pots on the way here!"

"How lovely that their careers work together."

Then Myrtle grew more serious, remembering the mystery surrounding Daffodil Clivesfield.

"I have been wondering if you might help enlighten me Mrs Merryweather… I found out that Miss Clivesfield…." she began, "Well I was up at a lumberjack's lodge in the mountains between here and Winspern. There is a great waterfall that falls into the Giant's Eye and on a tree surveying the waterfall I found the initials D.C. and M.S."

Mrs Merryweather nodded, "Oh yes, Daffy and Michael loved to frequent that spot. It's very romantic." She laughed, "Yes, I am sure that you could spend several hours up there finding all the initials couples carved into trees, and even then, you wouldn't have found all of the spots!"

"Oh-" Myrtle was surprised, "So you knew then about Mrs Clivesfield and Mr Strawby?"

"Oh yes, everyone knew about Daffy and Michael." She lowered her voice to a whisper and dipped her head closer to Myrtle, "They were going steady!" And then she chuckled again.

"Have you heard, then, that the Clivesfields disagreed with the match?"

Mrs Merryweather paused mid mouthful frowning, but then continued her bite.

"Yes, we all knew that they thought Michael was… a little beneath her."

"Have you thought that perhaps her family disapproved so much of the match that they might even send her away?"

Mrs Merryweather's frown deepened even further as she chewed the stewed lamb she was eating more briskly.

"Perhaps that's why the Clivesfield's were acting so strangely before she disappeared. Because they knew that *they* would be the ones making her disappear." Myrtle went on.

"Oh Myrtle, you're so full of imagination." Mrs Merryweather laughed, "You are such a dear girl!"

Myrtle was a little put out by this response. Perhaps Merryweather was hiding something to discredit her claims so quickly, but perhaps the elderly woman just didn't want to think creatively. She went back to her plate, cutting into a soft butternut pumpkin slice. After a moment, she heard a soft sigh from Mrs Merryweather.

"I'm not sure that they needed to send her away." the older lady suddenly grew very quiet and serious, "Daffodil rejected Michael's proposal all on her own."

A Basket Full of Pie

Sunlight filtered in through the window, falling in dapples across the wooden table and floor of the little cottage.

"It's perfect." Myrtle breathed.

The cottage was an inviting home. The walls of the room were lined with bookshelves, a fireplace in its corner, chairs and stools sat about the place beckoning visitors to rest. One might find it cluttered, the bookshelves were still packed with books, the table a messy array of pens and papers both blank and ink filled. Crumbs too were scattered over the table and under a cooling rack, although they were barely indistinguishable from the thick dust that covered everything. At the table's centre stood a stain-glass vase with crumpled roses and daffodils. The cottage looked as though it were frozen in time. It was clear that Mrs Clivesfield's parents hadn't wanted much to do with their daughter's belongings once she had disappeared.

"Well, it's yours if you want it." Mr Strawby smiled and handed Myrtle two metal keys on the palm of his hand.

Myrtle took the keys and turned back to the room sighing, a big, long happy sigh. She could have only dreamed of such a place as this to call her own. Finn stood in the light of the doorway, peering into the cottage but not setting foot inside. He wore a blank expression on his face. She felt a flicker of annoyance, though he was mostly expressionless, that said more to her than a condemning glance would have. He suddenly spoke.

"It'll need a lot of cleaning."

Myrtle rolled her eyes, at the wall of course, not Finn, "Never mind that,"

"And we can, of course, offer our assistance with such a clean, I'm sure." Mr Strawby stood scratching his beard, "Although, I suspect that my wife might be a little better help with all of this dust."

"I'm sure I'll be quite alright, Mr Strawby, I'll get this place cleaned up in no time." Myrtle started, "It's a gift enough that the village has given me this place to have all to myself!"

"Alright then." Mr Strawby nodded slowly, "Let us know if you need our help with anything. -And of course, our farm will always be open to you."

Finn shuffled his feet outside, fingering the rim of his flat cap and then pulling on his suspender slacks. He said nothing, but looked for all the world as if he was barely able to contain himself. Mr Strawby made his way out through the door, but Finn lingered there a moment.

"We're berry picking by the river today." He announced then he remembered himself and stuttered, "W-would you come?"

Myrtle blinked in surprise, it took her a moment to answer as she hadn't the faintest idea how too.

"Well-" She pursed her lips, "It depends how much time it will take me to clean."

*　*　*
*

The dust rose, filling the room with haze as the afternoon sunlight streamed through an open window. Her bees had come to join her, as she sat sprawled on the floor sifting through papers, caught up in the world of Daffodil Clivesfield. Most of the papers were disappointing, many were cooking lists and recipes. A great deal were also ledgers filled with numbers. Some scrawled with haste and others written in careful checklists and equations. A small pile of coins on the table indicated that perhaps she had been counting money. Perhaps she had recently received an inheritance? Or perhaps the ledgers were not for money at all, but maths required for new recipes. There was nothing that barred a Beekeeper from receiving inheritances, or even small amounts of money from sponsors, family or friends, however payments from patients were out of the question. She had also come across a handful of poems. Most signed with the initials M.S.

Like lilies from the fields,
Thy hair a brightness yield,
Daffodils could not in all their splendour,
Be as beautiful or as tender,
For you are a treasure by a chest concealed,
My Daffodil Taylor Clivesfield.

She turned over the poem to reveal its blank underside. This particular one had no initials, but she had found several others in a similar style signed off as M.S. It was now almost beyond question, M.S. was certainly in love with Daffodil and M.S. was almost certainly Michael Strawby. As the papers were shifted, her fingers found something metal beneath.

She rifled through the pages and clasped at what had been hidden, It was an earring. In the shape of a delicate silver teardrop and porcelain white, that depicted bright daffodils at its centre. The painting was so small that she could scarcely believe such a tiny painting was humanly possible. It wasn't a messy daffodil either, but with shading and detail. The kettle whistled on the stove, and Myrtle stood to attend to it. The earring would be a mystery for another day, she folded it in a handkerchief and placed it within a drawer. Perhaps she would uncover its missing twin as she cleaned. It had been hours, and the sunlight now was growing orange as it glanced through the window. She poured the water into a cup and glanced out the window surprised to see the orange glow of sunset. Leaving the steaming kettle she rushed to the window. The sun was indeed beginning to set between the walnut trees and behind the forest of pines. *Am I too late to go berry picking?*

The thought came with a startling disappointment. The scent of the apple pie left to go cold on the cooling rack wafted through the cottage kitchen. She hadn't meant to bake the pie all for herself but hadn't been quite willing to decide who she might want to share it with.

Was there any harm in checking whether the girls and boys were still by the stream? She decided, for curiosity's sake, that she would go and hurriedly began stuffing a wicker basket with the pie and a flask of tea. She then whisked off to the yard where Hodgepodge was happily grazing and upon seeing Myrtle in a hurry, the complete buffoon galloped off. She huffed angrily.

"Come back here Hodgepodge Eveningswood!" She yelled after him, but he paid no heed until she resorted to apple pie bribery and produced a thin slice. Only then did he whinny and trot back over to her. The bridle went straight over his head.

"Ha! I've caught you!" She gave him a mocking grin and climbed onto his back hoping for the best as she clutched the wicker basket tight with one arm and the reins, extra tight, in the other.

"Now, let's be nice and sensible Podgy. Absolutely no galloping!" Hodgepodge immediately broke into a trot down the driveway, threatening to ruin the apple pie in the basket. Myrtle decided she would have to settle for a slightly smoother gait, the canter and so urged him into the faster pace. For once the pony made her feel like they were gliding, the wind rushing through her hair, yellow dress billowing behind them like a cloudy sky. Before long the rush of the stream filled her senses and she drew Hodgepodge to a walk, as she scanned through the bushes. The path became rockier here, loose stones clacked as the pony stepped on them. The bank of the stream became visible for just a moment through the thick undergrowth, and she spied thorny raspberry bushes. She halted Hodgepodge as she contemplated scrambling down the bank to pick the berries by herself for, she could neither see nor hear any of the others.

Down the road a white blur raced, she flicked her attention to the path and heard the panting of a shaggy haired dog It stopped as it drew near Hodgepodge and whined.

"Biggans? Biggans?" a voice called from down the road.

She could just make out a figure scrambling out of the bushes.

"Biggans? Biggans! Oh there you are-!" The figure had sighted her dog and then, surprised by the company, stopped her frantic run. "Oh- H-Hello."

Myrtle's heart leapt into her throat, this was a girl she had not seen before, and the sudden thought of making a new acquaintance was…

"Miriam, did you find him- Oh hello Miss Beeswood!" It was Miss Pineswood that appeared out of the brush, her blond hair had acquired some leaves and twigs since last time she'd seen her.

"Miss Pineswood." Myrtle nodded.

"Oh, I'm so glad you came, Finn said he had invited you!" Then she looked at the young girl who had finally secured her dog, "How rude am I-! You have not met Miriam-I mean Miss Smith."

"I am pleased to meet you, Miss Smith." Myrtle drew her attention to the girl once more, who had dark hair tied in a ponytail. She was tall and had tanned skin, hinting that she may have had eastern ancestors.

"Happy to meet you too." Miss Smith called back as she patted her dog.

"We're all down by the stream, you must come! There are just far too many berries for our own good. I'm afraid my brother is already practically sick with them!" Miss Pineswood grinned, pushing back her tousled hair, and frowning as she realised just how much of a mess it was.

Myrtle let Hodgepodge loose to chew his own way through the raspberries though she gave his smacking lips a harsh glare as she disappeared down the path, knowing he would probably end up in some kind of trouble. The path declined steeply from the roadside, the prickly raspberry bushes pushing on either side and finally ended in the pebbled stream.

"If it weren't for all these raspberry bushes, a former Miss Farthington, who lived in Wendermere a great many years ago, would not have invented the most delicious pudding in all existence." Miss Pineswood informed her.

"I haven't yet had the chance to taste Wendermere Pudding." Myrtle answered.

"Oh, it's good." Miss Pineswood's eyes became wide, "Very, good."

"I assume that's where the stream got its name from?" Myrtle asked.

"Indeed!"

Once down by the stream Myrtle was surprised to see both boys and girls ankle and even calf deep in water. The girls had knotted their dresses just below the knees or left them to trail in the stream. She wasn't bothered by the prospect of mud, after all she had spent many nights camping when she first arrived in Wendermere, but for some reason the picture before her of the girls in the stream incited an uneasy feeling. Their laughs echoed, like the gurgling stream as they slipped on the smooth worn stones and splashed through the stream's dappled surface. The raspberry bushes were so laden with rubied fruit that they drooped over the stream's edges, over-shadowing the glassy water in tantalising reflection.

"Martin! Stop it! Hahahaha- Stop that!"

It was the abrupt giggling of Miss Jenson that caught her attention further upstream. As Master Fodderhill was proceeding to flick water at her face, and then dash out of reach when she attempted to splash him.

Master Farthington was filling a basket beside Master Strawby, they too were conversing a little more quietly than the others, both boys' hands were stained a brilliant red. Even the shy Miss Cobblinghill was chattering in excitement with another girl she had not met. Myrtle was disappointed to find Master Pineswood standing on the bank's rocky side, with another boy who she did not recognise. They were both periodically throwing berries on the girls and boys in the stream. With all these new faces, it suddenly dawned on Myrtle how many people had not attended Mr Taskin's ball.

"I see that you've come prepared." Miss Pineswood jolted Myrtle out of her thoughts as she gestured at the basket Myrtle was carrying.

The basket was of course concealing the apple pie and a flask of Mary Grey tea, both were steadily growing colder, but the thought of producing them felt awkward… nevertheless she handed the basket to Miss Pineswood.

"Oh, I brought some apple pie and tea, I hope there is enough for everyone."

Miss Pineswood's blue eyes lit up and her smile deepened as Myrtle opened the basket lid to reveal the pie and flask.

"Miss Beeswood, what a delight you are!" And then she added, "And I think I know at least one boy who has already eaten far too many berries today…" Then in hushed tones, "And I don't think it would be a travesty to *anybody* if he missed out on your apple pie."

*   *   *
*

Nine figures lined the bank of Wendermere Pudding stream. Their bare feet dangling in the water. Miss Pineswood had somehow made the apple pie into nine satisfying slices, which each boy and girl was presently enjoying. Master Pineswood had barely chewed the pie before swallowing it down whole and Myrtle made her contempt known to him with an icy stare.

"How we have the same mother…. I'll never know." Miss Pineswood shook her head,

"Do you have a brother Miss Beeswood? I sure hope that you haven't been subjected to the special kind of chaos that a brother brings."

"No, I only have sisters."

"Oh! How delightful, I would give anything to have a sister. How many do you have?"

"Three, two older and one younger than me."

"What are they like? I've always wondered what it is like to have sisters." Miss Pineswood sighed wistfully.

"I'm not really sure it can be described." Myrtle frowned, "I have never been without sisters, so I wouldn't know what makes it special."

"I see," Miss Pineswood looked taken aback for a moment, "Well, what do they do? Do they have professions? Are they married? Do they have children?"

"My oldest sister, Gwendolyn, is newly married, but she barely seems to return to her own home. Tara the second oldest works as a teacher at the Wattleshire orphanage and Penny is only eight, she spends most of her time playing with dolls, or chasing 'fairies' in the garden."

"I wish Derek had never spoiled fairies for me!" Miss Pineswood chuckled, "I used to play hide and seek in the garden with fairies. That is- until Derek came upon me one time! He gave me such a fright that I fell over backwards. Then he poked me with sticks until I conceded and told him what I had been doing. Once I explained about the fairies… well he stood there and laughed at me. He then told the other boys at school, and they all came over to mock me. It was enough to ruin fairies for me, forever."

"I am not sure I ever believed in fairies." Myrtle fumbled with the tea flask and the six little cups she had brought.

Miss Pineswood looked as though she were going to say something, lips pursed, but then nothing came out.

"Would you like some tea, Miss Pineswood?"

"Yes, please!" Miss Pineswood smiled.

Myrtle proceeded to pour Miss Pineswood a cupful of the floral tea. Miss Pineswood took a sip, and her smile grew somehow even wider, how she did that Myrtle had no clue.

"Oh, Myrtle! This is truly the best tea I have ever tasted!" She said, perhaps a little too loudly, "And this apple pie is just to die for!"

"I'm glad," Myrtle mustered a smile for the ecstatic girl, "The tea has my bee's honey in it, so I have their hard work to thank."

"Honey! Why yes, I thought I could taste something a little different, how lovely." Miss Pineswood murmured, "I must confess that when Finn first told us about you, I was very excited to meet you. - Even without Finn's *alluring* description of a magical girl who commands the bees! - I wanted to meet you from the moment we saw you riding down the road in your cart. And, well Miss Beeswood, I hope that we can be great friends."

Myrtle had no idea how to respond to such a statement, she never thought that the life of a Beekeeper would allow her to be in possession of 'great friends'. She wasn't even sure she knew what a 'great friend' was.

"I think that Master Strawby's description of me, is greatly exaggerated Miss Pineswood. Yes, I talk to bees and sometimes they listen, but I am just a Beekeeper."

"Yes, but a magical one!" Miss Pineswood took another mouthful of the pie, sauce dripping down her fingers. She attempted to lick the sticky droplets before they threatened her green dress and apron.

Myrtle had almost forgotten that beekeepers existed who kept bees that produced honey without healing qualities. When her parents had told her of this soon after beginning her training, she could hardly believe such a thing. She remembered her mother explaining that while all bees could produce healing honey, not all beekeepers knew how to draw out their magical qualities. The Beekeeper's creed came to her mind, and she found herself mumbling it under her breath.

"A Beekeeper's duties are sacred
and what is lacking will be given,
Our power does not come from within us, we will not flatter
ourselves with such thoughts lest they be our end."

She was startled to find Miss Pineswood peering incredulously at her and realised that perhaps the girl had been able to hear her words. Her cheeks grew hot.

"Beekeepers only borrow the powers of the bees, they do not possess any power themselves." Myrtle coughed a little awkwardly.

"But then how do they find these magical bees? Why aren't all beekeepers magical?" Miss Pineswood frowned and then laughed, "If I was a beekeeper and had the choice, I would most certainly want to have magical bees rather than the regular boring ones."

"I…" Myrtle hesitated, she was about to say that the bees were granted power through the vows and tender keeping of their Beekeeper, but then you could argue that perhaps Beekeepers were magical after all. Her mother had taught her that while all bees could produce healing honey, it would often take a long time, patience and perseverance on the Beekeeper's part. Even then, the bees may never produce honey with healing properties. This was why many 'magical' bee hives were kept in families, each family producing new Beekeepers of their own to pass the hives to, some of these Beekeepers would tend to a nest left at home while others would travel to villages in need. If there was any girl in the village who wanted to become a Beekeeper and take up the vows, they would be trained by an existing Beekeeper family and a portion of that family's hive would be given to the new Beekeeper once they had taken up their vows.

Then the words of the creed came to her again '*Our power is lent and borrowed from the Wild King*'. Her mother had spoken of how a Beekeeper could do everything right, be self-denying, kind, always tending to the sick and the hives, but in the end, it was the King who granted the honey its healing abilities. But she felt silly saying that. She didn't know anyone who had ever seen the King, only legends and stories of deep magic, a still voice in the dark. It was important for keeping the Beekeeper's legacy alive, but an ancient part of it. She knew that her parents believed that there was a King, after all he was supposed to be fighting for all of Evermone on the Northern Front. She had often wondered how much her parents truly believed the King really influenced the Beekeeper's life. She would hear them sometimes pray to him late at night when she crept past their room. Though she knew the books on their shelves about the legends of the Great Wild King, she only read those stories as a young child. Perhaps there was something in that strange whisper she rarely heard, or the way the bees knew which herbs would heal the sick. But, perhaps, the King had died centuries ago in battle, and the voice she heard was just an imagining. She gave a grimace. It would be pointless to try and explain where the magic came from, it felt silly.

"I suppose some Bees are just magical. I believe it has something to do with how a Beekeeper treats their bees, and so perhaps not all Beekeepers know how to care for their bees to achieve this magical quality." Myrtle finally answered.

"Oh…" Miss Pineswood's frown deepened, "So… Theoretically, all bees could become magical?"

"In theory, yes I suppose." She took a sip of the tea, "But, I have personally never met a Beekeeper who has tamed their own bees."

"Laur-Miss Cobblinghill told us of how you healed her brother." Miss Pineswood grew sombre, "He surely would've died if you hadn't come to Wendermere."

"He was not *that* close to death."

Vivid images of the man who *had* in fact died in front of her bubbled up, she found herself getting lost in the frightening event once more. It seemed so long ago, but yet the horror was seared into her mind. The man lying, chest heaving, pale face scrunched in agony. Once more she saw him gasp and die. Had she really heard the Wild King's voice? At the time, she was sure that she had, quietly, in the awful stillness of death. She had cried out to him and perhaps he had answered.

"You have seen worse then?" Miss Pineswood asked, taking another bite of pie, the apple-cinnamon sweetness filled the breeze around them.

"Yes, much worse."

Clearly someone had been listening in on their conversation for she was surprised to hear a boy's voice exclaim loudly.

"Of course she's seen worse, she saw a man die."

Unsurprisingly, it was Master Pineswood who spoke, a queer smile upon his face, viridescent eyes flashing as he stood knee deep in the stream. His cheeks were stained red from the raspberries.

"Or rather, she *let* a man die." He added.

"She's a witch." his eyes locked with Myrtle's, "Who else could raise the dead?"

The bankside was oddly quiet. Not one of the children whispered. Not a pie was heard being crunched, nor the squish of baked apple or the sloshing of tea in a cup.

"Miss Beeswood is *not* a witch." Finn abruptly leapt from the bank, his feet sinking into the smooth stone bed of the stream.

"Prove it then *Myrtle*, show us you aren't a witch. A necromancer." Derek mocked, "I'm sure she only raised that man from the dead to become her slave."

"Miss Beeswood has nothing to prove." Miss Pineswood spoke, "In fact, Miss Beeswood was just telling me that she in fact does not possess any power."

"Well then how does she do magic? Has she sold her soul to Narsh."

"Derek! Don't be ridiculous, do you really still believe in those fairy tales? Oh! Must you have such an overactive imagination brother!"

"Bugs and Beetles, twigs and needles. She will take your soul from you. Tread the paths of thorn and stone that end in deepest darkest hues. There you'll find her moonlit form with nothing in her gouged-out eyes. If you hear her silvered tongue cry out, you'll know her wicked lies." Derek chanted.

"I can't *do* magic." Myrtle finally spoke, though her heart thudded so hard she could barely hear her own voice, and there was a slight wobble to her words.

"Then how did you raise the man from the dead? How did you heal Romero? Laura's baby brother?" Derek demanded, "You know she thinks she's better than us, don't you!"

Derek's voice was almost at a shout as he turned to the boys and girls on the bank, his teeth gritted now in a look more worrying than the smirk. Myrtle tried to regain some sense of composure, reminding herself that this was just a boy, a young boy at that, who threw raspberries at girls and made cruel jokes. Finn looked even more infuriated, his hands gripped into fists. His brow drawn into a long frown, but as he turned to look at Myrtle, his fists fell open. She caught his brown-eyed gaze and found something she had not expected as she drowned in their intensity. A deep and tender wound, one that sought answers in her own eyes.

"M-My bees produce magical honey... I cannot do magic without them!" The words came out far more uncertain than she wanted, but she managed to turn them into words of defiance.

"And I am sure that's just the kind of cover up a witch would use. You're all the same, your kind. Everyone else might be too scared to say it, but you're just a greedy hag, who came to the village to suck us dry!"

She found herself in disbelief, of his vulgar words. They felt searing. Like the lick of a whip against her chest. Tears pricked at her eyes, but she held on. He couldn't see her cry. It was a weak response, with little evidence, surely he would back down. But the bank was quiet. When her gaze found Finn again, he looked defeated, all the anger had disappeared from his composure and his eyes conveyed something more; disappointment. *Why?* Had her defence not been good enough?

"And this is the way you thank Myrtle for making us all pie?" Miss Pineswood's voice was now a low growl, her chiding had turned from that of a teasing sister to that of an enraged mother, she looked ready to spank him, "Clearly your ego is as big as your stomach! And you'll grow fat, old and die alone because of how arrogant you are!"

There was real shocked silence that accompanied her words. All of the children were dumbfounded at the trembling Miss Pineswood, fists balled ready to knock her brother over the ears. The dappled sunlight swayed as the breeze shifted in the trees, making the light dance across the stream and for a quivering moment upon Miss Pineswood's face, now streaked with tears. An angry sob rose from her throat.

Myrtle barely knew what she was doing. The moments that it took for her to run from the stream to the dirt road flashed past like the memories of a bad dream upon waking. She could hear the girls and boys behind her, the children exclaiming as she got up and left. It made her run all the more faster. Her feet skidded on the gravel, branches along the trail snapped at her shins. Her focus was fixed on trying to find her pony. She reached the road.

"Hodgepodge!" She yelled, hands around her mouth as she shouted.

For a moment she was motionless, panting on the wide road, wildly searching the bushes. A crack sounded deep in the forest on the other side of the road. The children were there behind her, they were calling. She turned, hesitating. The panting figure of Master Strawby stood crouched at the entrance to the path that led down to the stream. Then, she darted towards the other side of the road, running blindly, twigs whipped at her face. Trees became indistinct as she raced past, eyes squinted. She pushed further and further into the forest until the trees obscured her view from the road and she was sure that the children had stopped following her. But now she didn't know where she was.

Somewhere through the haze of panic the thought occurred to her that Hodgepodge could not have come this far. He wouldn't have fit through these trees. But, still she went on. The trees grew closer together here, thin trunks crowding around her. She pushed on through them, puffing hard. A cool breeze hit her face, and she gasped from the sudden cold. With it came the realisation that she had gone too far. *There will be a short-cut. The forest will meet the river somewhere through here.* She continued on shivering. Bending back branches now to push past them. Breaking twigs to stop them from scratching her. There was something through the trees.

She breathed a sigh of relief. There was a break through the trees, a small clearing. Carefully, she shimmied through the trunks until her feet found grass and-.

A figure was bent down in the clearing. Her heart skipped a beat. Bathed in golden sunbeams was a kneeling statue framed in twisted vines. Its head bowed and crowned in writhing green. A gust ruffled the flowers of weeping purple, they bounced in the air. Myrtle's heart thudded within her chest. Glistening red thorns. A statue just like the ones in Romero's Garden. Why was this one deep within the forest? She leaned closer, feeling the whisper of cold wind on her cheeks. There was something different about this one. She bent to peer into its stone face. Beneath the mess of vines was the vague imprint of a woman's face. Eyes closed, lips downturned. Hair of tumbled vines falling over her shoulders. In her lap, something yellow was hidden, where vines clasped hands in a messy embrace. Something odd. Myrtle crouched down. It was a singular stem of daffodil. The flower's frilly edges peaked from the tangle of vines. How odd.

A shiver ran down her spine and a sweet stench washed over her. The hairs on the back of her neck prickled. She had gone too far. She had to turn back, the forest was too dense to continue. Besides, the children would have likely forgotten about her and Hodgepodge had probably eaten through all the raspberries in Wendermere by now. He would be wondering where she was. She turned away from the queer stone figure. Leaving it forever to kneel alone in the gap between thick trunks. Her feet crunching on the forest litter as she made her way back to the road. It took so long that she was scared that she wouldn't find the dirt path again. Finally, it appeared through the trunks as the spaces between them widened.

"Podgy!" She exclaimed, spying the rounded rump of her steed.

The Breathing Forest

The gentle clip-clop of Podge's hooves resounded from the road down the mountainside. It was accompanied by the crunch of the wagon wheels. Myrtle was on her way to spend the week in Pinesdale, a town that lay to the north-east of Wendermere. She was looking forward to the time away and, though it would be more work, the thought of a new town was refreshing. They passed the bridge into Wendermere and the sound of Podge's hooves became sharper as they hit the stone. The town square wasn't busy this early in the morning, but the townsfolk were starting to emerge. Her eyes found the bright blue of Miss Pineswood's as the girl stepped from her house. Seeing her made Myrtle's cheeks burn, and she ducked her head down.

"Miss Beeswood!" Miss Pineswood called, her eyes alight as she stepped toward the cart, "I had been so hopeful that I might bump into you!"

Myrtle brought the cart to a halt, though she wished dearly to hide. The girl's gaze searched her, but Myrtle was mute in reply.

"I wanted to say how sorry I am for my brother's behaviour. He is a fool of the worst kind." A deep sigh came from her, "But, I hope that even if you cannot forgive him, you might still be willing to be friends with me."

"Would-. Would you like to have tea with me? I have just put on the kettle and Derek is out with the boys. Yesterday I baked a vanilla and raspberry cake, though I am afraid it is a poor substitute for that apple pie of yours."

"Sorry Miss Pineswood, but I am on my way to Pinesdale and I cannot delay as it is a long journey. I likely won't return to Wendermere until the end of the week." The words left a bitter taste in her own mouth.

"Oh." The girl was downcast, her gaze turned to her toes for a moment before looking up again, "Well, I will just have to look forward to tea upon your return. And you can expect a full feast! I'll do my best to bake something as scrumptious as your treats."

"Alright then." Myrtle nodded politely.

Miss Pineswood's face was a full smile as she waved goodbye to Myrtle, wishing her safe travels.

* * *

*

Honey pooled in Myrtle's wooden bowl reflecting the concerned face of a woman in the amber. She took the bowl gratefully but could not hide the fear in her granite eyes. The woman hadn't seen a Beekeeper before, as her family had recently moved from further north. A bee flitted over to the bowl she had now accepted from Myrtle and landed on its tapered edge. She watched and listened as the woman drank the honey. Her breathing slowly cleared from its crackling rasp to a clear long sigh. Her granite eyes grew bright, and a rosy blush returned to her cheeks. Somehow even the woman's dull brown hair seemed to become lush and shiny within an instant.

"I-" The woman gasped in surprise, "H-How…. How did you do that?"

Myrtle couldn't stop a smile from spreading over her face as the bee alighted on her hand, "It's their magic."

The woman sat for a long moment, the realisation washing over her. Myrtle watched intrigued as the woman pinched herself, then frowned, rubbing the skin.

"I'm not sick." She whispered, and then turned and exclaimed to what seemed like nobody, but was most likely intended for the whole house, "I'm well!"

"Mother?!" a call came from over the other side of the room, and a youth appeared.

"John! Fetch your father!" The woman suddenly leaped up with fervent vigour, not in the least bit wobbly.

"Just be careful, Mrs Ravenswake." Myrtle scrambled to stand as the woman was already dashing into the kitchen, "You'll still need to take a spoonful of honey every day, for a few weeks."

The youth raced from the room, flinging the front door open with such a force that it soon crashed shut behind him. A distant "Father! Father! You must come now, Mother's been healed!" could be heard.

The woman, however, did not seem to have heard Myrtle as she began diving through her cupboards. After finding a ladle and pot she turned back to the forgotten Beekeeper in her living room.

"Oh, how can I thank you Miss Beeswood! I feel as though you've added years to my life, I have scarcely been able to leave that chair for a decade…" Mrs Ravenswake stood pensive for barely a moment, "I have so much work to catch up on!"

She grabbed a cream apron that had been slung over a chair to collect dust, she shook the garment out, which resulted in a momentary cloud of particles that made Myrtle sneeze.

"It's quite alright." Myrtle coughed as a tickle in her throat threatened her voice.

"You must stay for dinner, we'll have so many lovely things…" Mrs Ravenswake drifted off, "We'll have lamb stew with buttered potatoes… and corn…. Cake! I-I'll make a cake!"

And just like that the Mrs Ravenswake was off again, down the hallway this time. Myrtle hadn't the time to object to the invitation, though she knew she would need to leave well before dinner. Pinesdale was a long trot from Wendermere and an even longer trot back up the mountain to her little cottage.

*　*　　*
*

They were headed home, down the narrow valley path between Mt. Mappleleaf and Mt. Plowman. Soon they would skirt the edge of a large forest, known as the Breathing Forest, and then after stretches of paddock and farmland, they would arrive back in Wendermere. It had taken her the better half of an early day's travel to get there, and she, along with Hodgepodge, had spent five days camping in Mr and Mrs Peartree's fields. The work had been exhausting, and she had needed to stay up well past her normal bedtime every night, in order to visit all the sick in the small town before the end of the week. When she had finally emerged from the fifth house Hodgepodge had regarded her with a curious expression. He had sniffed her thoroughly as if to make sure that she had not gotten herself into trouble, then he sighed a long hard sigh as if to say, 'Oh, so you've really got absolutely no excuses for keeping me up this late then'. She had offered him an apple as recompense, and it seemed that all was well with the world once more, "Oh well I suppose if you're giving me an apple!" Myrtle had mocked the silly pony.

While in Pinesdale, Myrtle had also attempted to track down the whereabouts of Mrs Cloverfoot, Daffodil's former Beekeeper mentor. Most of the townsfolk's memories of the senior Beekeeper were hazy, many could recall a town healer who used honey, but few could say anything meaningful about her. One elderly woman could remember her visiting with a younger woman in tow, this must have been Daffodil. None of the townsfolk could give any accurate accounts of Mrs Cloverfoot, of her appearance, where she lived nor relatives, with many saying that they believed they hadn't seen the healer in several decades. Myrtle found this all a little disturbing. In fact, if Mrs Cloverfoot left Pinedales a few decades ago it would mean that she wouldn't have been living there while training Daffodil. All this begged the question, where was Mrs Cloverfoot? No one could say. It was as though she had vanished, but unlike Wendermere, Pinesdale couldn't care less about their former Beekeeper's disappearance.

Now they were on the road once more - the pebbly road to Wendermere. The bare valley echoed the steady clopping of Podge's hooves. The Beeswood bees buzzed gently in the cart, their winged forms slowly drifting with the breeze inside of the fluttering curtain that separated them from the outside. Myrtle found her eyes heavy, her hands slowly sinking down to fall on her crumpled buttercup dress. The reins now loosely lying within her aproned lap. Her head began to tilt, her flaxen curls tumbling across her eyelids like a curtain.

* * *
*

Myrtle awoke blurry eyed to the soft squish of hooves on moss and a splattering of rain on her forehead. She startled suddenly, eyes wide as she took in the road. The road she didn't recognise, for this was not the way they had come before. Then she gasped as she saw the trees. Trees so wide you could fit a whole room inside them. Maybe even a whole house! They towered above the little rickety wagon like mountains, the leaves so high up that their individual shapes were now too tiny to spot… and the sky, well why… the sky just wasn't there. It disappeared under the dense canopy, but somehow the rain still reached the forest's floor. The leaves were like slides, the rain's droplets slipped down, plopping from one leaf to another, gathering momentum and volume before falling to the forest floor. And with another jump, Myrtle realised that the floor was not just moss, but riddled with deep puddles. She leaned over to peer into one as they passed. Something swished into the dark cover of the yawning tree roots which enclosed the pool's sides. She turned her attention to the distant forest and found that the puddles were *not just* puddles, but whole lakes! "Hodgepodge Eveningswood, where on earth are we!"

The pony turned an eye to glance at Myrtle but gave nothing more. The trees were silent, no branches rustled, no

131

leaves crunched, but only the dull plop of rain as it thudded into the dark pools and dropped onto the ferns and moss that covered the forest floor. She could tell that they were on some kind of road, though clearly an ancient one that was not heavily used. It had been cleared of any large obstacles and at one stage had been laid with gravel and stones, but moss had reclaimed the path. It had evidently sucked up its fill of water and was now spreading out, claiming what little of what wasn't part of its soggy empire.

An unexpected rush of wind swirled through the moist forest, stirring ferns and causing the rain to veer off its downward fall. The gust swept up Myrtle's hair, with the force of a gale and sent her dress ballooning around her. She closed her eyes tight. Her hair swayed back against her shoulder, she shuddered and opened her eyes. The air around her was still once more, but only for a moment. Then the wind moved upwards with even greater force, making the formidable tree trunks shake, making them sway and creak and….

Myrtle once again could not stop a shocked gasp from escaping her lips. The trunks themselves had come alive, expanding as the gale moved through the forest trees circling up and up, breaking the silence with its low grumbling of branches creaking and scraping and thudding. Leaves clattered way up in the sky, and then, it was gone as quickly as it had come. All was still, aside from the gentle plip, plop of rain. A droplet fell on Myrtle's eyelash as she stared up at the sky. She moved to brush it off.

With a terrifying force, wind swept down from the top of the trees to the very bottom of the forest's floor, with such tenacity that it thrust the surface of the pools outward, splashing the water everywhere. The low growl of wind subsided once more. Myrtle could feel her heart pounding in her ears as terror seized her. But her pony kept plodding along. He was clearly unbothered by the gale force winds that had just catapulted water from the ponds and made the tree trunks bulge.

The trees now appeared relatively normal, their large trunks still once more. Podgy dropped his head for a moment to sniff the ground as he walked, but there was no grass for him to chew. *Then why would you have come this way?* Myrtle sighed.

"I know this is what I get for falling asleep and letting you take the reins, but could you be *any* less infuriating Podgy!"

She looked back at the cart's precious cargo, her bees. They buzzed softly, apparently, they were also relatively undisturbed by the gusts. One of the winged creatures flew to land on her nose, she picked it up on her fingertip. The bee was an older one of pale yellow, one from her family's hive. It perched and licked its feet with curled proboscis and antenna swaying.

"Do you have any idea where we are?" She asked.

There was no reply. Of course there was no reply. But she couldn't help feeling a little disappointed, she had no idea how they were going to get home before dark. She didn't know whether Hodgepodge had branched off their charted path following an existing fork in the road, or whether he had ploughed through a field and chanced upon this one. Should she turn back? Should she continue? For surely the path would eventually lead out of this forest? She was so tired from all the work in Pinesdale that she was sure she must have slept for many hours, her mind was still partially in that fog of sleep even with the anxiety of the situation creeping upon her.

The clop of Hodgpodge's hooves turned to the harsher crunch of stones. Myrtle peered once more over the edge of the wagon to see that they were walking over a little stone bridge that spanned another large pool of water. Dark shapes scuttled away as they saw her face. She was sure they must have been fish, but how the fish had come to be in the middle of a dense forest she knew not. She supposed that if they continued, they might be able to find some place to pitch a tent for the night. Her hands found a woollen blanket folded beneath the cart's awning and she wrapped it around her shoulders.

"Have it your way then." She grumbled to the pony, Hodgepodge flicked his head in reply and then stopped to shake the droplets of rain from his fur.

"But if this rain keeps up, I'll be climbing into the cart, and you'll be on your own again!" She grunted at her pony, who in return picked up a jog. Once on the other side of the stone bridge, Myrtle leaned back over the wagon seat to try and spy the creatures that lurked just below the surface of the pools. One by one the creatures slowly swam out from beneath the tree roots they were hiding under.

They were definitely fish. But they were not fish. They had heads that were oval shaped, with big black eyes. Two feathery fin-like appendages were attached to their head almost like ears. They were all different colours too, some so grey they blended into the dirt, others were green, and various shades of orange. She spotted one further up the back that was the most vibrant purple, like that of an iris.

They had tails that were longer than a fish and shaped like the paddle of a boat. Instead of fins, they had two front legs and two back legs, she wasn't sure whether the limbs ended in fingers because they were so small.

The forest around her was suddenly caught up in a growling gust of wind once again. Swirling the forest floor, making the trunks of trees bend and undulate with its tremendous force. Sweeping Myrtle's hair in front of her face and making Myrtle's bees land abruptly on the cart's floor silencing their hum. But as suddenly as it came it left, lifting up through the trees, chattering branches and a final tinkle of leaves as it left. Myrtle frowned and looked upon the towering trees around her, they were unmoving, but bloated, rounded as if they were…. And then like a gasp the air rushed back down, giving the pools life and animation, as they splashed outwardly.

As if they had been holding their breath, and let it escape again.

"We're in the Breathing Forest." Myrtle whispered aloud.

Of course it made perfect sense. She had heard rumours about the curious forest but had never supposed that it actually *breathed*. Interestingly enough the strange water creatures were not perturbed by the sudden rushes of air, and neither was Hodgepodge.

"Why am I the only one who thinks this is unusual?" Myrtle glanced at Hodgepodge who continued along in his squelchy jog.

The bee's hum caught her attention once again as they went back to their business as if nothing had ever happened.

"Huh." Myrtle nodded and then shrugged her shoulders. The forest and its curiosities would have to remain a mystery. For now, she would need to preoccupy herself with how to get back to Wendermere.

* * *
*

The forest seemed to go on forever, although the rain did at least periodically stop. Myrtle found herself being pulled into sleep's tender embrace, the forest's rhythmic low grumbling breath became like some kind of lullaby. Before long she was forcing her heavy eyelids to stay open. The moist forest grew slowly dimmer. The light of the world's sky, though unseen, was still a part of the strange forest. Which didn't seem fitting to Myrtle, because all other aspects of life's regularities seemed to be stripped away here.

But as the sun left this side of Evermone, far above the canopy, the forest began to show another of its oddities. It began to glow. Luminescent lights flickered beneath the giant trees' trunks. Not all at once, but gradually they dotted the forest, until it was light enough for Myrtle to see the pale outlines of trees and pools, ferns and moss once more. The glow came from mushrooms. She must have drifted off to sleep altogether, for suddenly she was aware of the pitch black of the treetops, and strangely bright illumination of the forest floor. The light was so bright it highlighted details she hadn't noticed in the dappled shade of the daytime.

A smell wafted through the air, it was sweet, like maple syrup only somehow sweeter. Myrtle's eyes darted in search of the source. The forest, up until this point, had only smelt of damp earth and wood. The scent stuck out like a thorn in a bed of harmless chamomile. It was faint like a splash in the air, maybe it came from some bush down the path. She breathed in deeply, trying to pinpoint why the scent was so familiar. Hodgepodge paused, it was the first time he had stopped since she had awoken from the unfortunate nap that started the whole situation. He turned his long shaggy head to look at Myrtle, dark eyes glinting in the light.

"What's wrong? We can't stop now. You brought us into this mess, and you'll have to help get us out of it." She murmured to him.

He snorted in reply, then sighed and continued. Myrtle shrugged, he probably just wanted a carrot. But something strange had come over the forest, and it took a few moments for Myrtle to realise that the forest had stopped breathing and instead a chill breeze was rattling the branches like hollow bones. Unlike the breath of the forest, it was starkly unrhythmic. An Inky smudge flicked across Myrtle's vision, through the trees. She jumped, eyes trying to follow where the impression had disappeared to. Hodgepodge continued his clop through the forest, she looked to his ears, which were pricked forward, perhaps he had heard something.

A chill gust swept some leaves up from the forest's floor, ruffling Myrtle's hair. A prickle went down her spine and she shivered. The dark shape darted again through her vision. This time Hodgepodge flicked his pricked ears and stopped abruptly, turning a wary eye. Was it a coincidence? Could Hodgepodge have also seen the shape? Myrtle felt her heart leap, thudding in her throat. The shadows of the giant trees cast against the glow of the fungus waned and skewed. Hodgepodge threw himself into a gallop.

The breath was flung from Myrtle's lungs as the pony launched himself. She found herself gasping as his hooves thundered on the ground beneath them. The lights of the mushrooms flickered past them like stars in the night. Hodgepodge slipped on the mud, and for a frightening moment they found themselves stumbling down a deep murky bank into midnight waters. The glow of the mushrooms didn't reach into its depth, it yawned open like a monster's mouth ready to swallow.

Hodgepodge reared away from the pool snorting and bucking.

"Slow down!!" Myrtle yelled, but the words were snatched from her mouth by the pony's speed.

Trees like giant walls seemed to hedge them in, and the ancient road had long since disappeared. Myrtle squeezed her eyes shut as they hurtled towards moss covered bark, but at the last moment Hodgepodge squealed to a halt sliding on his back hooves, his face was just inches from a tree. Myrtle took the opportunity to gather up the reins, as tightly as she could, but he still tried to take a swift turn to gallop off in another direction.

"Settle down!" Myrtle's voice quivered, "Stop this nonsense!"

The shadowy figure had clearly been some animal. Perhaps the strange fish could move on land? Perhaps they had a cousin? There were many logical explanations, she was sure of it. There were certainly no large cats or wolves living in the forests near Wendermere and its neighbouring towns. But… perhaps there were bears. Myrtle grimaced but tried to keep her fear to herself. No, it was more likely to have been a deer, or a rogue sheep. She urged Hodgepodge on, in a much more orderly fashion, brushing through the ferns and back to the now barely visible path, giving thanks that they had only strayed a few metres from it.

"Hodgepodge Eveningswood, if you start any nonsense again, there will be *no* carrots waiting for you on our return." She muttered to him, "And don't expect *any* extra apples, or berries either! After the stunts you've pulled today, you'll be lucky to get plain old hay!"

The pony flicked his ears agitatedly, and though he continued down the road, Myrtle had to keep him from trotting off on multiple occasions. Eventually he seemed to settle, though his ears remained pricked and alert. The light of the mushrooms, now fell unwavering on the ground, spotting the forest in the ethereal glow. The chill breeze swept through the forest, but it was little more than a whisper. Ferns barely rustled in its wake. But Myrtle still felt a persistent and nagging fear. It wasn't enough to make her heart pound, but it was enough to raise the hairs on the back of her neck. She kept glancing over her shoulder, though she wasn't sure what she was expecting to see. As the night went on Myrtle noticed huge fungi shelves growing on the giant trees, now also glowing with ethereal light. The shelves were so large that she could easily stand or even lie down on them. She gasped in wonder at the glowing staircases that wrapped themselves around the trees, up and up into the deep night sky.

It was like she had chanced upon some fantasy kingdom, something from the books of the Wild King and the children's fairy tales. She wasn't quite sure how it could be real. But then another thought came to her, suddenly as if it wasn't quite her own.

How then, could bees from the wild be led by a child?

She found herself nodding, the magical bees of a Beekeeper were definitely not the only curiosity in this world. Something sweet wafted through the air again, but this time it wasn't the strange too-sweet smell, but the smell of something cooking, and something warm. Down the road, a pinprick of warm yellow appeared and as it got closer, she saw that it was the yellow glow of a window, just through the trees.

"Hodgepodge!" She quivered with both excitement and fear, "Maybe you weren't quite as daft as I first thought!"

The prospect of spending a night in someone's comfortable, warm house, safe from bears or strange shifting shadows overwhelmed Myrtle, bringing tears of relief. *Thank the Wild King,* she whispered. As they drew closer to the little cabin, smoky trails drifted in the air, and sparks flew from its brick chimney. The pale-yellow window illuminated an old hunched figure working busily in the kitchen.

Sweeter than Honey

The amber glow from the window fell like dripping honey on the outline of Myrtle and her pony, the light stirred a dancing twinkle in their eyes. From here the glow of the luminescent mushrooms winked dully behind them, through the trees and undergrowth. It seemed that the strange pocket of glowing fungi did not grow here. They had trotted up the cottage's cobblestone driveway feeling the weariness of a long day…and an even longer diversion. Before Myrtle could knock on the pine door, she saw it crack open, the warm light spilling out like a sunrise.

"Why hello there! Come in, come in! Oh, you poor dreary thing! And your gorgeous little pony, he must be ever so tired after your long journey. Here I'll take him to the stable for a rest, but you just head right on inside and go sit on the armchair beside the window."

The woman was old, but had aged tenderly, with hair like spun-silver streams, and face wrinkled like thin leather… the kind of well-worn leather that you might find in a trusted old purse, so reliable that you wouldn't have noticed any holes, until all of the coins had slipped out.

"-Oh… But-" Myrtle stuttered, about to protest, but she could already feel her grip loosening on the reins as the woman offered a kind hand. She was suddenly hit by a wave of exhaustion that made her sway. *How long had she been travelling? Surely only a day?* It felt like weeks since she had seen another face, the thought came with tears that threatened to cloud her vision.

"Oh, my dear-." The woman's brow was drawn together in concern, her grey eyes glistening, "How frightful the journey must've been! You'll be alright, you're with Melinda now and I'm going to take good care of you! Just head on right inside, I'll be with you in a moment."

And with that the reins were handed over. Hodgepodge's head hung low, and his steps were heavy as the woman walked away with him. Myrtle stepped toward the inviting cottage, but not before the woman looked back toward Myrtle. Her face was caught in the light cast from a window, it made her eyes glitter and the creases in her face deepen like cracks in pottery.

"There's already a spare bed made up for you, young Beekeeper." She smiled and then walked off into the shadows around the cottage's corner.

Myrtle glanced toward the cart down the road, hidden by the long driveway and behind bushes. Her bees would be fine there for now, she sighed and walked through the doorway into the cottage. It was bright, so bright it took her eyes several moments to adjust. A kettle steamed on a crackling fireplace. On the floor beside the fireplace a fluffy tortoiseshell cat lounged, its tail flicking lazily. Next to the fireplace was a narrow staircase spiralling steeply upwards. In the corner beside the window a dark green armchair stood, its plush pillows reminded Myrtle of sleep, and she found herself snuggling into its arms, pulling the blanket from its neatly folded place on the side. She spotted drying herbs strung near the fireplace, and a delicious scent drifted through the open doorway of the next room, which was the kitchen. The scent was candied.... like honey... but somehow sweeter. It was intermingled with the smell of toasted bread, freshly baked and out of the oven. She spotted another doorway as she turned to look over, and past the fireplace. The room it led to was pitch-black, she assumed it must be a bedroom perhaps, or cellar? Maybe a sewing room? Her eyes flicked back to the kitchen and its enticing scents, her stomach grumbled. She sighed, closing her eyes for a moment and let the warmth of the cottage ease her restless heart.

*   *   *
*

Myrtle opened her eyes to swirled oak panels above her head. Dark knots from which branches had been cut stared down at her like large black eyes. Like horses' eyes in the moonlight, she smiled and stretched ruffling the patch-work quilt. Her last memory had been on the armchair. Had the woman really carried her to bed? *How embarrassing,* Myrtle grimaced. And her sleep had been so deep that she didn't have the faintest memory of it. She sighed, grabbed hold of the quilt and nestled down into it. The bed felt like a cloud compared to the cart and tent she'd been sleeping in the past week. Light filtered through a curtain drawn window accentuating the A-Frame roof above. She lay in silence for a few more moments, not wanting to get up and to start the long journey home. *Home.... Was Wendermere really home?*

The memories of her time in Wendermere, now that she wasn't there.... Well, they felt lonely... She was startled by how removed she was from those images in her mind. The images of her bees humming on the gentle breeze, busily pollinating flowers. Juicy strawberries brought to her in a basket by a freckled boy. The Ball, a flurry of brilliant figures floating like clouds to the rhythm of dance. The children sitting, legs dangling from the bank. Something black flicked at the corner of her bed. She sat bolt upright, eyes darting wildly about the room, they came to rest on the black tail of the tortoiseshell cat. Its green eyes half-slits and its tail lazily swished as it lay at the bottom of her bed.

"And who are you?" She whispered to the cat.

It jerked its head to peer up at her. Eyes regarding her features, taking her in as if examining her very being. It blinked once at her and then turned away. Myrtle didn't have much experience with cats. She removed a hand from the blanket to stroke the cat, but as soon as the shape of her hand hovered over its patchwork back it leapt, and jumped down from the bed onto the floor boards.

"Oh? You don't want a pat?" She asked.

Irritation glinted in its green gaze, as it stood, tail flicking like a striking snake.

"Alright then I won't pat you."

"How did you sleep, dear one?"

She hadn't heard the steps of the silver-haired woman. She felt her cheeks grow hot.

"Enough that I've clearly forgotten myself and the time!" She hurriedly began throwing back the covers of the quilt.

"None of that now," Melinda tsked and pulled up a stool to the bed's side.

It was only then that Myrtle's gaze found the tray that the woman held in her long fingers, a tray with an ornate little pot of steaming tea, and a plate full of buttery pancakes. She set the tray down on the stool and stood back to pat down her apron.

"Now…. you wouldn't happen to be getting out of bed after I've brought this tray all the way up here?"

Myrtle grew scarlet and lay there blinking up at the woman like an owl fledgling, not knowing how to respond. The woman in turn laughed.

"Don't worry yourself, it's much too late to leave today anyway. You won't make it out of the forest before dusk fall, particularly if you're travelling down Wendermere-way."

Could she really afford another day away from Wendermere? Had Mr Merryweather been taking the honey for his cough? Had Mrs Cobblinghill been waking up with a sore back again? Not to mention the villagers who had no doubt gotten ill or injured while she'd been in Pinesdale. They needed her, she was the only Beekeeper in the area.

"I was due back…. Two days ago."

"They managed without you before, and they can manage without you for another day." Melinda shook her head, "But the question is will you manage, without needing to manage someone?"

Myrtle frowned at this, *will I manage without needing to manage someone?*

"It's alright to stop worrying for a day, the world will still be waiting for you tomorrow." Melinda came and sat herself at the edge of Myrtle's bed, "How about you think about yourself for a change?"

Myrtle nodded slowly, her eyes darting to the delicious steamy breakfast waiting for her. Well, she'd certainly be no help to Wendermere with an empty stomach.

"Thank you, you have been too kind." Myrtle finally spoke, she grabbed hold of the delicate teapot and poured the floral scented tea into a teacup with edges framed in golden vines.

"Let me know if you need anything and once you're done I'd love your help in the kitchen with baking." With a last smile Melinda left Myrtle to finish her tea and pancakes.

*   *   *
*

The kitchen was already producing the most mouth-watering scents, of lemon, thyme and lavender. Myrtle breathed in deeply savouring the smells.

"And how did you enjoy the breakfast?" Melinda's smile lit up her wizened face, a silver ringlet fell across her cheek as she worked dough on the table.

"It was delightful! You must teach me how to cook, I've never tasted such fluffy pancakes. And- the tea, do you mix and dry your own herbs?"

"I sure do and grow them." Melinda gestured for Myrtle to come over and handed her a rolling pin, "We're making potato bread. Now, do you know the secret to the best loaf of potato bread?"

Myrtle shook her head, taking hold of the wooden pin she scooped flour from an open bag and dusted it liberally.

"Lots and lots of butter! Mashed to fluffy-buttery perfection!"

"I don't think I've ever tried potato bread," Myrtle began rolling the dough carefully, as to not let it tear or let it stick. She then gathered the dough up into a ball to knead it once more. Melinda directed her instead to use the rolling pin like a meat tenderiser, and pound it into the dough.

"Well, you're in for a real treat, potato bread is the best kind of bread!"

Once they had finished with the potato bread and it was baking in the oven, Melinda beckoned Myrtle to come see the garden. The path was overgrown cobble stone that had sunken with age. It was almost swallowed by the moss, but at intervals the stone re-emerged like the shiny hump of a dolphin's back before diving. The garden itself consisted of several stone rimmed beds with all manner of vegetables and herbs. Cucumbers, snow peas climbing up lattice, butternut squash and tomatoes. They collected anything ripe and juicy, placing the produce in a small wicker basket, which was overflowing by the end. It was a wonder how the garden managed to produce such an abundance of vegetables, as the trees towered high above them and blocked out the sky.

"Do you know how to weave a basket?" Melinda asked as they opened the cottage door to go back inside.

"I've done a little weaving, but never baskets. Oh! -" Myrtle caught a falling tomato before it hit the ground.

"Good catch." Melinda beamed, "Perhaps that's a task for tonight, it looks like this basket will be far too small for the harvest ahead."

They headed to the kitchen and took the now golden potato bread from the oven to cool. But it looked so good that Melinda decided it was best served hot anyway, and with a hefty portion of butter and fried tomatoes. Myrtle was grateful, as her stomach was rumbling, even though breakfast had been enough for three! They sat overlooking the garden, with cups of tea. The dappled light that spilled through the giant trees constantly quivered and danced in the unseen breeze. The glow of winged insects, lazily clustered around a fern here or a puddle over there. They looked almost like the tiny, winged fairies of old tales, an instant later she chided herself on how silly a thought it was. The firm back of the wooden seat behind her felt warm, though she wasn't sure how, the light shifted and changed so much down here on the forest's floor, it barely rested on one spot before dancing to the next. The scene of giant trunks and ferns, and luscious undergrowth looked deep and endless, you couldn't see far into the distance before it faded to a mesh of grey green. Instead of feeling the fear that yesterday's diversion had left she found a certain peace at being wrapped in the forest's embrace, nestled in its web. Then a thought came, was Melinda the only living, soul in this forest? If such gardens could grow and water was aplenty, shouldn't more have found the sanctuary of The Breathing Forest?

"How was our potato bread?" Melinda asked, "Do you believe it was a success?"

"It makes plain bread taste *very* ordinary." A little laugh escaped Myrtle and Melinda joined in the chorus.

"I do believe I would like another slice, if I may." and Melinda handed her another two slices, "Are you the only one who lives here, in the forest?" Myrtle murmured, taking a sip of the spearmint and chamomile tea.

"Yes, I believe so." The woman had a listless expression as she gazed far off into the forest.

"Has it always only been just you living here?"

Melinda seemed to hesitate, or perhaps she was just thinking, reaching back far into that long, long memory. The rustling of a faded purse, counting its coins. Myrtle turned to watch the forest once more, the distant shimmer of bugs ever fading and moving.

"No…. I wasn't always the only one." Melinda pursed her lips, "But, I have been alone for a long time."

"Do you ever feel… lonely?" Myrtle instantly regretted the question.

"I used to live in a village, but then I had enough of all the hustle and bustle. I got sick of it all, people everywhere all of the time. Sticking their nose in everyone else's business. They'd never leave me alone. I find the emptiness quite pleasant after that life. But I do get visitors here." Melinda replied, "and I welcome all who come to me as guests." She gave a laugh, "Most are quite lost when they find me, far more lost than you, Myrtle. Strangely enough all of them seem to need… rest and I see to it that they are given plenty of what they need."

"Well, I was definitely exhausted when I arrived yesterday." Myrtle nodded, but she felt a prickle of discomfort at Melinda's first words, which village had the woman lived in? Dare she ask?

"And how are you feeling now?"

"Honestly, I am still a little tired."

"Ah… well It looks like you might still need more time then." Melinda gave her a smile and sipped at the tea, "The ordinary life of a Beekeeper sure does take its toll, especially on such a young woman as yourself."

Myrtle nodded and took another bite of the squishy, buttery bread, it almost seemed to melt in her mouth, "I was… very displeased with Podge's detour into The Breathing Forest yesterday. But…. now I'm happy to say that perhaps it was probably just what I needed."

"You came through the Breathing Forest?" Melinda suddenly looked taken aback.

"Yes," Myrtle frowned, "I thought that's where we were?"

"Oh-" Melinda started, "No, the Breathing Forest ends a while back East of here. This is Ambling's End." She shook her head, "I can't imagine how you must have felt lost in that awful forest, with the tree's constant growling."

"It was alright, we got used to it, I was just concerned with getting home." Myrtle sighed, "But, I suppose I hadn't imagined it then? Do the trees… well… breathe??"

The woman nodded, something sparked beneath the surface of her gaze.

"Why do they breathe?" Myrtle replied, excitement bubbling up within.

"Magic." Melinda's eyes twinkled for a moment, "And by that, I really mean, nobody knows. The trees here don't do it. I know nothing of any other 'breathing' trees."

"Oh…" Myrtle thought for a moment, "Which way do your guests come from if not from the Breathing Forest?"

"Usually from the South, that's where the Coddling Swamp is and also from the West, from Ellendale."

"What kind of visitors?"

"Oh- well all sorts. Merchants, travelling through to Winnow Lake, messengers, doctors... You, however, are the first *lost* Beekeeper I've had the pleasure of welcoming."

"It must be interesting to hear of their different stories."

At this Melinda chortled, a loud, but not too pertinent laugh, "Of course, the stories are the best part. Once I lodged a manservant, of a Duke, no less. He was in such a hurry, travelling through both day and night, galloping on his midnight steed. He had fallen asleep in the saddle and his horse had wandered right into Ambling's End. He was very lucky to not have fallen off! But the nature of his haste was very intriguing." She leaned into Myrtle, eyes alight, "He was delivering a love letter to a lady who lived at Willow's Pier in Winnow Lake. Apparently, the servant was expected to make the long journey in just two days as the young lady was betrothed to be wed to a man whom she did not love. The Duke had not known that the lady returned his affections and for years he had tried to push all thoughts of the woman aside. Only when the lady had confided in a maidservant did the gossip finally reach the Duke's ears. She had revealed to the maid that her heart belonged to a man who had upheld her reputation when a scandalous situation had arisen at a ball. The lady had been getting out of her carriage when her dress got caught in the spokes of the wheels and tore the entire skirt away, all the way to her thigh.

"The Duke, having just come outside to welcome guests and seeing the dress rip, cooly took the woman from the manservant's arm and quickly whisked her away around the back end of the manor before any other guests could see. He then found her an elegant dress for the evening, one which his sister had left forgotten in the back of the wardrobe and escorted her back down to the ball. She was received by the rest of the guests with whispers of awe, as both having caught the Duke's eye and having one of the most beautiful dresses. Since that day she had been in love with the duke, though she hadn't the courage to say it. The Duke too had fallen for the lady, but for a different reason, firstly because she was very lovely to look at, and secondly because he noticed scratches on her arms, and light bruising. He realised that these marks mean one of three things either, she was an adventurer at heart, she was clumsy, or she was a victim. Any of these possibilities were intriguing to him and as the night went on, he found reason to believe that perhaps all three were true. She was a little shy, and the ripped dress suggested clumsy, which the Duke found endearing. But the shyness masked a fear, was she running from something or someone? There was also a strong independence about her, as soon as the Duke had escorted her to the other end of the manor she had attempted to leave, thinking it would be better to walk down the road a little way and flag down a carriage to take her home. And so, the evening went on and the couple danced away… but neither having the gall to say what they wanted. The lady and Duke parted ways at the end of the evening and never saw each other directly again."

Myrtle sat enthralled at the story's abrupt end. Her tea had been left to sit on a log stool and was steadily growing colder.

"What became of the duke and the lady? Did the messenger deliver the letter to the woman on time?"

"Oh," Melinda seemed strangely taken aback by the comment, "Unfortunately, I shouldn't know, for the manservant did not get lost twice."

"Oh, how frustrating it must be," Myrtle sighed, "To never know the end of the story."

Melinda swirled her tea with a tiny spoon, the delicate china clinking, like chimes in the wind.

"I wouldn't say so." Melinda took a sip of her tea, "What makes a story interesting is… how different it is… How… unexpected, or surprising, sometimes even shocking. A story is interesting when it is so different from everyone else's that it ceases to seem like real life… in fact sometimes it isn't real and that's what makes it so captivating."

Myrtle found herself frowning at this. She cast her eyes down, finding her tea, she took hold of the cup's slender stem and its saucer, moving the two to her lap.

"Take your life for instance." Melinda smiled, "It is like very few people in Evermone. You are a young woman, living away from home, making her own way in the world. And most remarkable, a Beekeeper, able to use magic to make bee's honey so powerful that it heals wounds." She paused, gaze intense as Myrtle sat, "And can even raise someone from the dead. It can overcome the one thing that mankind has never been able to overcome, the mystery of the next life…" A half smile came upon her face, but was gone in an instant, "Or the absence thereof."

"Myrtle, your story is the most remarkable of all stories. The power to give life even after it has been taken. This is like the power of kings, for who can save someone from death but a King? Only he can pardon a criminal from the death penalty, only he can acquire enough wealth to save the poor, to feed the starving, to pay a doctor to heal the sick. But you are even more powerful than a king, for you can pardon anyone, save anyone. A King's power only extends so far."

Myrtle felt a sudden cold chill, like a breath of sea spray. She shivered. *The power of kings?* She had thought of Beekeeping as noble, as sacred, but…. *The power of kings?*

"Well, we best get dinner ready, how would you like to learn how to cook rabbit stew?"

*   *   *

*

In the kitchen the warm glow brightened the whole house to an extent that the dappled sunlight high above the forest floor couldn't. The brick oven was smoking and flickering as they waited for the logs to burn down to amber coals. Then it would bake their maple cake to golden perfection. Over the table she could just make out the white, round belly of the cat, lazing next to the oven in the glow of the fire. The stew sat simmering on the other side of the kitchen where the iron stove was, the fire in its bottom cabin casting an ever-moving light through the cracks and grooves of its confinements.

Myrtle stood slicing carrots into small round pieces, Melinda beside her was taking care of the onions. Myrtle could feel the prickle of stinging tears and wiped an elbow over her eyes, sniffing. Melinda, however, with years of practice had calloused eyes, the onions did not affect her in the slightest.

"You've done this many times, I can see." Myrtle smiled as the tears freely ran down her face, she stepped away from the table to wipe her eyes with a handkerchief.

"Oh yes," Melinda chuckled, "I've been doing *this* a long time before you were even born. Surely you cooked with your mother?"

"Of course." Myrtle paused to blow her nose, "I often cooked with my older siblings, but I was always a lot better at baking, rather than…. Chopping the vegetables."

"Don't worry," Melinda looked up to Myrtle with bright, kind eyes, "It takes years to stifle the tears."

"Yes." Myrtle wiped the last of the tears and composing herself drew nearer to the table once more. As she went back to her chopping, she spied something on a cabinet in the back corner of the kitchen, nestled in next to the oven. It was a small figure, a statue of a horse and rider. She found herself walking over to it to take a better look and picked it up in her hands. The horse, its magnificent mane was swirled, front hooves leaping, tail sculpted like a wave. And… its eyes were furious, storms of rage and fear. The rider, a knight, paled in comparison. While the horse's muscles were moulded perfectly with tiny veins straddling the skin and wrinkles around the eyes, only a short nose protruded from the knight's face. There were not even eyes or a mouth. He also held a sword, but strangely enough from most angles the sword seemed to almost protrude from the horse's mouth, rather than from the knight's hand.

"I see you've spied my horse statue." Melinda turned around to see Myrtle.

Myrtle nodded, running a finger along its grooves, remembering suddenly why she'd been so drawn to it.

"I've seen a sculpture like this before." She turned to pop it back up onto the cabinet's topmost shelf, "It was in the garden of the richest man in Wendermere."

Wendermere… the sudden thought of Wendermere, why it… It felt hollow, lonely…. Alone. All alone-

"Do you know the artist behind the sculptures?" Melinda broke into Myrtle's thoughts like a splash of cold water.

"No, but I have wondered, they are very fascinating."

"Well, I found her, a travelling merchant. Some would even call her a mystic or a seer. She had the most luscious raven hair, striking green eyes, she was a very captivating woman. Even dressed differently, a mishmash of cultures, she wore a plain smock, that was cut off at the knees, shorter than I'd ever seen. The smock was embroidered with gems and beads from the deserts, and her raven hair was woven into this intricate braid, one of the likes I had never seen before. She was a very well-travelled lady, being a merchant, she had even crossed seas, all over Evermone. But, among all her exotic treasures, it was most definitely those statues which were the most famous. Because well, no one had seen anything like them before."

"Where did she find the statues?"

"Why, but that was the thing that made her story the *most* interesting. *She* was in fact the artist of these intricate statues." Melinda turned back to her onions with a mischievous expression on her face.

"Why was she a merchant if she was such a profound artist? Could she not have made a living from her art?"

"I asked her the same question, and her reply was that she would've never had the inspiration to create such art had she not travelled and seen the world. She's also now very wealthy because of it. I've been told many rich people commission her. Even though it costs a small fortune, that's why I just had to have one…. You see, it is a homage to humanity's individualism. A trophy for all the interesting stories." Melinda, finishing with the onions, picked up the chopping board and scraped them into the stew.

For all of the figure's details, the horse's rippling muscles, power and might, Myrtle couldn't shrug the feeling that the piece wasn't finished, and not only that the piece wasn't finished, but that if the knight upon the horse had been fully sculpted, the piece would've been so much more spectacular. But maybe she just didn't understand art.

*   *   *
*

After ravenously consuming a hearty bowl of rabbit stew, and then going back for seconds, Myrtle sat, belly warm, yet somehow still hungry, in the plush armchair by the window, bathed in the glorious orange light. She had been given a dress collar to embroider. The dress was a vibrant green that Melinda was sure would fit Myrtle if she desired. So now, Myrtle sat, fingertips pulling a silver needle through the white collar of the dress. Slowly coming to life, one stitch at a time, was a rabbit. Though, Myrtle wasn't really sure that it would indeed look at all like a rabbit in the end, or whether it would just be a swirled blob of browns and greys.

Melinda was more positive about the outcome, and Myrtle was thankful for the detailed outline of the rabbit that she had drawn onto the collar for her. Melinda sat only a few steps away on a couch by the fire embroidering her own project, a bag. Myrtle had caught a glimpse of it, and it was amazing, the stitches blending together like an oil painting, producing a rich and vibrant miniature garden. The old woman hummed as she sewed, Myrtle imagined the lyrics for such a little ditty would be about some grand legend or folktale, maybe a romance.

The light from the fire, candles and numerous ceiling fixtures filled the room with light brighter than day, and it was warm and toasty. It was beginning to remind her of home, her family settling into the evening… her mother to needle work, not often embroidery, but usually patching up somebody's clothing, whether that be her father's or siblings. But no… somehow this was even better than her family's evening, for that would often be filled with chores. Drawing a bath for her little sister, soaking a honey and lavender tea for her mother, applying a salve to her chest as she coughed. A heavy, heaving cough. One that seemed to crackle on forever without end. Finally exhausted, pale-faced her mother would slip into sleep, a sleep punctuated by rasping and gasping.

Just like the man who had died. clawing for his last breath... except at least in the end he was alive. Alive and well. While mother's sickness was end-.

"And how has your rabbit come along Myrtle?" Melinda had appeared, bag in hand, over Myrtle's shoulder.

"Oh-" Myrtle looked down to see the collared shirt, a rabbit's head now fully formed in the fabric, tiny nose, whiskers and all.

"How lovely! I knew you'd get the hang of it." Melinda smiled, "Such an accomplished young woman as yourself is skilled at everything she sets her heart upon."

But Myrtle didn't remember how she had come to create such an image. She had been lost in her thoughts, yet somehow her subconscious must have taken over allowing her to create this?

"I-I'm not sure how." Myrtle started.

"Maybe your magic extends to new realms?" Melinda laughed.

"Perhaps!" Myrtle found herself joining in with Melinda's laugh, "Perhaps there are more things I am useful for than just Beekeeping."

"Why of course-" Melinda drew another mischievous, playful expression upon her face, "I think that all Beekeeper's talents extend far beyond the hive, and many of those talents are in fact even more brilliant than the Beekeeping itself.

Sometimes I think it's the rest of the world that would like Beekeepers to see your talents as this; merely reduced to the healing properties of magic honey, because they want this magic all for themselves."

Myrtle nodded slowly, she hadn't ever asked whether the magic properties of honey could be extended to other talents, but perhaps.

"I believe you can do anything you set your mind upon Myrtle." Melinda leaned in, to whisper, "So why would you set your mind on something so small.... So small as a country village... when the power you wield could make kings fall on their knees."

With a Mask of Stone

Berry juice, the colour of deep scarlet, stained Myrtle's fingers as she accidentally squashed another ripe raspberry between her fingertips. The berries were practically falling off the bush, making its branches droop with the weight of the succulent juice. She absent mindedly popped one into her mouth.

"How many baskets do we need to fill to make the raspberry pie?"

"I'd say two baskets should make a couple of hearty pies indeed! Particularly with these large ones." Melinda patted the woven basket, which was large enough to fit even a few pumpkins, "You did well Myrtle, I knew you would take to weaving quickly. Perhaps this is another talent to add to your ever-growing skills?"

"Perhaps." Myrtle smiled, she couldn't help but feel proud of the two baskets she'd woven. They looked exactly like the ones Mrs Jenson would sell at market, and Mrs Jenson had most certainly been weaving baskets for a very long time.

"Well, I think that's enough from this bush, I always leave a little for the birds."

"Oh, of course." Myrtle felt a tinge of embarrassment as Melinda had been standing there for a little while now, surveying the bush while Myrtle had continued to pick at its branches. A pensive thought flicked through her mind as they harvested the next bush.

"I haven't seen many creatures in the forest… But in the Breathing Forest I saw these strange…. They were like fish but had legs and arms with feet."

Melinda turned to Myrtle with one of her mischievous smiles, silken curls swaying as she turned.

"You must mean the Fluges." Melinda spoke.

Myrtle nodded thoughtfully, she carefully picked her way back down the little slope, to the path. But she really didn't have a clue what a Fluge was.

"What are they?"

"They are amphibians, smart ones. Think of them as… the squirrels of the river. Very curious too, unfortunately sometimes they can be a nuisance."

"Oh? How?"

"They like to eat my vegetables! But luckily, they don't often travel this far."

*　*　*
*

Myrtle sat, having already consumed her slice of pie with ravenous endeavour. A steamy tea was in her hand, while she sat in the garden chair. Melinda sat beside her, although she had not eaten up her pie as quickly. Somehow, while she stayed here at Ambling's End, Myrtle's appetite had grown tenfold. She could eat a whole banquet of food and yet still feel hungry.

"I have another story for you." Melinda's hand moved to stroke the tortoiseshell cat as it brushed up against the leg of the wooden bench. "One, from another of the travellers who stayed here at Ambling's End."

"Yes?" Myrtle grew eager, Melinda would often recount stories as they ate, her memory was like a trickling stream and eating often seemed to dislodge a branch plugging her memory. Every story was new and vibrant. Each different, each unusual. Most seemed unfinished to Myrtle, but she was beginning to just enjoy the tale. Her eyes darted to the cat, its feline gaze gleamed at her curiously, tail snaking as the woman ran her hand along its back.

"'There was a man, his name was Ernest, he was blind, but had a good horse whom he was sure knew the way to Blackwood. Of course, his horse, a big black stallion, did not know the way to Blackwood and they both got lost at Ambling's End. Now when I saw them, I offered lodging, and the next morning he got on his way to leave, when I asked the obvious question, 'good sir, how do you suppose to get to Blackwood when you cannot see, and your horse has already shown that he does not know the way?'.

Ernest looked at me for a moment with an incredulous expression upon his face, 'don't you know? Did you not see the bees in my wagon? '

I replied, 'Do you mean to say that you are a beekeeper?' At this, Ernest chuckled a little, 'why of course not, but a Beekeeper gave me a few of her bees, I keep them in the wicker basket at the back of my wagon.'

It was then that I realised that he meant a Beekeeper of your kind, and not the ordinary one. 'And what possessed this Beekeeper to give you a portion of her magical bees?' I asked.

Ernest gazed off into the distance before replying with much pride swelling, 'Because she is the love of my life. Her bees will guide me home, for bees are always attracted to their masters. They brought me up the hills and through the Coddling Swamp and mark my words, they'll bring me through this forest to Blackwood.'

'But good sir,' I tried to reason, 'The quickest way to Blackwood Forest was already back through the Coddling Swamp and further up over the Great Plains.'

With full confidence he replied, 'There must be danger that way. The bees can sense it, they guide me to my love. I know it. They will. We will come upon Blackwood, and there I shall be reunited with the fairest maiden.'

'Perhaps, good sir, you have been duped? Are these bees really from the fair maiden's swarm? Can, you be sure?'

'I am as sure as the sun rising from the east and setting in the west. These are her bees, and they will bring me to her.'"

Myrtle sat quietly for a moment in thought, as she always did after Melinda's stories, "And did he make it? Did the bees bring him to the Beekeeper?"

Melinda shrugged, "I honestly can't say whether he did make it, for he got lost the first time." Then with a sudden little snort she went on, "I couldn't even tell whether the Beekeeper he was so smitten with returned his affections. After all, Beekeepers are attractive to men. Symbolising a magic so powerful, yet so unattainable, and if they can't have it for themselves, they want to control it, steal it. Let that be a lesson Myrtle, if you are smart you will never marry."

Myrtle felt a sudden blush come upon her face. Never marry? That wouldn't matter to her, she had always thought of herself as someone who would remain single. The life of a wife would be far too distracting, there were far too many extra duties to worry about, and she already had a great deal of things to worry about, never mind the thought of children running under foot, or even the ever-changing mood of a husband. Then a thought came to her, how peculiar it was that Melinda's stories were often of romance, whether it be unrequited love or a blossoming couple, and yet... she suggested that true romantic love, at least for a Beekeeper was unobtainable. The cat bumped Myrtle's leg, pushing up against her for a pat. It surprised her because up until now, the cat had regarded her with a certain coldness. She leant down to give it a stroke, letting her fingers brush back its ears and scratch underneath its chin.

"Why do you always seem to only meet such interesting people? And so many people in love?"

"Maybe it is because boring people don't find themselves on adventures that will get them lost and perhaps it is love that has blinded them so that they cannot find the right path home." Myrtle thought that Melinda had finished speaking but she went on, "You remind me of someone Myrtle, someone I knew not long ago. She was a self-driven, capable and talented young woman like yourself."

"Did you meet her here in the forest? Was she lost?"

"No. She wasn't lost. In fact, she was one of the few visitors who came to Ambling's End looking for me." Melinda answered, a look had passed over her, something unreadable.

"Did she come for a rest?"

"Actually, she came to me, to learn my ways. To increase her talents. She sought me out after finding I had left… left the village that I used to live in and managed to find me here, a clever girl."

"Well, you are a great teacher." Myrtle smiled, "I'm sure she found what she was looking for."

"That she did. Indeed, and I hope you will too, Myrtle."

*   *   *
*

A scarlet dress sat in Myrtle's lap as she embroidered sprigs of lavender on the cream collar of the dress. She was wearing the green dress with little rabbits that she had embroidered earlier. It fitted snuggly, and Melinda said it made her look mature. She was hoping the scarlet one might do the same. They were both of a less girlish fashion with stitched folds along the bodice, buttons ran up the centre, and the hem line was all the way to her ankles. Much like the rabbit, the lavender's slender stems, and swirled vibrant flowers came to life before her fingers, just like magic, creating for her an elegant dress. Within what seemed like mere moments, the embroidery was almost finished.

"I'd like to try something different, something more… challenging."

Melinda got up from the couch where she too was working and walked over to Myrtle to peer at her work.

"Why of course, and why shouldn't you test the lengths that your abilities can go? How about…" And she produced an ornate pattern, it was a wall hanging etched with the designs of a flourishing garden. There were sunflowers, poppies, and tulips. Ivy overflowed from a watering can and a birdhouse peeked from behind the grand garden beds. In the sky birds trailed and plumage flew. The scene was enough to get lost in, and it wasn't nearly finished. It was barely even started, the yellow sheen of a sunflower was the only colour on the bare canvas. Its threads were half pulled, probably from years spent being shoved further and further into some box or corner. But now Myrtle could use her newfound skills and bring the embroidery to life. Time went by like the steady clopping of hooves on a road, Myrtle found herself engrossed in the stitches, needle in, needle out, pull, check. Many of the flowers now lay embossed in the fabric, colours blending like a painting. She ran her finger over one of the roses and sighed a long, contented sigh. Turning the fabric over, she inspected the stitching work, she had been neater than expected. Her eyes caught sight of initials written in pencil at the far-right corner. A swirled *M.C.* Perhaps Melinda's? She was about to go on with the poppies when she found the smudged grey outline of a bee. It was flitting its way through the flowers. The sudden absence of bees filled the room with a silence that Myrtle had not felt before. Her heart leapt.

"My, my! You are making fast work of that panel!" Myrtle was jolted from her thoughts as Melinda appeared hovering beside the armchair.

"Oh, I suppose so." Myrtle muttered.

"You seem suddenly a little lost my dear, are you quite alright?"

"I-I think I might just step out to get some air for a moment." Myrtle found herself discarding the embroidery on the armchair as she briskly stood up.

"What has come over you, dear Myrtle? Are you feeling ill?"

Myrtle found herself walking toward the door, the wild thudding in her chest threatening her ears, hot and boiling.

"Is it your bees?"

Myrtle turned around to find Melinda's cloudy eyes staring back at her. The creasing of her pursed lips like soft leather. A well-worn purse, old and familiar.

"Oh, dear Myrtle, you have such a kind heart, always worrying about others."

Myrtle found tears welling up in her eyes, she didn't know why. But she couldn't hold her emotions at bay.

"Your bees are well and safe. Your Queens Petunia, Lavender and Rose are helping to organise their kingdoms, the worker bees are in turn finishing their busy day of pollinating, returning to make delicious, sticky honey. They are all safe, the guard bees have protected them from any foreign insects or animals. For bees will do what bees do, whether their Beekeeper is keeping a close eye on them or not. And a Beekeeper can even measure her powers by how efficiently her bees work when she is away. I believe Myrtle, that you and your bees possess great power. So do not worry about your flock."

Oh, but they are…. Well… they are safe and well. The thudding of Myrtle's heart became quiet.

"See this as another challenge… to flex your newfound skills, just like this embroidery. I am sure you will find hives overflowing with honey upon your return."

Myrtle nodded, she swiped at the tears. Silly, she had been so silly. Her bees were safe and well. She felt her cheeks grow red.

"After all, you have done what no other Beekeeper has *ever* succeeded in doing, raising the dead."

Myrtle found herself startled. The scene filled her vision once more of the man's gasping, clawing, dying. The stench of death and rot.

"Life, you could bring anything back to life."

And the man's chest rose and fell again, after a long anguished moment. His eyes flickered back to life. His flesh whole.

"A Beekeeper such as yourself has nothing to worry about. Such power does not have limits." Melinda's gaze was piercing, "Such power cannot be contained."

She had saved him. The sudden awe of the moment daunted her. She had brought him back from the dead.

"Now, how about we get you some warm milk and settle you down with a nice fluffy quilt?"

Myrtle found herself nodding as Melinda lay a hand upon her shoulder and steered her back to the armchair while she bustled around in the kitchen for some milk and a saucepan. She felt herself gazing out of the ever-lit house, bathed in its honeyed glow. The window reflected the light of the room back on itself, but if you peered closely, you could see the pitch-black of outside. Myrtle shivered. How cold and dark it looked, and the cottage so frightfully stark in contrast.

She walked to the bookshelf and let her hand stray across the spines. They were tones of muted greens, blues and reds, their titles embossed with golden lettering. There were titles such as '*A Hallowed Call*' and the '*The Dragon's Lair*', they would be old fables, but peppered in between were more intriguing titles such as, '*Herbs, a practical study*'.

Her fingers brushed against something metal, and her eyes met the dusty shelf to find a single earring. She picked it up and blew the dust off of it, revealing silver teardrop trim and- frowning she peered closer. Its china-white centre was detailed with miniature daffodils, their tiny bright heads opening like a sun. It seemed somehow familiar. But then she found something even more remarkable. Next to where the earring had lain was 'The King's Beekeeper'. The simple title was forest green embossed with gold lettering. She tore the volume from the shelf. It was unassuming, the front was plain, the back styling a shimmering bee in flight. It was a book that she had never seen before, a title not among her parent's Beekeeping collection. The pages smelled of rosemary, and lavender. Its spine was cracked from use.

She flipped the book open, letting the pages fall, words whizzed past like falling water, blending and blurring. The pages were stained, circular splashes in different colours, showing its heavy use. Myrtle rubbed a thumb over a large strawberry coloured stain, she brought the paper to her nose and smelled. Somehow, it still smelled faintly of rosehip and honey. She could sit and devour such a book, pour over it. What treasures did it hold? What secrets?

She flicked through the pages once again until she came to a chapter title: *The Beekeeper's Creeds.* The pages in this chapter were certainly in better condition than other parts of the book. They were stained dark cream from age, a milk-tea colour, but they were not splotched with the stains from herbs or honey. The words in ancient grey leaped out at her. The first creed. The Beekeeper's duties.

Beekeeper's Duties are to help others, above and before ourselves.

Never accept money, but only what the poor can give. A Beekeeper's duties are sacred and what is lacking will be given unto us. Our power does not come from within us, we will not flatter ourselves with such thoughts lest they be our end. Our power is lent and borrowed from the Wild King. We trust in him, for it is he who works in us and through our Bees. We shall not come to the end of ourselves, for he is our end, and he is infinite. When we hear his call, we shall answer it. Whatever he may ask of us, it shall be done as he wills it. For our lives, we live for him. And his call, and command is sacred above all.

Myrtle found herself frowning, it was very much like the creed her mother had spoken, and taught Myrtle how to speak… in fact the first four lines were identical, however there were extra lines. Extra lines that she had never heard. She read the lines over.

"We trust in him, for it is he who works in us and through our Bees. We cannot come to the end of ourselves, for he is our end, and he is infinite. When we hear his call, we shall answer it. Whatever he may ask of us, it shall be done as he wills it. For our lives, we live for him. And his call, and command is sacred above all." She whispered under her breath.

"Your milk Myrtle." The smiling face of Melinda appeared next to her.

The sudden interruption made Myrtle jump, as she turned to face Melinda, who held a cup of tea out to her.

"What book have you found there?" She asked, her gaze falling to Myrtle's hands and the book she clasped, "Can I see it?"

"I-I found a book about Beekeeping." Myrtle stuttered, "It's one that I've never seen before."

She showed the book to Melinda. Who took it from her, replacing it with the large mug, Myrtle smiled gratefully in return.

"Oh, I see. This old thing." Melinda chuckled, "Yes, I almost forgot that I kept such a tome in my collection!"

"I was just flicking through it, and I was surprised to find that the creed it mentions is a little different to the one I was taught." Myrtle replied, "Do you know how old it is? Could the creed be a modern version?"

"An updated version?" Melinda laughed, "More like, so old that the hills themselves have forgotten! It would've been written long before the Beeswood Beekeepers appeared. Long, long before."

"Oh." Myrtle nodded.

"Why don't we sit outside with some tea and enjoy the weather? It isn't raining, yet." Melinda turned to walk away towards the door, the book in hand.

"Do you still have use for it?" She asked the woman.

"What? For this?" Melinda looked at the book in her hands.

"Could I have it? Or even just borrow it really?" Myrtle asked, "I know such an old book must be special."

"I doubt that any modern Beekeeper would have use for such an outdated volume. Anything that you've learnt from your parents would be far more useful than whatever this can offer you." She leaned a little closer, "What could you possibly learn from these soiled pages?"

"You don't think it would be reliable anymore?" Myrtle found disappointment rising within her, "Surely some of those recipes would have merit?"

"Certainly not! I believe that your own information would be far more trustworthy."

"Alright then." Myrtle shuffled.

Melinda retreated from the living room, into the door that led to her own room, and reappeared just a moment later. Myrtle sat on the armchair, sipping the tea in cupped hands.

"We've been a little cooped up in here don't you think? How about we do some mushroom picking?" Melinda offered.

*   *   *
*

The strange, holed insides of the mushroom reminded her of honeycomb. She smiled as she plucked its thick stem and tucked it into the wicker basket. Melinda had told her that this mushroom was called Morchella, it was rare and delicious. Inside her basket was a bounty of other forest treasures. She had also found Saffron Milk Cap, Oyster Mushrooms and black truffles.

"I found a Morchella!" She called to Melinda who was obscured through the trees.

The leaves rustled and Melinda peeked out from behind a huge, gnarled trunk.

"That's three and counting!" She called back, "I'll have to teach you how to make Ambling's Pie."

"Is it similar to your mushroom pie?"

"Yes, but with more butter."

"Of course, you'd find a way to add more butter." Myrtle found a smile peeking from her lips.

"My dear, I am quite happy to inform you that I do believe that the more time you spend here, the more cheeky you are becoming." Melinda laughed, "But if there's a way to add more butter, you can rest assured I'll find out how to!"

"Then cheeky I will become." Myrtle laughed, "And fat too."

The afternoon sun peered through the tips of the trees to fall orange on the forest's floor. Though it should have been summer, it seemed that the warmest season of the year didn't make it to the forest floor as it was thick with crumpled leaves from autumns past. The trees were stuck in their autumn clothes of scarlet and amber as if they were stubborn children refusing to take off a brown winter smock for a vibrant spring gown. She moved through the trees, running a hand along their grooved surfaces, down to their bases. She rumpled the leaves, searching for any mushrooms that might be hidden below. When she couldn't find any she moved on. Her long dress swept the leaves as she walked, and they crackled and crunched like fire. The sound made her feel instantly warm and brought with it thoughts of the cottage upon their return.

The light that filtered through the trees streamed in beams onto the forest floor as it caught the dust lifting from the ground. There had been no rain recently to dampen the dirt. Myrtle coughed, as the musty scents caught in her throat. She must have walked into a denser part of the forest. Here the trees were more spindly, and they grew closer together. She stopped to feel the bottom of a trunk and was surprised to pull out another large black truffle, its bumpy edges like a blackberry but firmer. She slipped it into her basket and continued into the forest, hoping that she might find more of the coveted fungus. Then, perhaps Melinda and her might have enough to even make a pot of truffle oil to save through autumn, or even through the winter.

The leaf litter grew higher and higher, until she was trudging through knee-high piles. All around her the rustling of leaves resounded, filling the forest with noise. When she stopped it was dead quiet. Not even the wind stirred the tree's crowns far above. Animal noises had far since retreated, although she had seen many squirrels back where the forest became more spacious, now she didn't even hear a faint rustling in the distance when she stopped to listen for a moment. But as she hesitated, a cool breeze suddenly whispered through the inky grey that was the forest. A breeze like cold sea spray. It sent the back of her neck prickling and made her shiver. The leaf litter was so high that it seemed pointless to continue, for there was no amount of rummaging through the leaves that would help her find mushrooms buried deep within. Yet something pulled her on. Maybe it was the trophy of a large black truffle, or perhaps the queer way the trees grew slimmer and slimmer, and denser and thicker. She wondered whether if she continued, she might find that the trees grew so thick that they would touch. And if they did then she would be brought to a forced stop after all.

So she continued, the crunch of leaves growing harsher as she stomped through the forest's discarded skin. Soon she needed to snap small branches, for the trees had grown too close for her to squeeze past. The musty scents lifted from the leaf piles as she trudged on, and the air was filled with the earthy smells of slowly decaying plant matter. She brushed her hand past a trunk and found herself let out a yelp of surprise, her fingertips brushed against something sharp.

The tapered edge of a vine had entwined itself around the tree, with its red thorns protruding. Trumpet flowers of greying purple peeked from the trunk's base through the forest litter. Ivy-like leaves rattled along its green trails as another wisp of breeze snaked through the forest. The vine stuck out like embroidery on a blank white fabric canvas, a splash of green among the forest's autumnal hues. Myrtle shuddered, rubbing her hand. After a moment of peering into the forest gloom in front of her, she turned to leave this denser section of forest. She stepped back down, noticing for the first time the incline of a hill she'd been walking up. Leaves once again crunched under her boots.

Something flickered. Something black.

She stopped, heart pounding. But the world seemed still once more. Nothing stirred the leaves or snapped the twigs and branches. No obscure shadow hovered in the corner of her vision. She went on, trying to quieten her heart and her overactive imagination. Sighing, she turned her gaze to her feet to step over a long, fallen log. The breeze ruffled her hair again and she snapped her eyes up. Her gaze locked on something tangible and incongruent with the forest surroundings. More vines tangled and covered an object that rose from the ground through the trees. Perhaps it was just a broken tree stump, but it caught her attention.

Fading into childish imaginations she quickly found herself stepping over the log once more to head off towards the strange, vined mass. She made her way briskly through the trees, shuffling through the leaves with purpose. As she entered the lip of the hill and brushed past the strange semi-circle of thin trees, she came face to face with the vine covered sculpture.

It was a sculpture of a person kneeling, face upturned towards the light and covering its eyes was a blindfold. The vines obscured any features and ran along the sculpted folds of fabric. Red thorns and trumpet flowers smothered where detailed lines would have been etched. Tea-stained leaves after years and years of being left untouched had lazily drifted from the trees to fall upon the statue and lay in crumpled embrace with the encasing vines.

But why would such a sculpture be all the way out here in the forest? It had clearly been here quite some time. Perhaps it belonged to someone who used to dwell in the forest.

The cool breeze struck her face once more, flushing her cheeks red with the sudden cold. The breeze carried with it something familiar. Like the faint after toll of a bell, or an echo from far away. She listened for a moment, wondering whether it was Melinda calling to her, but as soon as the sound was there it was gone. Perhaps it was less of a sound and more of a feeling. She leaned forward to peer closer at the figure, noticing the vines curled around the head like short-cut hair. The breeze once more blew, this time a gust ruffled the purple flowers into flight, petals gave way and were torn from the vine, they swirled around her and then disappeared deep into the forest as they were carried on the wind. When she looked back at the statue, it was unharmed; the flowers unmarred. And there was that same faint echoing… Like a faint whisper of something that *Was.* Bla-

Just there.

It flickered past her vision, shadowy, shimmering, wavering along the ground.

But the forest was then still once more. She rubbed her eyes.

Her heart pounded in her chest, like a drum in her ears.

B l a c k.

Between the trees.

F a c e l e s s.

Wide yawning.

D a r k n e s s.

The basket thumped scattering leaves. Branches tore at her clothes as she ran. Stumbling, slipping, sliding across the crumpled leaves. Half rolling down the hillside. Leaves whirled, clinging to her like a shadow. She pulled herself up and continued to run. The ice-cold breeze prickled at her neck.

A branch whipped back at her with such velocity that she stopped, gasping for breath.

"M-Melinda?" She found her hoarse voice calling.

She coughed raggedly into her buttoned sleeve. Her eyes searched the forest, trying to figure out the way she had come.

Vines.

Another figure, clothed in green.

She spotted it between the trees up ahead, this figure had hands raised to the sky, as if pleading, begging for mercy. The twirling vines cascading down its leafed face.

She began to run again. This time with less stumbling. She caught branches and pushed them out of her way and took care when leaping over fallen logs.

Her heart raced as she came face to face with more green figures. Flowers peeked through green fingers that were covering the immortalised faces of ever-living plants.

Shadow shifted through the trees to the left of the statues.

She pushed on, stepping past the sculptures, but snagged a foot on one of the snaking vines. She picked herself up from the leaves once more. The shadow. She must be imagining it? Surely?

Was she also imagining the statues of snaking vines? But…. she had seen these same sculptures before…

The thought made her stop. *Yes, I have seen these sculptures before.*

In Wendermere. Both in Romero's Garden and in the valley's forest.

And the shadows.

And the forest was thinning. She slowed.

"Melinda!" She called, it came out as a scream, "Melinda?"

But there was no reply.

The forest was silent, no wind whispered through the trees anymore. So she ran on, trying this time to find trees with scuffed bottoms and disturbed patches of leaves. But she could find no evidence of their mushroom hunt. How far had she strayed?

"M-Melinda!" She paused to call again, cheeks flustered, red.

The trees were wider here, their trunks spanning her whole body's length. The thoughts of shadow flickering through the trees was beginning to once more feel so childish. But as one fear faded another arose.

Am I lost?

And then she noticed something so small and insignificant that she had not noticed it before. It was the absence of bees in this forest. Not her own bees nor wild bees. No wings fluttered by her, no tiny paws landing on her hair and shoulders in sticky delight. Not even the distant low hum of a hive, or of bees gathering their pollen. No, there was silence. The absence felt expansive, and somehow directional. Like the hollowness stretched throughout the forest, but like an echo, it began at one point where that hollowness first started and resounded outward until it enveloped the entire forest in eerie abandon. Though she did not want to, she found her heels turning toward the deafening absence, and straying from what she was sure had to be the path *home*.

As she continued into another realm of the forest, she noticed that the leaves felt softer here. Like there might have been moss underfoot. Something living beneath the decaying surface. The 'silence' crept down into a ravine, where the ground turned into pebbles and then larger rocks. Smoothed from years of water, but the stream bed now lay bare.

And then she saw it.

Standing upright, beside the dry riverbank.

The absence.

Three Stone hives.

A Whistling Kettle

The shrill whistle of the kettle sounded, jolting Myrtle out of her head.

"Myrtle, your tea is ready."

Myrtle got up from the armchair, and straightened her apron, before walking to the kitchen. The scent of lavender tea instantly eased her cloud of anxiety.

"Here, for your nerves dear." The old woman handed her a teacup and saucer.

Myrtle took hold of the china saucer, cradling it with both hands, the delicate forget-me-not blossoms painted on its rim, smiled up at her.

"What a frightful experience you have endured." Melinda placed a hand on her shoulder and began guiding her back to the armchair, "The forest can be an awfully daunting place, particularly when the sun starts to set. The bad light makes the trees look all the more taller, and not to mention altogether *different*."

Myrtle found herself sinking into the plush armchair once more. Her fears were beginning to dissolve as she took a sip of the tea, and it warmed her chest.

"But you need not fret, our trip was not wasted. We brought back a mushroom bounty and will be able to try out many fine recipes."

"I'm relieved." She mustered a smile, but the smile quickly faded. *Relieved.* How could she be *relieved?* A pang in the pit on her stomach followed. No bees were tangled beneath her hair. None flew lazily about the room or crawled from the furniture. As she stared out into the cobblestone yard, the light fading fast, she could see nothing drifting through the air… drifting down the road, towards… *Home.* There was only the dim wink of blue light from the distant luminescent mushrooms, in a sea of dark.

The sudden thought of her own hives washed over her, like silt unplugged from a drain allowing water to flow freely again. With it, came fresh anxiety, and she abruptly rose from the couch.

"Well, I am glad you are relieved." Melinda regarded Myrtle with a strange expression, "You must be tired too, why don't you head off to bed and I'll send you up some dinner when it's ready."

And suddenly, Myrtle did feel tired, so tired that she felt faint with the heaviness of her own feet. She found herself swaying.

"Oh, dear." Melinda exclaimed and grabbed a strong arm around her back and shoulders, "You've utterly exhausted yourself, poor thing."

"Yes…exhausted…" Myrtle repeated. Her tongue felt like stone in her mouth, it was hard to move, to speak.

"Come now, let's get you into bed."

Melinda escorted her to the little tent shaped attic room. Climbing the steep stairs proved to be most difficult, and Myrtle almost tripped, only to have Melinda catch her fall. Once in the small bedroom, Melinda tucked Myrtle underneath the patchwork quilt.

"I'll fetch you a hot water bottle."

The elderly woman's curls sprung as she turned and lifted her long apron to go back down the stairs. The light from the stairwell caught her figure and outlined her in scarlet red. The warm tones of the cottage vanished in the harsh hue. Myrtle's body tingled, like pins and needles running up her legs and arms, shackling her, immobilising her. With eyelids heavy, Myrtle gave in, succumbing to sleep's numb embrace.

* * *
*

Wake Up.

Myrtle jolted awake, sitting bolt-upright huffing. Her heart was pounding like a drum. Her head felt as though it were filled with mud, and trying to shift any congruent thought out of it was like trying to grab at memories half-buried and quickly sinking. She blinked, wiping her eyes. Through hazy outlines Myrtle could see that everything in the little attic room was still, and the house was silent. Silent.

Silent.

Silent?

No hum. No flutter. No bees.

Suddenly, the events of the previous day flooded back into Myrtle's mind like a roaring river. Lifeless hives. Cast in stone. The deep absence, echoing and resounding in the crumpled forest. Without hesitation she leapt from the bed, not stopping to slip on her shoes. The urgency to get to her bees took over everything, it banished the fog from her mind with a fresh, stabbing panic. She scrambled down the steep staircase. The living room was only dimly lit by the dying embers of the fire, she hesitated and glanced behind her towards the room in which Melinda slept. For a flashing moment bright green slits were illuminated, it was the glinting eyes of the tortoiseshell cat watching her. Its eyes moved to follow her as she turned back to the door. The hairs on the back of her neck prickled. She pushed on, across the living room to the front door. The door had a wide glass windowpane, looking out into the dark forest. It looked so uninviting. So cold. The distant soft glow of fungi had vanished, replaced with inky black. The cottage in comparison was warm and safe. It would be so easy to stay and to leave this silly notion, at least until morning. She shivered, and glanced once more behind her, to find that the tortoiseshell cat had stalked across the room and was looking up at her with its piercing gaze. Questioning her.

Don't you trust me, Myrtle? It said, *Why wouldn't you trust me? What have I done to deserve this betrayal?*

Myrtle turned back to the door and closed her hand tightly around its silver knob.

You couldn't leave me all alone? Don't leave me all alone again. Without another glance, she closed her eyes shut and opened the door. *Don't go Myrtle.* The blast of cool air was almost enough to send her racing back to the attic bed. She clenched her teeth against the night and stepped out onto the cobblestone, wincing, as her feet touched the icy ground. She could see her breath cloud in front of her. The wind whistled from deep within the forest, rattling branches and swirling leaves as it reached her, it lifted her nightgown, sending it flying behind her. She gasped, holding herself, white-knuckled with chill.

Now that she was outside of the cottage, the sense of deep dread reached the pit of her stomach, the urge now was no longer to see her bees, and to check on them… no. She had to run. The urge was inexplicable, and she found herself trying to command her body to calm down and go back inside.

But instead, she grabbed at the hem of her nightgown and ran towards the back of the house to the stables.

A weak nicker sounded.

"Hodgepodge!" She exclaimed, as she found her pony's shaggy head pop out from the stall. His eyes were sunken. Wrinkles on his eyelids showed worry. *How long had it been since she'd seen him?*

How long has it been?

How long have I been here?

Tears threatened to flood her eyes as she found his velvet muzzle, his soft, warm breath caressing her cheeks and face. He licked his lips and nibbled at her hair, sighing.

Run.

They had to go.

She felt around the wall of the stable stall until her hands grasped at leather, hoping with all her heart that it would be the wagon's gear she desperately needed. She heaved the leather straps into her lap, bits trailing, threatening to trip her up, but she couldn't stop to organise the straps and buckles. Dust rose in the gloom as she kicked the stall gate open and hobbled up onto an upturned crate in the corner of the stable. Then she launched herself over his back, all the while clutching onto the leather gear. She managed to sling her body over his back, legs dangling to one side, head and chest on the other when he took off, with such speed and velocity that Myrtle was certain she would fall. Hooves thundered on the cobblestone, clattering and shaking the ground. The earth peeled away beneath them, dirt flying wildly in all directions, it splattered against Myrtle's face. She managed to find a tangled clump of mane, and with all her might she pulled her legs up and over his rump, until she was sitting on his back, holding onto his mane for dear life. They passed the flickering light of the cottage, and flew down the driveway, the cobblestone turning to dirt and mud. Hodgepodge ate up the ground with terrifying speed. She stole one glance back. The cottage had vanished. Where it had once stood, a glowing beacon in the cold night, was now a hollow of complete darkness. The buckles and bit clanged like dissonant bells on Myrtle's lap urging them on. She shivered once more, the hairs on her neck standing up. Hodgepodge continued at a gallop, until they came to the end of the driveway, where Myrtle had hidden the wagon in some bushes so that it had been obscured from the road and the driveway. But Hodgepodge did not stop.

"Whoa!" Myrtle yelled, "Whoaaaa!"

He did not heed her call, in fact his ears did not flick back in recognition of hearing anything. She grasped Hodgepodge's mane higher up near the ears and pulled back with all of her strength. At this the pony slowed to a canter, but she could tell he would continue his run if she could not stop him now. She pulled at the mane so that his head had to swing to the side, and he finally slowed to an awkward bouncy trot that almost sent Myrtle off into the ditch beside them. He snorted, flaring his nostrils wildly, but she finally convinced him to stop.

"You have to turn around." She begged him, "I know you don't want to go back there, but I have to save the bees!"

The pony's reply was in his heaving lungs and wide-eyed look. As she tried to swing his head further around, he shook his head wildly, almost uprooting her from his back. Hodgepodge was not going to budge.

"Please!" Tears sparked in the corners of her eyes.

The pony stamped his feet, pawing at the earth, sending pebbles rolling.

"I'm sorry for leaving you in the stables, I'm sorry for not checking on you." She stroked him, "I need you to trust me again."

Hodgepodge jumped forward, she braced herself and pulled his head round and back, stopping him from galloping off.

"Please." Myrtle sobbed, "I need to save them."

"I need to save them if they are still alive."

But, the stamping of Hodgepodge's hooves, driven further into the dirt revealed that he wasn't going to listen. He flung his head and reared. Myrtle wrapped her arms around his neck to stop herself from sliding down his back. *Please…. Please. Wild King.*

There was a low whispering wind that swept through the forest, it lay a warm hand upon her cheek, ruffling her buttercup hair. Stirring leaves and branches in a soft chime. Then it was gone, almost as quickly as it had come.

Hodgepodge stood, breath coming ragged, snorting. She grabbed the mane once more, gently tugging at it. Though she could feel that Hodgepodge was still anxious, he conceded, and turned his head warily at first. Then as they continued down the road, his gait grew with speed, and he lifted his head like a proud war-horse ready to charge into battle. Myrtle mustered a quick smile, pushing him into a canter, they swept down the road once again, hooves thundering, this time not with speed but power.

In the dark she could barely tell where they were headed, the shapes of trees blurred past in shadowy haste. Finally, she saw a gap through the trees, a hollow gap, that seemed somehow darker than the surrounding forest. She knew that this gap must have been where the cottage once stood, its glow a welcoming sight in the deep forest gloom. Firmly, she tugged Hodgepodge toward it, and he complied, snorting at the darkness, perhaps it was out of fear or it could have been a laugh from this new found courage.

They came to the bushes once more. In the gloom of night, it was difficult to tell which bushes her precious hives and wagon were concealed behind. Jumping off Podge, she climbed to the ground and darted to the edge of the roadway. The leather harness slid from Podge's back and lay on the cobblestone behind her. She left it discarded for now, as she groped through the bushes, grabbing at branches feverishly and pushing them out of the way. Bending and breaking them as she scrambled through the undergrowth. The sticks scratched and tore at her dress. Her hand felt wood. She stopped pushing and felt the smoothness of the planks of her wagon. Carefully, she shuffled, squeezing through leaves to the side. Eventually she freed herself from the bush and pulled herself up into the driver's seat. Breathing raggedly, heart beating like a hummingbird's wings, she drew back the lace-awning and listened. All that could be heard in the still night was the thudding of her heart and the breath heaving in her chest. Her fingers grasped the thin curtain of the cart, and she climbed through into the back of the wagon. Hands outstretched feeling for the hives, for their warmth. *Please let them be warm.* Knuckles brushed hard clay. Her heart skipped a beat, she placed her palm flat against the hive. It wasn't stone. It wasn't cold.

Relief flooded her. Warmth. There was warmth beneath the soft clay. She found herself gasping and sobbing. Placing an ear against the hive, she stifled her sobbing. Within the hive, the deep thrumming of sleepy bees resounded. She pulled her arms around the hive and hugged it close to her chest, her sobs filling the cool air. Heart beating against the clay, echoing inside the honey-comb nest. It stirred bees. As if they knew that their master had finally returned. Tired worker bees awoke and drifted lazily through the air, they came to rest on Myrtle's arms and head. She felt wobbling antennae on her fingertip and bent to try to see the little insect. But in the dark, she could only feel the bee's warmth and its tiny sticky feet.

"I'm so sorry I left you." She whispered to the bee, "I'm so sorry I left you and your queen all alone."

It stayed, for a few moments on her finger, as if truly contemplating. Then it turned and flew back to the hive, the hum of its wings disappearing. Tears that had been rolling down her face, were beginning to dry in the breeze. She moved onto the next hive, placing a hand on the rounded clay, she found warmth and life murmuring beneath the hard surface. Myrtle sighed deeply and smiled up at the canopy sky before moving onto the third and final hive. Leaning closer, she felt a strange foreignness to the hive. She hesitated, feeling a heaviness drop to the pit of her stomach. Something was wrong, there was a clear distinction between this hive and the others, and it pulled her in closer, resounding like an echo. Her breath caught in her throat as she reached forward, placing a hand over the clay. Cold. It was Cold. The coolness of the hive made her flinch. She brushed an ear against its tapered edge and listened closely, breath lodged in her chest. Silence. A resounding silence. There was no hum. No quiet buzz. The hive was lifeless.

Her lips trembled, whimpering a soundless *no*.

She opened the hive's lid reaching her hand inside, hoping she might find some weak bees still alive. Her fingertips brushed crackling, stiff corpses. Hundreds piled on top of each other littered through the hive. Bees that would never fly again. Sobs arose in her throat, shock cascading through her like a frozen river.

She forced her hand down through the lifeless bodies of the bees and found wax, the edges chewed by tiny mouths as they starved. *Perhaps some were still alive further down?* She told herself. *I can find the queen. I have to find the queen.* The songs came drifting back to her. Coronation songs of generations of Beeswood Queens and finally the sweet notes of her own Queens, Petunia, Lavender and Rose. First, she hummed Petunia's melody, the notes passed from her lips barely audible above the warble of her tears. But the tune reached the hive to her side, as the thrum of large wings vibrated the clay. They lifted into flight, and Queen Petunia alighted on her outstretched palm. Myrtle breathed a sigh of relief and moved on to the next tune. This time her voice grew in strength as the memory of Lavender's coronation in Wattleshire flooded back to her. The soft hand of her mother's on her shoulder, as they welcomed the new Queen into her kingdom. And the second pair of wings answered the song's call. Soon Lavender's soft flutter had alighted also in her palms, she could feel tiny antennae quivering as the

Queen crouched against her skin, pulsing. Myrtle turned back to the third hive, her heart heavy. Rose's tune bubbled up within her, she forced the melody out between cracked voice, and shaking lips. Rose had been her first Queen, the first new kingdom that she had formed without the help of her mother, a hive formed from the broken remnants of Daffodil Clivesfield's bees and her own. But the young Queen did not answer. She sang louder, the notes drifting through the darkness around them. The hive was silent. Sobs racked her and she found herself slipping, against the hive, once warm clay now turned stone cold.

Memories of her time at the cottage flickered through her mind. It had felt like only a few days, but now she wasn't so sure. Her bees could not have run out of honey so quickly.

To bear the burden, the deaths of thousands of bees. She was a failure of a Beekeeper. The bees that so dutifully served her, gave their lives for her. And what did they die for? For her to live in comfort for a few nights? Through her sobs she heard a crack from behind the bushes that obscured the road.

"Hodgepodge?" She called out after a few moments.

The wind rippled through the air bringing an icy chill, Myrtle shivered. The leaves rustled, branches clacking together like bones.

Hodgepodge gave a frightened nicker.

We have to leave. *I must leave.*

Now.

But she didn't want to. She could feel her spirit slipping. How could she go back to Wendermere and call herself a Beekeeper after this? Not with the death of thousands of bees on her head. The forest would take her, and she would melt into it, let it fill her emptiness with its snaking vines, twisting until she became a part of it.

No.

Let it take me. I am not worthy to be a Beekeeper. I am not worthy to carry the Beeswood name.

She could feel the pull of the emptiness where the cottage once stood. Feel that awful nothingness calling. The silence of the hive resounding. Whispers of shadows melded to form nothingness.

The absence of life, the still dark stone.

Three hives.

Besides the riverbank.

Here there are no obligations.
    Don't you want to rest?
        Why not come back and sleep awhile.

Her nails bit into her numb palms, they came back wet from her eyes. Teeth clenched against tears.

I can teach you the impossible...
    how to turn dust into silver, rubble into gold.
      Bones could be a servant to you,
blood an ancient covenant, the wood your altar,
      the stone for your sacrifice. If only you would
        free yourself from those burdens.
          You could be the hero of your own story.

The whispers turned to the silvered voice of the old woman. Whose face was like well-worn leather.

*Turn back now, and you will **see** how **much** they **hate** you. Those children by the stream. Your story is nothing without me. A **Beekeeper** who has **killed** thousands of her own bees.*

Well-worn leather, like a trusted purse that should've been thrown out years ago.

You could not see the holes, Myrtle.

The holes big enough for coins to slip through, clinking noiselessly to the pavement. Their sound covered by your own footsteps. Because the thought of a trusted purse having been torn was a silly thought. Just like an unassuming cottage, full of bright warmth in a dark forest.

Hodgepodge's stamping jolted Myrtle, her fragile form curled tightly in the wagon.

Child, you must get up.

Myrtle shook her head, teeth gnashing, her frantic sobs reaching a new level, drowning out Hodgepodge's stamping on the stone pavements, as he beat his hooves against the rocks over and over again.

You must!

But the sweet voice in the silvered tongue of the woman of the forest urged from the darkness.

*I **can restore** you.*

It promised.

A Beekeeper so unique. So special. Different.

Its words dripped sweeter than honey.

What does the death of one hive mean? When you can give life to the lifeless. The power to give life beyond death. Yes, Myrtle, you are so very special, even more special than the other Beekeeper who came to me.

Shadows leered.

Myrtle's tear-stricken face drew together in a frown. The other Beekeeper?

An Enchantress!

That is what you could be, Myrtle.

Men would quake before you.

Silver hair caught in a moon beam and the sunken face of the woman, now seen for what she truly was. In place of her sightless eyes large black beetles shone. Their wings beating as she spoke. Hideous. Disfigured. She was a monster. Nothing of the kind woman remained.

You are stronger than she was, Myrtle.

Her story is a crumbling statue

forgotten in the forest.

But yours could live on forever.

For you can cheat death.

I can teach you to command death,

bend it to your will.

It was as if the woman wasn't talking at all anymore. Her sounds had become the beetles, their thumping wings melded into her own words. As she drew closer. Moving through the trees down the road. The light of the moon caught her disfigurement.

For a moment, the thought of a life without the fear of death overwhelmed her.

Get up, child!

Myrtle felt the sting of words like fire across her body. Prickling, rippling, the command struck her. The darkness seemed to lose its pull. Myrtle found the strength to uncurl herself, gasping. Knees wobbling, she crawled to the edge of the wagon and grabbed the leather gear. But before she left, a desperate question screamed from within her, it needed an answer.

"Who are you?" she whispered into the night.

The wind snatched her words as soon as they left her lips and swept them up into the trees' clacking branches. She dared herself to pause and peer into the night, though she knew that she should flee.

The lady of the wood's figure took shape once more, this time closer. Myrtle jumped, as her shiny black eyes appeared before her, flittering. A strange smile took over the figure's face, pale body naked in the moonlight. It was terrible. So terrible that Myrtle knew instantly she had made a mistake, but she was now rooted to the ground once more.

"I am the Witch of Ambling's End."

The reply came with the whistling of the wind, and Myrtle felt it tremble down her spine. She choked back tears of panic, it was too late now and it wasn't the answer she needed. She needed a name. Hands stretched towards her, gnarled like ancient oak. Twisted like thorns. Hard as stone. She would not be able to break free if the Witch caught her. But all she could do was watch helplessly as the monster stalked towards her. Its black beetled eyes winking from gaping eye-sockets. Thin smile drawn out by rubied lips.

The Witch was close enough to touch her. Fingers mere centimetres.

"You are banished from this place Melinda Cloverfoot."

A brilliant light flashed brightly as with the thunderous words, so loud it buzzed in Myrtle's ears.

Go!

The command sliced right through her. This time the voice hurt like the burning of a whip's lash. It made her let out a scream. But she heeded the words. Jumping up and scrambling blindly towards Hodgepodge.

Hodgepodge was already standing, already hitched to the wagon. Buckles glinting in the gloom. She didn't stop to think how he managed to buckle himself in, but instead flung herself into the driver's seat. Hodgepodge launched himself forward, dislodging the wagon from the bushes, the branches whipped back into Myrtle's face striking her on the cheek. The cobblestone rumbled as they flew down the road. The emptiness where the cottage stood. Where it once stood. Where it should have still been. Faded. Where the absence, the resounding lifelessness that echoed through the forest, was now filled with the faint murmuring of bees. But a small part of that absence still remained.

The third hive.

For it would not thrum with the same

multitude of a thousand wings.

Their sweet honey would never stain the air nor

wounds revive.

The servant-hearted bees would work no longer.

For they lay with their queen, slain and conquered.

* * *
*

Dawn cracked its gaze through the trees, shadows leant and made long translucent trails along the forest floor. They waned, as the sun rose, they grew slimmer. The trees thinned, as if parting like a curtain, they peeled further and further back. Myrtle sat, blank eyes staring as Hodgepodge plodded along. The pony's steady rhythm was now occasionally interspersed by a quick snatch of grass, which peeked in clumps from the tangled piles of leaves. Her heart ached. The scratches on her cheeks reminded her of the long night. It hadn't been a dream as she had hoped.

Her bees were awake now, and the smell of life rustling beneath the decaying leaves woke them from their sleepy stupor. The air smelt fresher, from the long stalks of green and bobbing yellow flowers. Sunlight. It fell now in large spots across the forest's floor. The canopy above them thinning with the trees. To feel the warmth of the sun again. Myrtle sighed as a beam found her face, its heat briefly alighting on her. How long had it been since she had felt the sun?

The next hours were interrupted by many stops, as more and more green appeared, waving now in a breeze. Not an icy one that would leave you with goosebumps, but gentle wafting, like air from an open oven. The yellow flowers were joined by scarlet ones, their petals opening to the sun, dancing on the breeze. Tiny purple-blue forget-me-not tumbled down the sides of the path.

The path had turned to dirt, which was somehow a more welcome sight than cobblestone. Hodgepodge certainly agreed, as his steps grew more bouncy. His mane became an animated wave as he walked, swishing and sloshing. A bird sprung up startled from the ground. Its high-pitched call was answered by its friends in the distance as it soared through the trees, through the-

Sky

Blue as the forget-me-nots, was in the distance, through the trees as they thinned and the lip of a hill too! Myrtle found herself leaning forward, hands clasping the rim of the wagon. And clouds too, wispy white ones floated through the sky, now visible.

"Myrtle?"

She whipped her head around in surprise at the call of her name. A familiar voice. And there through the trees at the edge of the forest, where emerald hills could now be seen, rippling across the forest down the hillside, stood Finn. His face a mess of dirt and freckles, farm clothes grubby from work.

"Finn!" She choked.

"Oh my- It is you!"

And he ran to the wagon's side. Rubbing Podge's velvet muzzle, he smiled up at Myrtle, with tears pricking his eyes.

"Miss Beeswood, we've been looking everywhere for you, we thought you had gone! Well- they did -they thought you had left us. But I knew you hadn't. I knew that you wouldn't leave us. That's why I came up here, it was the only place we hadn't searched. They didn't want to look here, because of the old tales of witches. But- I told ma and pa that this is where I had to go, and I was certain-. And. Well-here you are Miss!"

Myrtle didn't know what to think, but her eyes were stinging once more. Relief washing through her. She was safe.

"Thank you, Finn." Myrtle's lips wobbled, tears threatening, "You are a dear friend."

Wendermere Pudding

It was morning. Light streamed through the open windows and the breeze billowed in the curtains, tickling Myrtle's face as she lay in bed. The faint wind stirred the leaves of walnut trees outside. She had slept soundly and deeply after the forest ordeal and now it was late morning. After they had arrived back in Wendermere, Finn had taken her straight to the cottage. Of course, they had been stopped by many, all gasping in surprise as they saw the young Beekeeper's face and anxious to hear of what had befallen her. She had tried to be both polite, and curt. After a dozen or so such interactions, Finn had noticed her grow more and more fragile, voice shaking. He told her to pretend to sleep, and she did, convincingly so, because after all but a few moments of pretending, she had indeed fallen fast asleep, head falling to her side and then to Finn's shoulder.

The sun had dropped past the horizon when she awoke some time later. Embarrassment burned on her cheeks as she muttered an apology on her breath, but Finn had said nothing as they continued up the road. By this time Hodgepodge was starting to protest, tossing his head to the wind. He was weary, even though he wasn't pulling the wagon. It was only now in the daylight that Myrtle could see his coat had grown shaggy to hide his gaunt shape.

She sighed, a deep sigh. Pulling a hand up from underneath the thick doona covers and letting the light that spilled in from the window dance across her hand. How good it was to feel the light of the sun and not just the inferior light cast from a flame. How good it was to see the sky! She had almost forgotten how blue it really was. Beside her sat a glass of fresh milk on a stool, she took the cup in her hands and drank until the foam left an imprint above her lips.

She had been gone for twenty-six days. Almost a full month. When Finn had helped her down from the wagon, she had all but collapsed, he ended up having to carry her inside to her bed. But, by this point she had been too exhausted to care. After propping her up, he had given her water and waited until she had drunk the full glass, though she hadn't been sure why at the time. He then left in quite a hurry, and she again succumbed to sleep, waking later to the tender smell of stew and Mrs Strawby beside her bed. Finn leant on the doorframe, he looked anxious.

"Here, you must eat Myrtle." Mrs Strawby had said, "You have lost much of your strength, let me help you with the spoon."

And Myrtle's hands had shook too much to take the spoon to her lips, so she had let Mrs Strawby feed her, though she felt as helpless as a babe. Mrs Merryweather came through the door later, dropping off fresh bread. When the elderly lady had peeked into the bedroom, she had gasped at the figure she saw in bed. Myrtle knew that she must have looked frightful. Once Mrs Strawby was sure that Myrtle had eaten enough of the thin stew, she and Mrs Merryweather retreated to the kitchen where they stood whispering in harsh tones. Myrtle caught words and tried to piece them together.

"A whole month.", "So pale, so thin." and "How did she survive?"

Mrs Strawby stayed the whole day and the whole night. Myrtle supposed she was still here now even, in the kitchen perhaps. She had filled the glass with milk while Myrtle had slept. Clinking, and the creaking of floorboards beyond the bedroom door told her that she was indeed correct, Mrs Strawby was busy in the kitchen.

*　*　*
*

The sun told her that it must be afternoon, as it no longer glowed directly through her window, but was obscured by the roof of the cottage. Mrs Strawby had been in regularly to check on her and to give her more stew. She was thankful that she had recovered enough strength to use the spoon herself, however she still spent much of her time dozing. Her bees flitted through the open window to lay fluttering on her nose, her arms and the bed. It was as if they too were checking on her. It warmed her to see them and both her heart and stomach felt fuller. but there was still a piece missing. She was reminded whenever she saw the stripy bees drifting towards her, buzzing on the faint breeze, of the many bees she had failed, and of their Queen, Rose. The crunching of their lifeless corpses haunted her. The melody that was never answered.

As she lay, staring blankly at the window where vivid grass, fluffy trees and forget-me-not sky framed the view, there was a knock on the door. She could see the streaked wooden handle turning. The slim face of a blue-eyed girl appeared, her blond curls bouncing as she peeked into the room.

"Miss Beeswood?" She whispered, then spying Myrtle sitting propped up in the bed, she blushed a little, "Oh! You are awake!"

"Miss Pineswood," Myrtle dipped her head as the girl shuffled into the room, closing the door behind her and sweeping over the stool from the bed's side. The curious girl sat herself down with a fluff of her dress.

Miss Pineswood's eyes were alight as if a fire sparkled beneath, and she reached forward and clasped Myrtle's hand, which lay on the doona.

"Myrtle! I was so worried! I-I can't believe that you made it back from those ghastly woods! Every night when the search party came back, I told them, we *have* to keep looking- she's out there somewhere, I just *know* it! They all grew tired after a few weeks…" She trailed off, looking downcast for a moment, "But- Finn-! He knew it too, that you were out there somewhere in the woods. He tried to convince the rest to follow him into Nearne Forest, but they all forbade him from going." Her voice suddenly became a hushed whisper, "In fact, Mr and Mrs Strawby even forbade him from leaving the house for *five whole days*, not allowing him to do farm work or anything for fear that he would run off and try to find you."

The sudden flow of words from Miss Pineswood was like a cold splash to Myrtle's tired body. She wasn't sure how to respond, but she didn't need to wonder for long, because Miss Pineswood barely needed to pause before she continued.

"And do you know what he did, Miss Beeswood? The moment that they let him outside to do some work on the farm, he sprinted out the door, down the road, through the village and all the way up the hillside to Nearne Forest. That's where he found you- he said you looked as though you were on the verge of collapsing. Of course, that's what you would expect from someone who'd spent a whole month in the wilderness. And- Oh Myrtle, I do hope you are well. I hope it is not too inconsiderate of me to say that even though I cannot begin to understand the perils you must've faced this past month, you do look radiant this morning!"

Myrtle almost found herself laughing, she stifled it, then spying Miss Pineswood's ridiculously large grin, she couldn't help herself. Both girls erupted into giggles like a bubbling stream after a heavy rainfall. The sounds echoed in the room, and out through the hallway, into the house. The footsteps of Mrs Strawby were presently lost in the sound, or perhaps she had stopped to listen to the sounds of joy gurgling from Myrtle's room.

"I am so glad to have returned." Myrtle finally spoke.

Miss Pineswood nodded and leaned forward to look out the window catching a glance at Hodgepodge's figure, which stood on the sloped paddock. He was shovelling grass into his belly at an alarming rate. No doubt his chubby figure would be back to normal shortly.

"Can I ask- I can surely understand if you would not want to utter a word about the experience… but pray can you tell me. Were you lost in the forest? Or did you encounter the witch of Nearne Forest, as everyone has been whispering about?" Miss Pineswood had sympathy in her eyes, as though she could not believe such a fate would have befallen the young Beekeeper.

Myrtle hesitated, since she had left that dreaded forest, it was hard to slip back into the memories of her time there. Every time she tried to grab hold of a memory it seemed to wiggle away. There were snippets of memory, but never a full picture, and she couldn't tell what reality was and what was magic.

"Yes, I believe I did meet the witch…" She grimaced, her face becoming downcast, "She didn't seem like a witch though. Not at first."

Miss Pineswood nodded animatedly, "That's how witches are. They are kind to you, enticing you in, and then trap you in their web."

The silvered hair of the woman… the witch, bubbled up through the haze of memories. Her face was a mishmash of wrinkles, stormy eyes, and beetle's wings, but she couldn't piece together the full expression. Could this woman have truly been a witch? But then she felt something, cold, hard, smooth. In the recesses of her mind the one tangible memory that remained was of that dreaded moment when she had found the three stone hives, lifeless. Just like her own hive, where the gentle thrum of life had ebbed away. Starved.

Miss Pineswood seemed to notice Myrtle being drawn into her thoughts, the Beekeeper seemed suddenly unaware of her company.

"Well then Miss Beeswood, I must catch you up on all of the happenings of Wendermere while you were away." Miss Pineswood piped up.

Myrtle looked again to Miss Pineswood, catching her soft blue eyes. They conveyed a warmth that Myrtle squirmed under. It wasn't because she didn't want friends, she was sure of that. Something about the girl unnerved her. Miss Pineswood wasn't afraid, life beat from her just like the wings of a bee. Her enthusiasm fluttered out, tirelessly and Myrtle was oh so tired. But she owed it to Miss Pineswood to at least try to listen.

"Well- The mountain folk were all quiet as they always are, in their relatively ordinary lives. Mr and Mrs Cottonflower were among some of the most concerned for your wellbeing; they feared that you may have fallen to the same fate as that of poor Miss Clivesfield. And Mrs Merryweather even went so far as to suggest that there may be some conspiracy to kidnap all of the Beekeepers of Wendermere! The Jensons welcomed a new son into their homes and baby Jack, the Cobblinghill's son, has learnt how to walk, bless his little soul. Among other news, Master Strawby resigned from the coveted position of 'paperboy' leaving the job vacant for Master Farthington. But really the talk of the town has been about how Mr Strawby is courting a young lady, although… There is some speculation as to whom, as he has not publicly announced his engagement yet. I for one believe it to be Miss Woodsdale, because she was the young lady who held his affections at the ball, however, Miss Bottlebrush apparently caught him taking a stroll with Miss Merryweather, that is Tabitha, Mrs Merryweather's granddaughter."

"I am glad to hear that the Jensons delivered a new baby…But…" Myrtle could barely bring herself to ask, she didn't want to know the answer, "There has to have been incidents while I have been away. You need not spare me."

"Well…" Miss Pineswood winced, "Unfortunately, while you were trapped in that awful forest, Mr Farthington broke his leg fixing the shingles on the Woodsdale's roof. The wound was quite ghastly, and it got infected. Luckily, this was the worst of the instances, although Miss and Master Bottlebrush have complained about a persistent cough, and young Frankie Fodderhill has an upset stomach." She took in a low breath pausing, "However, it pains me to say that there has been wretched news… The Fodderhill's baby, Benjamin, succumbed quite suddenly to a terrible illness. They are laying him to rest tomorrow."

Myrtle couldn't help the shock from showing on her face. She had known that her delayed return from Pinesdale must have had consequences, however she had hoped to tend to those who had fallen sick as quickly as she was able to leave her bed. The baby's death was a sore blow, one that left her feeling torn up inside.

"Oh dear…" Myrtle began, she found her eyes brimming, the edges of her vision blurring and a blush staining her cheeks, as she attempted to hold the emotions at bay. Her gaze turned to the girl before her with golden ringlets that spiralled perfectly, just like a corkscrew. Miss Pineswood's dress of muted red tones, seemed to crease faultlessly, as it swept the floor. Her apron was pressed and clean. Myrtle was suddenly aware that she must look frightful in comparison, and smell hideous, as she had yet to muster up the strength to take a bath. These realisations left a sour taste in her mouth, she felt sick. Exhaustion swept back over her with its misty embrace, the energy that Miss Pineswood had managed to feebly draw out of Myrtle, with her kind eyes, words and hope of friendship, now vanished. The reserves had dried up.

"Are you quite alright Miss Beeswood?" Miss Pineswood asked, worry framed her words with a quiver.

"I am just tired."

Myrtle's eyes never left the quilted cover of her duvet, the thick blanket enveloped her like a cocoon. Its colours blended and blurred out of focus as she blinked away tears.

"Oh- that's quite understandable, of course you must be exhausted!" Miss Pineswood exclaimed and then she grew serious, "I'm sorry I hadn't realised... how inconsiderate I have been."

The exhaustion had taken Myrtle so abruptly that she felt as though cotton was wadded up in her ears and Miss Pineswood's voice sounded as though it were coming from another room in the house.

"I will take my leave from you at once." Miss Pineswood got up from the chair, "I am glad to see you returned, dear Myrtle, and I shall be thinking only of your recovery."

*   *   *

*

Myrtle's fingers came back hot and clammy with sweat. Her knuckles were glistening, she shook her hand, trying to shake the droplets from her fingertips. The ragged breath of the child ceased for a moment as the girl coughed and then wretched into a bucket. She was gaunt, the once beaming eyes of Frankie Fodderhill were cast in a glaze as she huddled over a bucket.

Though Miss Pineswood had described the illness as being mild, another week of complacency had given the illness a strength which no doubt Mr and Mrs Fodderhill had not been expecting. Myrtle could not afford to lose yet another life.

"I need chamomile… fresh." She riffled through her lambskin belt, her fresh herbs were dried beyond use, they disintegrated in her hands as she grasped for them. The dried herbs, which she stored in tiny bottles had fared a little better, but she had been low in reserves after visiting Pinesdale. Her fingers found a bottle, It was the large crackling leaves of basil. She rarely used this herb as it was one whose medicinal properties were largely in question. But she picked two leaves, crunching them together in the wooden bowl. Next, she picked yarrow, its tiny yellow flowers broke apart easily. Mrs Fodderhill returned with two fresh sprigs of chamomile. The large white flowers bobbing as the woman hurried through the front door. Her expression was worn, almost on the verge of giving in, her brows knitted together with dread at the inevitable. She knew what would happen if Myrtle couldn't save her child. The mother could hear the desperate, plaintive cry of a baby cradled in her arms. It gasped. And died. Just like the man, except Myrtle, hadn't been there this time. Mr Fodderhill's expression was similar, as he sat next to the sick child. This was a couple that she had failed before, and whom she could not fail again.

As Myrtle clasped the chamomile, another ingredient occurred to her, as if whispered through the wings of the bees that crawled around her. It was an ingredient, like the basil that she rarely used.

"Do you have any arrowroot?" She asked, ripping the chamomile flowers from their stems and hastily plucking the petals.

Mrs Fodderhill glanced uncertainly at her husband who was crouched next to the retching child. He met her gaze and shook his head.

"No, w-we don't." She stammered.

"Do the neighbours?"

"I'll go check." The woman was about to go and hurry out the door, when Master Fodderhill appeared, he had crept down the dark hallway, careful to not wake his other siblings.

"I'll go mum." He murmured, light touched his soft round features as he grabbed a green coat from its hook.

"Oh, Edmund, you're awake?" Mrs Fodderhill sighed, "Alright, I suppose you'll be quicker than me at any rate."

Myrtle brought her attention back on the child whose breath was becoming even more laboured. She had at least presently stopped retching. Myrtle cupped the child's face in her hands, feeling instantly the warmth of fever, she swept a lock of hair out of her eyes. When Frankie opened her hazel eyes, they were red, swollen and had sunk into her face, leaving shadows. The child's skin was pale, her lips tinged with blue. Myrtle dipped a spoon into the jar of honey, gently shooing a bee, whose sticky feet were crawling over the lid of the jar. Cradling the child's head backwards, she dripped the honey into her mouth.

"Can you swallow?" She asked.

Frankie licked her lips in reply, but Myrtle could see her struggle. She massaged the child's throat a little and propped her upright, finally the child gulped. Myrtle sighed in relief.

"We're lucky she can still swallow." Myrtle murmured.

"Does that mean you can help her?" Mr Fodderhill, was crouched beside Frankie, rubbing the child's back with the palm of his hand.

"I believe so."

It felt like an age before Master Fodderhill returned with the arrowroot clutched tightly against his chest. Myrtle took the root, dirt crumbling from her hands.

"I'll need some hot water." She picked more lumps of earth off the tuber, "And a brush."

Once the steamy bowl was brought, she set aside some of the hot water, spooning it into the already prepared ingredients. Then she scrubbed the arrowroot, as clean as she could get it, until its skin was white. Taking a knife, she sliced five thin slices, and added it to the bowl. With haste now, she crushed the ingredients together into a brown paste and dripped a heavy spoonful of the most important ingredient, honey. Its golden shine turned the mixture amber. The child was curled up again over the bucket. Myrtle again lifted the face, basked in a sheen of sweat, and delivered a spoonful of medicine. Myrtle could see a look of panic in the child's eyes, as she went to try and swallow it, but couldn't.

"You're alright." She carefully massaged the child's throat.

There was a gulp. The medicine had gone down.

"Thank goodness for that." Myrtle murmured, "Can you take another mouthful?"

Frankie nodded, dazed, but she could tell the medicine was working. Its warmth healing the child's raw throat. For the next mouthful, the child promptly swallowed it all on her own. Her breathing was beginning to sound less shallow and more quiet.

"And how are you feeling now?" She asked.

Frankie turned a face to her, hazel eyes, looking just a little bit brighter, shining in the candle light. She nodded in reply, taking a hand and feeling at her throat. Frankie swallowed again. Her breath caught, and she began crying, it was a loud cry, one of relief, one that showed she was alive and had enough fight in her to make noise.

"Oh, Frankie!" At this Mr Fodderhill wrapped his big arms around his daughter, bundling her up against his chest, weeping aloud. Mrs Fodderhill's cheeks glistened as she too hurried to her husband's side, cradling Frankie's head in her arms.

"You're going to be alright." Myrtle murmured, smiling through the tears.

Master Fodderhill let out a long sigh of relief and leant back against the door frame.

"We can't thank you enough." Mr Fodderhill choked looking back at Myrtle.

She had saved Frankie, but all she could hear was the chilling silence of a baby who could not cry. Whose spirit had given in. Of a baby who would never feel the safe embrace of her father's chest and her mother's supple arms cradle. Of parents who would never watch their son grow into a boy and a man.

*   *   *
*

Myrtle wiped the sweat from her brow, hands shaking as she walked down the cobblestone path and back through the lopsided gate of the Farthington's front yard. Mr Farthington's leg had been healed, though it had been broken in three places, and Myrtle had needed to push the bone back into place before she could even think of the honey. This had been a very challenging job, a sour smell had tainted the air with the tell-tale signs of infection. The man had howled in pain, though Myrtle had been as swift as she could in setting the bone back in place. His knuckles clenched a bag of wheat so hard it had burst, the grains spilling out everywhere. She gave a sigh as she closed the gate and managed a weak smile. It had been no small feat. Bees buzzed around her. They had been there, as always. Helping in their own quiet way, wings flittering, antennae waving. One landed on her dress's collar. Most would say, perhaps it had mistaken the embroidered flowers for real ones, but Myrtle knew that they were really much smarter than that.

As she clambered back into the wagon, the exhaustion of the last few days hit her, and when she took hold of the reins, she saw the horizon of dirt under her fingernails. There hadn't been the time to give herself a proper bath, but rather she had only managed to sponge her face and arms. Instead of her beloved steed, the Strawby's old mare, Marley, was hitched to the wagon. Hodgepodge was a distant blob lazily chewing in the field behind them, he still needed more time to recover. The mare, Marley, was in her senior years and didn't like going faster than a trot. Myrtle had almost resorted to scaring the living daylight out of the creature just to get her going. But she was thankful that Hodgepodge could have a rest. He had slowly been returning to his old self. Myrtle could still see fear in his eyes when she moved a little too suddenly, and he always sniffed at her palm before scoffing treats, when he had previously snorted treats into his mouth without any thought.

They took the climb up the mountain slowly, letting the breeze ruffle hair and mane alike. Everyone whom she passed now stopped and waved whenever they saw her. Though tired Myrtle always made sure to wave back, or smile and nod. Finally, they approached the little cottage on the hillside. It's red roof showing through the trees, and sandstone a gritty splodge in the forest of greens. She untacked Marley and led her into the field with Podge, who once seeing Myrtle, turned to walk over to her.

"Podgy," She called, and though he didn't trot to her, she knew he was beginning to trust her again.

He licked his lips and blew warm air through his nose into her outstretched palms. She in turn, blew warm breath into his soft velvet nostrils, laughing as he huffed back at her. She combed a hand through his knotted forelock.

"I've brought your paddock mate back." She whispered to him.

Though Marley wasn't a very exciting companion, she was a companion nonetheless and Hodgepodge was grateful to be with another horse. In Wattleshire, he had been used to a small herd. Myrtle's family owned two other horses, both were big bays called Lucky and Courage, and one of the neighbours' horses was also kept on their property and she knew he had been lonely all by himself.

"And now, I believe I shall go straight to bed." She breathed, closing the gate. But before she could even get to the doorstep a horse and cart was pulling up next to the cottage.

"Myrtle!"

She heard a girlish voice call, it was Miss Pineswood, she was with Miss Jenson and Miss Cobblinghill who were chattering loudly and giggling in the back of the cart.

Myrtle couldn't help but feel her heart sink when she saw the girls, no doubt they would be expecting tea and biscuits and, of course, then there was the matter of conversation, not to mention the sting of embarrassment still tangible from the last time she had been in the company of these girls.

Miss Pineswood's company she could endure, but she was on the edge of exhaustion's deep river, and she feared that if she fell in, there wasn't much hope in getting out again. Miss Pineswood, having no preconceived ideas of how Myrtle was truly feeling, skipped up the path, weaved basket in hand, braids swinging.

"We've come to bring you pudding!" She beamed, "Wendermere pudding!"

And Myrtle fell. Tears welled in her eyes and this time she couldn't stop them, they dripped down her cheeks, lips wobbling, chest heaving. She couldn't even stop herself from snivelling.

"Oh, dear Myrtle." Miss Pineswood dropped the basket to the ground and leapt to her side, enveloping her in a hug, arms wrapping around her, like a blanket.

And then the tears really came. And her lungs heaved, as she sobbed into Miss Pineswood's delicate sleeves, staining the pink fabric. But at least it was the pink fabric of a friend.

Forty-Spotted Pardalote

"Whatever is the matter dear Myrtle?" Miss Pineswood asked, but the only response was the young Beekeeper's continual sobbing, interspersed with coughing.

Miss Coblinghill and Miss Jenson were still standing by the wagon and peering intently at the scene besides the little stone cottage.

"Let's get you inside." She turned back to Myrtle and gently guided the crumpled girl, ushering her through the red-toned door and into the cool kitchen.

"You go hop into bed and I'll start a roaring fire to get you warm!" She smiled, leading Myrtle to the bedroom.

Miss Pineswood then hurried back out to the wagon to tell the other girls that they could make the rest of their rounds without her as she would be needed at the cottage for some time. Myrtle could hear the wagon pulling away, its wheels crunching on the earth. Miss Pineswood returned to the cottage with an armful of wood to start a fire. She was practised in keeping fires and shortly had flames bursting to life within the hearth. The glow of the brick fireplace danced across the shadowed floorboards and the sun winked through the kitchen windows. Its rays were vibrant orange like nasturtium blossoms, its petals folding outwards through the tall pine trees on the forest mountain. Finally, Miss Pineswood took two large spoonfuls of Wendermere pudding, and placed them in delicate china bowls on a tray before shuffling into Myrtle's bedroom.

The young Beekeeper was already fast asleep. The tears staining her red-flushed cheeks were a sticky glow in the fire-light cast from the doorway. Miss Pineswood sighed, a long sigh. She darted back to the kitchen and wrote a quick note.

Dear Miss Beeswood,

I hope you should find the Wendermere Pudding that Miss Coblinghill, Miss Jensen and I have made for you. Do not worry about your image being tarnished, the girls shall know only that you suddenly took a turn and needed to go straight to bed. They will understand, especially after the ordeal you have had in Nearne Forest! I wish for you to know that I am always here for you. Your affectionate friend,
Sincerely Samantha Pineswood.

And with that Samantha tucked the note next to the Pudding, which she had covered with a tea towel, and latched the door behind her.

* * *

*

Dear Mama and Papa,

I am so sorry for worrying you both, but I can assure you that I have quite recovered. I have many people here making sure that I eat, and that I rest. I am already beginning to feel like myself again! However, since my time away the work has piled up and there is a great deal of catching up for me to do and unfortunately, I don't believe that I will be able to return until mid-winter at this rate. I hope that Mama's health is still improving and that my sisters are well also. I hope that Gwendolyn has settled into the new homestead with Timothy, and that Tara is still enjoying work with the orphanage. When I return, I know that I will find Penny a great deal taller, but I hope that she is still chasing fairies in the garden. I am missing everyone and think of you all often.

With Love Myrtle Beeswood.

And with that Myrtle closed the envelope, it would be ready for a wax seal upon her return back to the cottage at nightfall. The letter was smudged and a little messy from the cart's stumbling along the less-used dirt road, but it was the best she could do. Her days had been filled with tireless work, far more work than the incidents Miss Pineswood had relayed while she was recovering. Common colds had turned into pneumonia, upset stomachs had turned children into hollow shells of themselves and broken bones into festering wounds. Today she was visiting the Wrens, a family that lived at Forty-Spotted Pardalote, almost a full day's travel out of Wendermere, on a wool farm. Since the sheep weren't readily used for milk, or cheese, the family would only visit Wendermere perhaps once a month, for supplies, or at shearing season to sell their goods. Myrtle had not yet met the rather elusive family, and she had been told that they preferred to keep to themselves. Yesterday evening, she had received a very urgent message that one of their children had fallen gravely ill. The family were already preparing for the worst when a traveller, passing by on his way from Berrydale, had stepped in for quick refreshments. Seeing as he was travelling to Wendermere they had asked him to fetch for Myrtle or anyone who might be able to help.

So, while the cartwheels whirled, she'd taken this short space of quiet to write her parents the hasty letter. Sighing, she turned her attention back on the road. The saggy bay rump of Marley wobbled with each footfall as she plodded along. Myrtle hated not being able to take Hodgepodge out on adventures, but at least he would be recovered enough for short trips soon. The leaves arched overhead, obscuring parts of the sky, and framing them in speckled greens and yellows. A few browned leaves drifted to the ground lazily. It was already the turn of the season, in the past week autumn had brushed its hands over Wendermere and the surrounding countryside, leaving it shivering in morning frosts. Crystal-like dew sparkled from the hillside paddocks as Myrtle left every morning. The water from the pump hurt if you drank too quickly, or too slowly, numbing the whole body with icy fingers. Tea was a much better alternative, and Myrtle didn't need the excuse of ice-cold water to drink it.

The only problem with long cart drives was that it gave too much time to think. Myrtle sighed, she hadn't wanted to turn her thoughts to the embarrassing scene she had caused while Miss Jenson and Miss Cobblinghill stood there watching. Two times now she had made a fool of herself in front of the other children. It had taken her being lost in the forest and captured by a witch to make her even begin to forget the first time. It calmed her nerves to know that at least this time not all of the children had been watching. At least this time, Finn had not been there, to turn away from her, disappointment plastered on his face. She was grateful for Miss Pineswood's kindness, making the fire and leaving pudding (which she had unashamedly eaten for breakfast the next morning). She was certain that Miss

Pineswood would stem the seed of gossip where she could, however she couldn't help but be concerned at how far the news of her untimely 'episode' would spread.

What if the news was brought back to the children's parents? One childish outburst could be forgiven, but two? It was unprofessional. Beekeepers were supposed to be level-headed, mature, and have wisdom well beyond their years.

A chirp sounded from ahead and there, sitting on a little worn, and crooked picket fence was the Forty-Spotted Pardalote. Myrtle pulled Marley to a halt as she spotted the little bird, only a few paces in front of them, on the side of the road where the woods met the dampened path. Its black beady little eyes peered at her and as it turned its head the subtle yellow blush on its cheeks became visible. Apart from the muddy-yellow cheeks, the bird was quite ordinary from this angle, the rest of its body was earthy-grey. She willed it to turn its body, hoping she might catch a glimpse of the black wings and bright white spots. Myrtle was sure she had seen them, when she had first looked up. Then suddenly the bird flew off, beating its wings so quickly that Myrtle wasn't sure whether she had really seen the spots or not. She sighed, pausing for a moment before encouraging Marley into an ungraceful trot. The Forty-Spotted Pardalote, for which this region had been named, was an extremely rare sight.

She reminded herself that she had not the time to delay, not even for a rare bird, and pushed Marley into a canter. It took a lot of clucking, wiggling of the reins and even growling, but finally the old mare launched herself into a surprisingly smooth canter. Although, it was short lasting and soon poor Marley was quite spent. Myrtle let her walk for the last hour.

They arrived at the edge of the Wren's long windy path and Myrtle grabbed her things quickly, a jar, her belt, and she hesitated for just a few seconds to still her thumping heart. Within the last hour anxiety had set itself upon her, and she needed to recompose herself. Whatever it was that the child suffered from, it could not be worse than she'd already seen. She had brought a man back from the dead. She had done what no Beekeeper, that she had heard of, had ever accomplished. To give life, even after death. And that meant she could do it again if she needed to.

The garden outside of the large woodland house was unkempt. Tomatoes tumbled over broken lattice work, their leaves withered, though bright red tomatoes still shone from their stems. Pumpkins were growing and their leaves made a canopy which the small green pumpkins peeked from. The garden was also a mishmash of herbs and flowers. She was surprised to look a little closer and find that the pumpkins' dominance over the garden was so great that their leaves even harboured chamomile and feverfew underneath them. As she drew her gaze up to the front door, she was made aware of the silence. By all accounts the Wrens were a large family with many children of different ages… but she could hear no children playing, not even little feet tottering on old floorboards.

She frowned, perhaps the family had gone out? But she knew that the thought was silly, unless the child had miraculously recovered, and besides, the only place to go was the sheep fields. They wouldn't leave an ill child by herself. Before she let her thoughts spiral, Myrtle knocked, A hard, confident rap on the wood of the door frame. The window in the door had sheer curtains that were drawn, and she couldn't see inside. She waited. Nothing happened. No movements. No footsteps, not even a groan on the floorboards.

She knocked again, this time louder, and with a longer pause between each knock. Still nothing. She sighed and glanced around the veranda. There were other windows, and she stepped over to them, cupping her hands to peer in. Her breath fogged the glass, obscuring her view, but she could still make out the sheer curtain drawn in a dark room. The hazy shapes behind the curtain told her that it was likely a kitchen, with a large table, chairs and stove, with lots of blurred shadows on top of them. A messy kitchen. There were no people, for none of the shapes moved. She went back to the door, and this time knocked loudly, and for longer. If truly nobody were home, then they couldn't think her ruder for knocking louder. The thumping of heavy booted steps sounded. She almost dashed back to her cart in surprise.

A man opened the door, his face was red and grey stubble bristled from his cheeks and chin. He had clearly expected to see someone taller than Myrtle for his gaze pierced the air above her, before finding its way down to her height.

"And who are you?" He asked, crossing his arms, frown deepening on his face, "We don't have anything for travelling strangers today. You'll have to tell your parents to go to Wendermere."

"O-Oh." Myrtle stuttered then she went on more confidently, "Well, I am not a 'traveller' I'm the Beekeeper you called for. Can you bring me to the sick child?"

"A Beekeeper?!" The man erupted angrily, his face growing even redder, "No… No! We have no use for your thieving lot!"

And he went to slam the door, but not before Myrtle managed to grab the handle, startling him. She didn't know what she was doing. It was as if her hands had a will of their own for everything inside her was screaming for her to run away.

"*Please*, you must let me see the child. I can help." Her voice was unwavering.

"No!" The man snarled, "You're already too late."

Fear, like a snake, slithered, clenching Myrtle's insides. *No.* She thought, *not too late. Never too late.*

"I can help." And she held the man's gaze confidently, hand clenching the knob of the door, white-knuckled, "I can *still* help." she repeated.

The man leered closer, teeth clenched in hatred.

"Martin!"

There was a call from behind the man, a woman's voice. It was strained and desperate.

"Martin, who are you talking to?"

The man turned around to face the woman, "It's nobody Charlotte. Don't bother yourself to get up. I've already dealt with it."

But the footsteps quickened, before the man could shut the door, the figure of a round woman appeared, her cheeks glistening as she hurried to the door. She pushed past her husband's towering figure, face alight with a teary smile clasping Myrtle's hands.

"Thank you for coming. It must have been such a long way." Her eyes became half-moons, and she sniffled.

Myrtle found herself blushing with surprise, and glancing awkwardly to the man, whose face grew darker and darker and as realisation hit him.

"*Charlotte-*." His nose was scrunching, as his brows knit together. "*YOU* sent for this girl!" He boomed.

Mrs Wren's hands were on her hips in an instant as she turned to regard her husband.

"*Yes!*" She hissed, "I sent for the Beekeeper! Because our little girl was dying, and it doesn't matter about past grievances and past Beekeepers when your daughter is on her deathbed! A smart man would KNOW that!" Her tone, though quieter than his, sent shivers down Myrtle's spine. This was not a woman to be trifled with. And Mr Wren, clearly agreed, for his shape cowered under her words and he sank backwards. Mrs Wren drew her attention back to Myrtle and softened. Her eyes were puffy and red.

"I'm afraid that… There's nothing that can be done now. But I hope you might stay for some tea and lunch for your troubles." But the woman couldn't hold her tears back any longer, and she choked down a sob, bringing a hand to her mouth and retreating into the shadows of the doorway.

"I'm sorry."

Her voice came between sobs. Myrtle knew she must see the girl immediately, if there was ever any hope, in her being revived.

"Please. I must see her."

"Now, see 'ere-!" The man regained his voice but was interrupted.

"Don't you understand, child?" The woman willed her grief to part, and for a moment she returned as the ferocious mother, "It is too late. Lilly is dead!"

And the grief soared back in like a wave, taking her in shaking sobs, she hunched over and turned away from Myrtle. But she was not about to be sent away, or to be given tea when such a grave job was at hand.

"I do understand." She pressed on, "And I would like to see the child."

The man was still frowning, but he had something else on his face. They were both shocked.

"Do you mean to say that… you could still heal her?" The woman murmured.

"Perhaps." Myrtle chewed her lip, "But, only if I should be brought to the girl right this very moment."

And with that, they hurried her inside, but not without Mr Wren muttering under his breath that he 'didn't like this, not one little bit'. The house was cool, and a fire had not been lit despite a chilly morning. The floorboards groaned under each step as they shuffled down the hallway. Myrtle spotted a thin little face peeking from one of the rooms that they passed. It was the face of a young boy with ash-blonde hair and dark brown eyes. His face was as pale as the moon, and his eyes loomed large as he watched. They took her to the last room at the very far end of the house and Mr Wren fumbled with a key to unlock the door.

"I shall need hot water." Myrtle whispered.

"Then you shall have it." With that Mrs Wren was off, scuttling down the hallway again, as she passed the side rooms, a door creaked, it was the boy, his hand clutching the sides of his trousers as he fumbled, another even younger curly haired child had joined him now.

And the door opened. The scent of dust made Myrtle sneeze. This room was clearly not often used or cleaned.

She wasn't quite sure what to expect as she stepped into the room. There was a bed with a patchwork quilt and a window, which would have looked out into the forest, had the curtains not been drawn closed. On the bed was a white sheet that concealed the figure of the girl, Lily, the Wren's daughter. Her outline of white splashed against the dark green curtains and the colourful quilt.

Through the thin, almost transparent sheet the child's nose, and toes poked upward, a hint of blond hair tumbled down over the pillows. Myrtle moved slowly to the child's side, clasping the honey jar tightly against her chest. Her breath came out raggedly as she sighed, preparing herself for the face that lay beneath the cloth. She was beginning to realise how different this situation was from the man in Winspern. Pushing herself on, she took the top edge in a shaky hand and folded it down to reveal the face. The girl looked as though she were sleeping. Blond lashes turned down, pale face cold, yet gleaming. light freckles showed where the sun had kissed her face like a mosaic. Myrtle was surprised to find that the girl looked much like herself. For one moment she almost felt as though it were own figure lying on the bed, the breath of life fading fast from her chest.

Instead, she was here, gazing upon the girl, whose spirit had long since left her body. No Beekeeper could heal her, the girl couldn't be fixed. Myrtle almost stumbled, as she realised the magnitude of what she was doing, of what she was trying to accomplish. Perhaps she had brought a man back from the dead once, but had he really been dead? Had his spirit totally left him? Perhaps it was just his heart that had momentarily stopped. This girl had been dead for many hours, possibly the whole night. Myrtle couldn't call her spirit back to her, not any more than she could will a wild bird not to fly, or wild horse not to gallop.

A bee bobbed into her vision, as she gazed at the wooden floor. Its wings hummed in the silence of death, striped yellow and black like a tiny sun meeting earth at dawn.

She can be healed. I can do what you cannot. Her spirit can be called.

The bee landed on the face of the girl, the husk of Lillian Wren. Its sticky paws crawled over her cheek, its legs were heavily laden with orange pollen. Antennae waved in anticipation.

Myrtle clenched her fists and sucked in a breath. Then she flicked open her eyes. Mrs Wren returned with a sloshing jug of water. She stood anxiously by the door, Mr Wren had also returned beside her, he was quiet.

Myrtle unrolled the lambskin, and the bee immediately took flight landing over on her pouch.

"Which ones? I haven't a clue." She whispered under her breath to the bee.

In return the bee began crawling over the herbs, Myrtle watched patiently until the bee found a jar of dried petals. She took the jar with gentle hands, it was chamomile. She frowned, surely not just chamomile? It was a good herb, one she used often, it had many properties, such as calming nerves, and aiding digestion. She took a heavy spoonful of glistening amber honey and crushed the petals in her fist sprinkling them onto a bowl with the honey. A few splashes of hot water and then she mixed. The sweet scent of honey wafting through the air as the vapour rose. The bee was still, its antennae waving on the glass jar. *Shall I add anything else?* Myrtle hesitated. *Was that enough chamomile?*

"A-Are you... able to heal her, Beekeeper?" The voice came from Mrs Wren by the door.

They had caught her pausing, Myrtle sighed and unclenched her hands. Their trust of Beekeepers would be destroyed if she could not do this. Perhaps their trust had already been destroyed.

She is sleeping. I will wake her.

Myrtle turned to the bee again, it had risen in the air and was floating back to the lifeless figure.

"She is only sleeping." Myrtle found her voice reassuring the couple.

Just chamomile it shall be then. Though her heart still thumped like heavy hooves on hard stone she stilled her trembling hands and lifted the bowl to the dead girl's lips. The steam rose from the medicine, flickering over the girl's face, its tendrils snaking and then vanishing. The vapour collected and droplets formed like tiny pearls on her skin. Myrtle didn't know exactly how to give her medicines to the dead, but she had to try, so she began to tip the bowl ever-so-slightly.

Lillian's eyelids fluttered open. Fawn eyes bright. Breath rose and fell from her chest in a gasp. The Wrens in turn, exclaimed loudly, jumping up and rushing to their daughter's side.

"Lillian! Oh, dear Lillian!" Charlotte wept, her tears coming now in far greater quantities than before.

Martin was more sceptical, he stood, dumb founded above his daughter, the frown had been wiped from his face and was replaced with shock. He shot Myrtle a look, it said, *this must be a trick.* But he knew that even if it were a trick, it was a very good one.

"Oh, mama and papa-" Lillian frowned, "Why am I not in my room?"

"You've been dead child," Martin spoke, taking her hand in his, "But, you're here now. And that's all that matters."

And with that, even the burly man with callouses as deep as steep riverbanks could not hold the joy back from his face and the tears.

Myrtle smiled, and just breathed. She stepped back, and quietly walked down the hallway. Wondering to herself the mystery of what had unfolded, for the honey hadn't even touched her mouth before her eyes had opened. Sensing that the family needed much time alone, she walked back to her cart waiting beneath the trees. They need not be troubled with her tea or lunch, for she had taken provisions for the trip. Myrtle climbed into the cart's seat, just as she caught sight of Mrs Wren's wide figure hurrying as fast as her legs could take her, arriving breathless before the cart.

"Please, we don't have much, but take this- we can't afford to be in debt. I hope it might be enough." The woman produced a pouch, and the clinking of coins followed.

"O-Oh." Myrtle stammered, "I-I can't take this."

The woman frowned, her eyes flicking from the bag to the young Beekeeper in front of her.

"Whatever do you mean?" Mrs Wren huffed, "do you mean to say that we'll need to pay you instalments? I-Is it not enough?"

Myrtle was taken aback.

"Mrs Wren, I'm a Beekeeper." Myrtle gave an awkward smile, "I have taken a vow to never accept money as have all Beekeepers. Whatever gave you the notion that I should need payment?"

"You don't accept money?" Charlotte paused and a nervous laugh escaped her, "What do you accept then?"

"I won't accept anything from you Mrs Wren, you should go back and celebrate the return of your daughter."

"They were right," She had tears in her eyes, "Oh Wilds- you are a good Beekeeper."

Myrtle smiled back at the woman, as she made her way back to the house, where all of her children had now clambered out from their rooms and were stomping about the house with such glee. Marley picked up a trot as the driveway met the dusty road. It would be a long way back to Wendermere, but the joy of the family reunited would fill her hours with peace. As they trotted away from the house, she turned back... there was the bird again. It stayed perched, on the fence, just long enough for Myrtle to count the spots, all forty of them on the little Pardalote as it turned from the picket fence post and collided with the breeze.

Spread Thin as Honey

"Beekeeper." It was the voice of a man, a ragged beard framing his face.

His hand was on the shoulder of his son, a young boy with sandy blond hair. A large growth covered his right cheek, pushing his eyelid closed. Myrtle hadn't ever encountered such a large facial growth before.

"He has had it his whole life, and it has been steadily growing. The doctor said they couldn't do anything-" The man's brows knit together, "-and that he would not live long."

Myrtle began smoothing together a paste. A bee flittered over to a brightly coloured turmeric root. This was a new ingredient that Myrtle had been able to add to her honey remedies, it had been a gift from Mr Pineswood from his recent trades with other merchants. She crushed a sliver of the root into a vivid orange, adding mint and feverfew. Then she drizzled sticky honey and mixed.

"I believe that will do." She gave a spoonful to the boy and proceeded to wait.

The boy, though he had been grimacing as Myrtle pounded the ingredients, now took the spoon, the syrup medicine disappearing into his mouth.

"Mmm, it doesn't taste like medicine." His voice was slurred and muffled by the growth.

And then, before their very eyes the growth shrunk, its edges receding, until the boy exclaimed in excitement.

"Papa! I can see through my right eye!"

But the growth was not entirely gone. Myrtle could see it would take a few doses, and a little bit of patience. She ladled the medicine into a jar and handed it to the father.

"Here, give him two doses a day. Both in the morning and the evening until the abscess is completely gone."

He took the jar, eyes smarting with tears, one hand grasping the shoulder of his boy.

"Thank you, thank you so much."

And as they left, Myrtle sighed and turned to regard the long line. It wasn't dwindling, but instead was growing longer. People from further than even Pinesdale had congregated in Wendermere, all with ailments for Myrtle to heal. The news of the first man Myrtle had raised from the dead had spread to all surrounding provinces. Nobody had ever heard of a Beekeeper... no... not even a witch who could raise the dead after a full night and day. And nobody had heard of a Beekeeper who could raise the dead not once but twice. People from far villages had begun arriving in droves in the last couple of weeks. First there were only a few and then a trickle, stream and then a torrent. She couldn't turn them away, so many had come, most with chronic illnesses that were progressive or illnesses that would eventually lead to death if left untreated. There were so many people that she had needed to station herself in Wendermere's town square so that she could see people as quickly and efficiently as possible. Every night she trudged through her cottage door later and later and left so early that the sun's rays were not visible over the walnut orchard and distant pine forest.

Once, it had even been so late that she had needed to spend the night at the Strawbys.

Hodgepodge was finally back by her side, his rounded flank shifting as he happily munched on a hay bale that the Farthingtons had dropped off to her. He blinked lazily in the sun and snorted as a grass seed got caught in a nostril. Then he went back to chewing slowly and yawned, his muzzle becoming a show of teeth as his eyes rolled back. Even though Myrtle was beyond tired, she couldn't help but muster a smile. The next couple in line stepped forward. They were young, the woman was beautiful, her skin glowed, and her cheeks blushed with a faded red. Her striking green eyes shone in the sunlight and beat with inner emotion. Her brunette hair fell in ringlets down her back, it too shone when the light hit it, reflecting the shine like a stream caught in a ray of sunlight. When she opened her mouth to smile, her teeth too were so white, like caps on a mountain. Myrtle almost gasped, the woman was so beautiful that she could've been a princess, however she was not. Her dress, though fitting, was simple faded blue and worn floral embroidery on her collar hinted at the garment's many past adventures.

"And what can I do for you?" Myrtle asked before the couple could speak. She realised that she must've been just a little bit too animated, for the woman looked taken aback for a moment.

"-Oh." She started, looking suddenly embarrassed, "I… well you see."

The man beside her, was a less striking character though he still had charming features, and a well-groomed appearance. He placed a hand on the woman's shoulder and stepped forward.

"My wife and I, you see… we've been married for five years." He started, and then too hesitated, meeting Myrtle's gaze unwaveringly.

Myrtle frowned a little, unsure what the man was wanting from her. After a few moments of awkward anticipation, she couldn't wait any longer.

"Yes?" She prompted

"Well…" He motioned to his wife and then his voice lowered at a whisper, "There haven't been any children."

Myrtle's eyes raised and she leaned back a little nodding. *Children, of course they want children.* She continued to nod sifting through her memory, of her mother's instructions and her training. Had they ever healed a couple of infertility? Then again, she had never raised anybody from the dead with her mother, nor had she ever heard of her mother raising the dead. Perhaps it can be done. There were many things that remained a mystery in the ways of Beekeepers, and Myrtle was learning more and more that sometimes you needed to just get on with things.

"I have to be honest." Myrtle sighed, "I'm not sure it can be done."

The couple looked on eagerly, hope sparkled in their eyes, as well as a distinct fear of the unknown. Bees crawled around her, they buzzed from the wagon where the hives were concealed to the flower beds besides the town houses and shops. Some briefly alighted on her arms and head and on the jars of honey besides her, sticky legs clambering around the lids trying to find a way to the sweet syrup. She turned to her herbs before her and the bowl, which had already been used many times today and held the residual of many different combinations of honey and herbs. No bees flew to her aid as she wondered what she might use. None turned to land on the fresh flowers and dried herb bottles. Perhaps all that was needed was honey? She waited a long moment, feeling the couple grow nervous when they could see that their Beekeeper was hesitating. What could it mean that she had raised the dead but could not help a couple procure a baby? Surely raising the dead was a far harder task. She frowned. Just honey it would be then. She grabbed a jar from the box and handed it to the couple. Then she paused again wondering about the specific requirements to give them.

"You will both need to take it," She began, "One spoon-"

She trailed off, "One teaspoon a day, and for a whole month."

The couple took the jar from her hands and the man handed it to the woman, who clutched it tight against her breast.

"You are a most kind and blessed Beekeeper!" The man grinned, "Thank you."

Myrtle nodded and smiled at the couple as they left. Was she giving them a false hope? She couldn't be sure.

With each new person she saw, it was beginning to feel as though she gave another part of herself away. And she was dwindling. The sun seemed to pull at her face and the corners of her mouth, as though her features were melting. Each time she smiled, it became harder, like stones had been tied to her lips.

The next man in line had a boy, pale and limp in his arms. For a moment Myrtle was worried that the boy might be dead, but she breathed a sigh of relief when the man explained that his son had fallen sick with fever and had fallen into a deep sleep. She set to work fumbling through the dried bottles of herbs and the fresh sprigs. Bees fluttered around her, two crawled down her fingers, their paws tickling her skin as they walked.

She picked feverfew, echinacea, and arrowroot after listening to the boy's breathing and finding that he was congested. Then honey was drizzled in, and the medicine was mixed. Once done she promptly handed the bowl to the father with a spoon.

"Perhaps you would like to feed him a few spoonfuls for me?" She asked, unable now to keep exhaustion from seeping into her voice.

"Oh-" The man looked startled and visibly uncomfortable, "Surely not I? I am not a Beekeeper? I am no healer?"

"But the medicine has been made by a Beekeeper." Myrtle retorted, "It wouldn't matter who gave the medicine, but only who made it."

The man would still not take hold of the bowl from her, in fact he flinched away from her outstretched hand.

"Are you afraid?" Myrtle frowned.

"O-Of course not. Forgive me Beekeeper, but I would not want to risk the medicine in my untrained hands."

Myrtle sighed, pulling back and swirling the bowl's contents once more, "Alright."

The man lifted the boy's head, and he stirred a little, opening his eyes for but a moment he muttered something between chattering teeth. She cupped his chin and spooned a mouthful of the medicine into his mouth. He swallowed. She wasn't convinced that just one would be enough to break the fever and she took another spoonful of the medicine, waiting for him to stir. And he did, his eyes opened for a moment as they met Myrtle's.

"One more spoonful- " She told him and scooped the syrup into his mouth.

The colour slowly returned to his face, red to his lips and his teeth stopped chattering.

"Oh, father-" He called, "I could see people- faceless people- shadows. They wanted to take me." He gripped his father's shirt.

"It's alright, it was only a dream." His father smiled.

Myrtle stepped back to clean the bowl in the trough of water beside her.

"I wasn't sure that this would be enough- We don't have a lot. I hoped perhaps what others were saying was true, that your lot had changed, but I didn't want to take my chances."

She turned back to the man to find him proffering an upturned palm, six copper coins glittering in the light.

"I cannot accept coins." Myrtle mustered a thin smile.

"Cannot or will not?"

"Cannot, it's in our oaths." Myrtle explained, "We will not accept money, those are our ways and have always been. Where are you from? Have you ever been treated by another Beekeeper?"

"Always been?" The man shook his head, "I haven't, but a woman in our village was so sick they took her to Winspern while a Beekeeper was there some years ago. The Beekeeper did her job, but nearly bled our whole village dry. The woman's family was so poor they didn't have enough to pay for the healing, and so our whole village was paying instalments for the next year."

Myrtle was left struck and unable to speak, and the convergence of many different memories came to light.

"I don't suppose you know where this Beekeeper originated from?"

"I'm unsure sorry Miss, all I know is that once a month she travelled to Winspern, for it was there that she would collect payments."

"I am so sorry that your village was treated in such a way by one of my kind." Myrtle looked at the man with compassion, "The Beekeeper who you describe has made a grave mistake."

The man nodded and shook Myrtle's hand before he turned to leave. As she watched them turn back towards their cart she shivered. For a vile feeling was enveloping her. The Beekeeper whom the man was referring to would not be worthy of that title, they would be more comparable to a witch. Though she could not quite grasp at the memory, she knew she was missing something. A memory lost within Nearne, if only she could discover it again.

*　*　*
*

Dear Myrtle Beeswood,

I hope that you have found time to recover from both the ordeal that the Nearne Forest was, and the state that the experience left you in. I called in today and found once more that you were off healing the many sick that have gathered in Wendermere's town square! You seem to have your hands quite full, and I hope that you are managing. The Strawby's sent me along with an apple pie, it smells delicious! As I was writing this note and waiting for you, a story came to mind, from a book that I have been rereading... I am not sure why I feel the need

*to share it with you, but perhaps it is a story for such a time as this.
With love from Miss Pineswood*

The Horse and its Rider

There once was a horse, on whose back sat a royal and gallant knight, in silver armour shining. The horse was as black as the deep dark night, its eyes were as wide as a dinner plate and the strands of its tail were as thick as a bullwhip. The horse's muscles were like fine sculpted clay rippling as it carried its rider to wherever he wanted to run. This horse was a beast among the cavalry, and the other horses shied away at his splendour. When he broke into a trot the ground quivered and when he galloped the earth peeled away. When he leaped, it was as though he had the power of an eagle and soared over every obstacle. And the knight who rode this horse was no ordinary knight. He was the King.

The kingdom was preparing for a battle with the enemy, a strong legion of shadowy monsters from the south who wielded a dark power of poisonous thorns and vines. The horse would practise the battle charge with his rider, the King, every day. He would flick his tail eagerly and swing his head like a viper and then when the horn sounded, he launched himself forward with a shrill whinny, always ahead of the rest of the cavalry. But when the day of war came, and the scent of battle filled the horse's nostrils, excitement entered his heart like an ignited fire gone wild. Such delirium filled the beast's heart that he thought suddenly of his rider as an impediment. The lines of the army stretched out beside and behind them, so numerous they were like ants on the hilltop, waiting until the monsters hiding in the valley below showed themselves. Waiting for the blasts of golden horns. But the horse of midnight would not wait. He stamped at the dust and threatened the squire boy with bared teeth.

"Wait." The King commanded him.

But he would not wait. He gathered his loins under himself with the strength of a lion ready to pounce, but before he could leap the King took his reins and gathered them tightly to the side so that he could not turn and run. The horse then reared, pounding the air with his hooves. He wanted for the wind to be in their faces and to feel the earth rumble as he galloped down the rocky hillside. He wished to be racing ahead of the calvary so far ahead that the army would become a splash behind them on the mountain. He longed for the thunder of his hooves to make the rocks on the mountain above tremble.

"Enough!"

And the horse halted with such force from the reins and he reared up once again. The horse was so furious to be denied by his rider that he threw his head down between his front legs and bucked sideways down the slope, throwing dirt into the air like a sandstorm. The King knew his horse could not be calmed and so he dismounted onto the ground. If the horse could have talked, he would have said, 'Ha-! Without you holding me back, I can finally charge into battle!' For he thought he had at last rid himself of the rider that was holding him back. The horse gathered himself to launch down the hillside and into the forest below where there was surely an ambush awaiting. So the King slid off a gauntlet, exposing the leather glove beneath. Then, the King struck his mount on the chest. A thunderous clap, resounding through the air. The horse was so startled that it turned and leaped into a gallop, away from the King and the valley below, instead galloping across the slope far away from the battle and into the mountains.

"Though you may be out of control dear horse. I am always in control. And I am always trustworthy."

Myrtle's hands clasped the paper, her shivering brought creases to the note, making pockets of shadow where the ink looked almost as though it were bleeding. She pulled her duvet cover up to her neck and sighed. It had been another long day, and she had come home too tired to light a fire. Instead, she cut a wedge of apple pie and stumbled straight into bed. The sun had long since disappeared beneath the forest's horizon. In the town square she had watched as its fiery orange bled across the mountain's peak and then the mist descended, its tendrils burning a chilly path down her throat. Perhaps tomorrow she would watch the sunset from her cottage on the mountain's side. But the hope quickly left her when she thought of the travellers, so many in fact that the town could not find a bed for all of them. Many would stay in the streets tonight, sleeping on the back of their wagons or on the cobblestone with a rolled-up jacket as a pillow. And they were sick. Some were even dying. Many were children and babies. They all needed her.

She let out a raspy breath. Fear was slinking from beneath the mirage of exhaustion. Its huge talons pressing her chest, weighing her down. Squeezing her. She took another shaky breath, but air wasn't enough. Tears pricked the corners of her eyes and soon she was crying. Smudging her tears with the back of her wrist, crumpling Samantha Pineswood's note with her other hand.

*　　*　　*
*

"Myr-Miss Beeswood."

The call came from behind Myrtle, and behind the line of people in front of her that trailed from the square, out from the town perimeters, and past houses, as brick turned into field. The people looked like ants in the distance, trickling out of their underground home to come lap at sweet honey. The line had only grown since yesterday. She turned to try to find the noise, though she initially couldn't see anyone, and so went back to her work -a woman with her tiny premature baby.

"Beeswood?"

This time she was sure she had heard her name and whipped around to find the freckled face of a boy, Finn.

"-Oh Master Strawby." She trickled honey into the medicine that she was mixing.

"I gave Samantha an apple pie- to give to you. Mother made it."

"Yes, it was lovely, you must thank her for me." Myrtle gestured to the mother to hold the baby up to her, and she spooned the medicine into its mouth.

"And… are you well Miss Beeswood?"

"I'm quite alright Master Strawby." Myrtle paused and sighed, turning to him once more, "Just busy."

"I can see that." Finn murmured, nodding slowly as he squinted against the sun and the long line of people.

Myrtle mixed the bowl on her lap once more. The amber honey was so stiff this morning that little bubbles trapped in the liquid would not break the surface, even when stirring slowly.

"Some of us are going down to the creek again today. The Merryweather's say this'll be the last warm day before next summer." He rocked back on his feet as he spoke.

"And- well I thought that maybe you'd want to come." He continued, "Samantha will be there."

A Frown crept onto Myrtle's forehead, and she clenched the spoon in her hand a little too tightly. The spoon, already sticky with honey, suddenly slipped and flicked out of her hands, tumbling through the air and hitting the pavement.

"Ag! Look what I've done!" She exclaimed, exasperation bleeding into her words, she leant over to pick it up, but Finn already had the spoon in his hands.

"Here." He said, handing it back to her.

"Thanks." She mumbled, sighing once more.

She moved to the trough to wash the dirt and sticky honey. Finn followed her as she went.

"Will you come?" He asked.

"Can't you see that I'm busy?" She met his gaze

Finn recoiled visibly, his expression gave her pause. She hadn't meant to sound angry, but as the frown melted from her face and the glimmer of passion faded from her sharp gaze, she realised that she had, in fact, been angry, furious even.

"I have a lot to do." She continued.

"Y-Yes," His voice faltered, "Can I help you?"

"No." She met his gaze again, his hazel eyes were searching her features, but she didn't know what he expected to find. Perhaps he was just disappointed.

"Samantha said you might have that answer."

This time it was Myrtle who flinched back. The scowl returned to her face for a brief moment.

"This is my duty. There are no other Beekeepers- for miles apparently." She bit her lip, "I thought that there were more, but there are not. And so- Who else will tend to their needs?"

There was tense silence, Finn stood, searching, for a few moments more and then he drew out a breath. He gave up. What he was trying to find, evidently, wasn't there.

"Alright then, well I hope you are able to rest easier soon. Good day Miss Beeswood." And with that he dipped his cap to her and was off.

Myrtle found herself more worn from the conversation, than even from the many needy people that she spent all day healing. She came back to the woman and the baby, with nothing left to give, she couldn't muster a smile for them as they left. Though colour had returned to the baby's complexion as it wiggled in its mother's arms.

*　　*　　*
*

Another day dawned, the sun's rays yawned through the pine trees on the horizon, piercing the grey. Myrtle shivered as she shook the reins.

"Come on Podge."

Over the course of the last few weeks, the weather had turned sour, Autumn had approached with frosty mornings and rubied leaves. As they clopped down the road littered with the tree's discarded summer outfits she was reminded quite abruptly of the crumpled leaves in another forest. One perpetually stuck in autumn, never ready to move on to the bleak winter, but always rejecting the warmth that summer would bring. That forest was Nearne Forest. Over time, her memories of the place were trickling back in, but they had a habit of doing so especially in the moments when she wanted to forget the most. Melinda had called the forest Ambling's End. Perhaps because it was a place where travelling would end. The witch had made sure of that, spinning a sticky web across the forest, catching lost travellers like flies. Those stories that she had told of other travellers… Myrtle shivered at the thought. The whispers of the night she had escaped came tumbling back to her. Whispers of another girl who had come willingly to the witch. Was it her imagination, or had the grotesque figure even called this other girl a Beekeeper? It couldn't have been a coincidence, but the memories of that night were still too hazy to fully unravel.

As they continued down the winding mountain path, she passed Mr Farthington and Mr Fodderhill, heading out to the fields for a day's work. They both smiled at her and waved. Mr Farthington even asked whether she needed anything. She had already packed a lunch, bread and cheese. The long few weeks had taught her well to bring a meal. A few bees hummed lazily in the back of the cart, they were still sleepy. And soon they would sleep. Over winter she would have to conserve her jars of honey, for they would barely be able to produce enough to keep themselves alive. There were duties that needed to be fulfilled before the cold truly set in. Fear sparked in her chest. She wasn't sure what she would do if the droves of people continued over winter.

She finally made it into town, and she untacked Hodgepodge leading him into the Jenson's paddock, which was a conveniently short walk from the town's square. She grabbed as many jars of honey as she could carry in a wooden box, grunting with the effort as she trudged down the street into the cobblestone square. Another loud grunt escaped her as she set the heavy box down. She brushed off her skewed apron and then promptly sat down. Pairs of blinking eyes were already in front of her. A yelp startled her from in the crowd.

"Help me! Someone please!" Cried a woman's voice, "We've been waiting for so long!"

"Make way! Make way!" A man's voice hollered, "This boy needs help now!"

The crowd parted, everyone turned around to witness the commotion. A woman trailed behind a large man who carried a boy in his arms. They made their way before Myrtle where she could see fear in their eyes, wide and yawning. Like a gaping wound. The woman's face was streaked with tears and the man's brow creased with a permanent furrow. He held out the boy.

"Please, please." The woman whispered, and then continued, "Is he dead? He isn't. He can't be." Her voice quivered and broke as she returned to sobbing.

The boy's mouth was opened, lips blue. His arms drooped, his body limp in his father's arms. Sweat was beaded on his brow, and it trickled off his forehead, tumbling down his cold cheeks.

Myrtle moved around the table, taking the boy's pulse. It took her a while to find it, but it was there, weakly pattering.

"Lie him down," She instructed, taking a jar of honey and a wooden bowl from the table.

She had to work quickly, for the boy was barely holding on. The woman was on the verge of hysterics, she crouched sobbing, muttering and interjecting with louder screams of help. The man was more focused, but could hardly support his wife, as she could not be calmed.

Myrtle grabbed for dried chilli, the boy needed warming up. Hot water… This time she needed hot water.

"I need hot water!" She called, "I need someone to fetch me hot water!"

The man was soon echoing her call, yelling louder than Myrtle's exhausted voice could muster. She prepared the other ingredients as she waited, checking the boy's forehead, there was no sign of fever. She guessed that perhaps the boy could be poisoned. She added fresh yarrow to the bowl, crushing it to a paste. People began thumping on the doors of homes around the square, asking whether the families inside had recently boiled water. A young man finally dashed through the crowd, a jug of steaming water sloshing as he ran.

"Here Miss," He set the jug down on the table, huffing.

Myrtle took the jug and poured the water into the wooden bowl. The honey gleamed and sparkled as it began dissolving. An aroma of chilli hit the air as the steam wafted, it stung her eyes. She stirred the honeyed medicine until it had all fully incorporated and then took her attention back to the boy.

"Prop him up." She commanded.

The man bent to hold the boy's skinny frame upright, his eyelids flickered briefly before he became entirely still again- too still. Myrtle took a large ladle this time, instead of the spoon she usually used and scooped the liquid up. It looked almost like a thin broth with all of the herbs floating and the steam. Carefully, she poured the medicine into his mouth, stopping at intervals. Then she took a step back. But the boy was still, he did not wake.

"What's wrong?" Asked the man.

The woman, now in a crumpled heap on the stone ground, looked up with terror in her dark eyes. They were pools of anguish. She let out another blood curdling scream. It split the air and threatened to break Myrtle's concentration. She shook her head to clear the sound and scooped up another ladle of the medicine to gently feed the boy again. But he refused to comply with the honey's tender call.

"He's not waking!" The woman screeched, "He's gone! My boy is gone!"

"Is the medicine not working?" The man couldn't keep fear from his words, as his wife fell apart behind him.

Myrtle tried to think, she looked over her herbs. Something must be missing. But she felt paralysed. The noise of the screaming filled her ears, and her senses- and she couldn't feel her bees. She couldn't think.

"Stop that noise." She hissed under clenched teeth, her eyes flicked to the families who were now peering out of their doors and windows at the commotion unfolding in the street. A few men came running and then slowed as they realised that there was nothing that they could do to help. The screaming reached a new pitch, its frequency made Myrtle pin her hands against her ears and grit her teeth.

"I need her gone." Myrtle whispered, but nobody could hear her, "Someone, take this woman away! She can't be here!"

Though her call was not loud she saw Mr Pineswood make his way through the crowd and take hold of the mother's shoulders. She tried to shake him off, but he coaxed her gently and she finally conceded. Myrtle let out a ragged breath as she disappeared inside the Pineswood's house down the road. A few moments passed as she collected herself, letting the ringing in her ears subside and the gentle hum of bees wash over her. She checked the boy's pulse again, his heart still fluttered softly beneath his chest. The herbs' scents mingled in front of her, the smell a cacophony almost as loud as the screaming. She clenched and unclenched her fists. Though she could hear the bees, none of them came forward, there were no tiny paws pattering to her side, no wings fluttering to her.

Ask me.

How do I ask you? Myrtle thought, *you are but a whisper on the breeze, I don't know who you are.* Her brow was knit together, she gripped the table, she couldn't look up at the man. She couldn't allow herself to see the pain in the face of the boy's father. She couldn't allow herself to confront failure. Not again. Not while her mother's lungs still fought to breath. Not while the third hive lay silent. She wouldn't live with another failure. To ask felt like a fantasy. The Wild King but a legend.

"I refuse to fail again." Myrtle murmured, "Not when I was just beginning to have a grasp over things."

Ask.

Myrtle felt her vision blur, the film of her eyes diluting until the hard cracked stone could no longer be seen. Bees crawled over the glass jars in front of her. They hummed quietly, but she couldn't hear their whisper. The man was talking, but she couldn't hear him. He put a hand upon her shoulder. Her lip wobbled as she exhaled shakily.

"I-I canno-" Her voice sounded foreign as she addressed the man, she tried to find the words.

I can.

And the whisper became a roar, rushing like rattling leaves swirling to the forest's floor. Trees shedding their skins, new buds of vibrant green sprouting in their wake. For a moment she was swept up in this world. It was undeniable, could such a sound come from the bees? Surely not. For a moment, she was caught up in the roar. That moment was all that she needed.

"Please." She choked, to the roar.

I will.

And the boy spluttered out of sleep. A fit of coughing wracked him as he sat upright, eyes wide and startled. The crowd was a mixture of shocked gasps, people fighting to see what had happened, stumbling forward. Then the street erupted with cheering.

*   *   *
*

If all that I truly need to do is ask, then I should return home now. Myrtle thought as the gentle crunch of wheels on gravel and the clop of hooves lulled her. She had flung the blanket over herself and curled up, eyelids heavy with sleep's embrace. But still she felt restless- nights of unease- days of tireless work… It felt as though everyday she poured a little more of herself out, gave part of herself away to each sick person. Would she have enough of herself to give? The day had long since ended and the sky turned to dark. Leaves crinkled as the wheels of the cart rolled over them. Then a thought came; she *had* asked for her mother's healing. While the sting of defeat had long accompanied the many times, she had tried to heal her mother this memory came with a new wash of shame. For she had forgotten the words. A few years ago, standing beside her mother's bed, she stirred a bowl of honey with a splash of lemon and chamomile. Her mother had told her to recite words.

'*O Wild King. If you are willing, please heal your servant. Restore this Beekeeper to health with your life. We ask for your strength, let it be given through the honey of bees.*'

How could she have forgotten the words? Once she had attended to the travellers, she would return home.

The sudden yearning was urgent. She needed to study the words again- even perhaps the old stories. The ones that her parents used to read. Passion like fire washed over her and gave her unwavering courage. *If I can raise a child from the dead... or a man, I can heal my mother.*

Mark of the Flower

A man came forward from the line of travellers. He was alone, he had no family, nor any companions with him. Myrtle could see from his eyes that he was gravely ill. They stared out; grey and sightless from their sockets. Though he appeared blind he had retained some amount of vision, as he did not stumble when he walked. He seemed to be able to recognise Myrtle as the Beekeeper, but his gaze never met her's, nor did they focus on anything, but stared blankly ahead.

"Beekeeper." his voice came exhausted, hollow from shallow breaths.

It was here that Myrtle suddenly noticed how young the man was. His hair was thick black with no signs of thinning or greying. His frame, though stooped with pain, was sturdy and muscular. Fear prickled on the back of Myrtle's neck, this sickness didn't look ordinary.

"Can you-" He grimaced with pain, "Can you heal me?"

Myrtle searched the man's milky eyes, she couldn't see anything obvious pointing to the cause of the sickness- perhaps it was a widespread infection of some kind?

"Can you see?" She asked

"Just, barely. I can…. Make out the shapes."

She held up three fingers, wavering them across his vision, trying to find any movement in his eyes. But there was none.

"Can you see how many fingers I am holding up?"

"No…"

Next, she felt his forehead, it wasn't hot with fever, in fact it was quite the opposite. It felt almost like touching glass… or stone. A wave of fear raced through her. His lips were purple-grey and now that she was closer to his face she could see the thin vine-like veins that ran underneath his skin, they were accentuated around his eyes. She leaned in closer and ran a thumb over the veins, she could almost feel them beneath the skin. They branched and snaked away through the skin tissue- as they should. But there was something different about them, they were all tinged green, not blue or red, but green. Green like new sprouts, growing from the earth, weaving their way through the soil until they finally broke forth from the dirt.

"What is it?" The man asked

"I am not sure." Myrtle admitted, "Can I see your arm."

He buttoned the cuff of his shirt and pulled up his sleeve to expose an arm where pink skin faded to a lifeless pale. Myrtle couldn't stop a gasp from escaping her lips as her gaze landed on something that shouldn't have been there. A stem was protruding through the chalky-grey skin near his elbow. At the end of the stem, a leaf was unfurling into a tear-drop shape, its edges waxy and gleaming in the daylight. Hanging next to the leaf was the drooping bud of a flower yet to bloom. It's head heavy with purple petals. The stem of the plant punctured the man's skin but did not leave blood or any evidence of a wound. Myrtle drew back in alarm and quickly pulled the fabric of the man's sleeve down.

"Beekeeper what is it?" The man asked.

Myrtle inhaled sharply, she couldn't treat this man here. The new disease could bring mass hysteria. It was unlike anything she had ever encountered.

"You must come with me."

She grabbed his arm tightly and pulled him towards a house down the road. It was the Jenson's house, and there she knew she could find a quiet room. The pounding of her fist on the door brought a maid, who let them in.

"Do you have a quiet room? This man is very ill, he must get some rest from the crowd."

"Of course, Miss Beeswood."

The maid led them to a dusty room at the back of the house, she passed Mrs Jenson on the way, to whom she explained once again the need for a quiet space. Mrs Jenson offered tea, and she politely declined. Myrtle sat the man down in a chair and asked him for his arm again.

The stem of the plant attached to his arm sprung outward as it was released from the confines of fabric. She inched closer and prodded the stem, feeling around the incision for any evidence of a previous wound or scarring. Perhaps this was a new kind of infection? Instead of mould could plants now infect a necrotic wound? Gently, she grasped the stem and pulled.

"Ow!" The man exclaimed.

Myrtle reeled back frowning. *Has the plant become a part of him?*

Fear throbbed deep in her chest.

"S-Sorry." She muttered, blinking away the panic.

The musty stench of the room filled her lungs and made her splutter, she forced herself to breath and a new wave of sickness came over her, suddenly, she felt an overwhelming urge to wretch. The door flew open as she hurried to get out of the room, to find a basin, toilet, bush-. The front door was just down the hallway, and she blindly darted towards it, swinging the metal handle down and flinging her weight to push the door open. But as she stumbled outside and let the air fill her lungs, the wave of sickness left as quickly as it had come.

"Myrtle?" She heard the sweet familiar voice of a friend.

Still doubled over and heaving, she lifted her gaze to meet the eyes of Samantha Pineswood. Her blue eyes held a look of deep concern, her brows furrowed into a bowed shape.

"I'm fine." Myrtle straightened herself and brushed down her apron, "I just needed a little air is all."

"You don't look fine." Miss Pineswood's frown deepened.

"There's been a lot of work for me to do." Myrtle gripped her forehead with her fingers, "I just needed a moment."

"I think that you need more than just a moment." Miss Pineswood tsked impatiently, "Have you had lunch?"

"Umm…" Myrtle leant her back against the rough sandstone, "I believe I have."

"Oh Myrtle-! It is already late afternoon."

She flicked her eyes to the sky, and saw that Samantha was indeed correct. The sun was making its way across to the western horizon at a steady pace. She could feel the adrenaline leaving her body, making her legs wobble and her temples ache. Perhaps a short break would do her well. The man was still alive even in the state that he was in, even though he probably shouldn't be. Presently, she couldn't bear the thought of going back inside to treat him. Whatever that disease had made of him, brought a feeling beyond disgust, beyond the grimace of the sour stench of a wound. No. This disease, whatever it was, left a feeling of utter revulsion. Even the thought of the plant's stem twisting beneath his skin brought bile to her throat.

"Alright." She sighed a shaky sigh, "I guess I could use a short break."

* * *
*

The two girls sat on the edge of a little stone bridge, feet dangling just above Wendermere Pudding stream. Their reflections were ever changing blobs of shadow in the waves of the current. Flickering like a candle. Myrtle had forgotten to grab lunch once again before heading out the door. Or rather, it had been too cold and too dark for her to be bothered with groping around the kitchen pantry. She was thankful for Samantha's kindness in preparing a sandwich for her as well.

"I was going to drop it off to you anyway, and check that you had enough to eat."

"Thank you," Myrtle did her best not to scoff the sandwich down.

"Who were you treating just now?" Samantha asked, her straw-hat casting sunshine in freckles across her face, they danced as she tipped her head back letting the breeze ruffle her blond ringlets.

"A young man." Myrtle hesitated, "I believe he was a traveller from up North."

"Did you find the right medicine for him?"

Myrtle paused mid mouthful, kind though Miss Pineswood was... She often was also quite nosy. She kept chewing and swallowed.

"I'll find a way." She murmured, "I always find a way."

Samantha tugged off her shoes and jumped down off the bridge into the shallow, ankle-deep water. Myrtle flinched as water splashed on her legs.

"Oh- Sorry Myrtle!" Samantha exclaimed.

"It's alright." Myrtle straightened her apron and fluffed it down.

Samantha held up the hem of her dress in one hand and used the other hand to balance as she stepped on the slippery rocks of the stream's bed. The sun gleamed through a gap in the trees and spilled out like honey over Samantha. The rays caught her blond hair and turned it to gold. Light reflected off her blue eyes and turned them into deep mirrors where Myrtle could, for a brief moment, see her own haggard face staring back at her. A sudden gust of wind made leaves quiver and ferns along the stream's banks bounce. Samantha grabbed at her hat just in time before it became airborne.

"Isn't it cold?" Myrtle asked

"Yes, it is so very cold." Samantha smiled, though it was more of a grimace.

"Why are you standing in the stream then?" Myrtle frowned

Samatha shrugged in reply and took in a long breath of the chilly afternoon air. The scent was earthy down in this gully, like the air after a long rain.

"It's refreshing, you should try it." Miss Pineswood continued, "Uncle always said that there was nothing quite like standing in an icy stream. It was something about how washing your feet in the cold water would cleanse your soul better than any bath could… But I could never figure out if he meant the soles of your foot or the other kind."

"I'll take your word for it."

There was silence, accentuated by Samantha kicking her feet through the water and wading back towards the bank. She scared a fish, which darted quickly for cover.

"Did you get my letter?" Miss Pineswood's voice came as she struggled to find a hand hold.

"Yes, thank you, it was lovely." Guilt prickled to life in Myrtle's chest. Samantha had delivered that letter two weeks ago, and she hadn't replied, nor had she come to call on Samantha. She had seen Miss Pineswood in passing, and the girl had attempted to catch her attention, but Myrtle had brushed her off as she had been so engrossed in healing the travellers. Finally, numbers of newcomers had begun to drop off, and the line slowly shortening. She had been hoping to leave social endeavours until her work with the travellers was done.

"I'm sorry I haven't found time to reply yet."

"Oh, that's okay." Samantha pulled herself up the bank and brushed herself off, "I just want to know that you are resting and being looked after."

Myrtle nodded, as the blond-haired girl came once again to sit down beside her on the hard stone.

"Have you been managing?"

"I will be fine, I just need to see these travellers and then I can rest." When Myrtle met Samantha's gaze, she saw… disappointment? Concern?

"But there will always be more travellers, Myrtle."

"Yes, but there are less coming now, and if I can just see a majority of them…" She trailed off, suddenly feeling the stupidity of her logic.

"And what will happen when the people that you've already treated return home and tell the whole town of how the miracle worker that they had heard rumoured of, *is* real and healed them of all their ailments?"

Myrtle let out an exasperated sigh. Silence once again enveloped them. She squeezed and unsqueezed her fingers feeling the steady pitter patter of anxiety sweep over her.

"I just want to be ready."

"Ready for what?"

A frustrated hiss whistled through Myrtle's teeth, and she rocked back to rest on the palms of her hands.

"I don't know."

"In my experience no one is *ever* ready." Samantha muttered, and then she grew louder, "But, surely getting a good night's sleep is the first step, if there is one."

"Have you been able to recover from Nearne Forest?" Samantha came again.

She's incessant! Myrtle thought.

"Well, It's certainly been long enough."

"Yes, but that doesn't mean anything, if you haven't had the time to reflect."

"I've had some time, I didn't work for at least a week after… remember, I was too weak?"

"Do you remember what happened in the forest?" Miss Pineswood's gaze was piercing, expectant.

"Some things." Myrtle thought that it was finally her turn to ask a question, "Do you know what the name Nearne means?"

"Oh-! It's from an old language that cattle farmers in the mountains used to speak. Nearne means, Nowhere. My father has told me stories of them, he knows a little of the language because many Wendermere families are descended from them, they were here before us. Most of our parents would know a little of the language."

Myrtle nodded, the name seemed to fit the forest… Afterall, 'nowhere' is the name given to a place when you don't know where that place is. For a moment Samantha seemed placated, but it was only for a moment.

"What happened in the forest?" Miss Pineswood poked.

Myrtle found her last ounces of will-power leaching out. She could handle Samantha on a good day, but not today. The girl was unusually pushy. Anger like a red-hot whip lashed inside Myrtle.

"Nothing happened." It was a lie so obvious that it almost wasn't a lie.

"What?!" Samantha exclaimed wounded, "But you were captured by a witch!"

"I didn't know that she was a witch." Myrtle sighed, trying, poorly, to control herself, "She was actually very kind."

"And nothing else happened?" Samantha's words grew in passion, "You were just living with an old lady for a whole month who happened to be a witch and when you came back it suddenly occurred to you that you hadn't eaten or rested in all that time?"

"-And that Hodgepodge hadn't eaten either?" She added with frustration.

"*I guess so.*" Myrtle found her eyes rolling.

"And *nothing* else happened?" Samantha frowned, "That's it?"

"*That's it.*" Myrtle widened her eyes with exasperation.

"Right then." Samantha huffed.

The silence grew between them like twirling vines, slithering and clinging with barbed thorns. It was pervasive. The stream gurgled, as though it were making a mockery of the dismal conversation. The swaying leaves which had made light leap upon the surface of the water, had also lost their gleam. Myrtle couldn't sit in the discomfort any longer, she made a quick movement to gather her things.

"You haven't rested. I can see it in your face, Myrtle."

Myrtle paused, letting the surprise of the comments sink in. She turned to Samantha, knowing all too well the look that would accompany the girl's words.

"You won't even talk about it!" Samantha's voice rose.

There it was. Her lips quivered, her blue eyes glimmered like the rippling surface of the stream. Her brows knit together like the string of a washing line hung down with the weight of sodden clothing.

"Why won't you talk to me?"

Samantha's words caught in the back of her throat.

"Am I not good enough for you?"

She choked.

"I only ever wanted to be your friend, but you won't let me!"

And she cried. Burying her face in the palms of her hands. Her face scrunched as the washing line snapped. Myrtle had made her cry. And suddenly Myrtle leaped up, without even gathering her things. Tripping, scrambling, running. She was running away.

*   *   *
*

When she returned back to the square, she had managed to keep her own tears in check, but the payoff had consequences. Her face was plastered with a look of rage, eyes pierced with fury. She gathered herself, as if she could bring her wilted spirit back to life. Then with fists like a tightly bound book, she knocked on the Jensons' door.

"Uh…Oh. It is you, Miss Beeswood." The maid stammered.

"Yes. I have come back for the man."

"Oh, but he left a while ago, dear."

"What?!" Myrtle's anger bled into her voice, raising it a little more than she had intended.

"Why yes, I am sorry dear." The maid replied, "I thought you had finished treating him? He seemed in quite a hurry."

She had to bite her lip hard to stop the tears. *That man could die because of my mistake.* She hurried away from the Jensons' house back down the street.

"Has anyone seen a man!" She called to passersby as she ran. The crowd of travellers now became visible.

"A man with a northern accent… he-ah… he had very pale skin, short brown hair?" She was met with blinking eyes. There were so many men that could fit that exact description. It was useless, the man would be long gone.

Defeated, she took her place on the little wooden chair and turned to the next patient. She could not smile, that capacity had been torn from her entirely. And now she could not even meet their eyes. But she had to keep going. So, she smacked away a fly which had crept up one of the honey jars and continued with her work.

* * *
*

The end of the day was fast approaching, the sun was giving Wendermere its last glimmer before letting the moon take its place. Myrtle knew that if she did not leave earlier today then she would not make it home, nor would she have any strength left to untack Podge and put him in the paddock. Even now the thought of that menial task weighed heavily on her mind. She wished to be in bed already, with the duvet scrunched right up to her ears. The rest of the day had not gone well, she had been clumsy and broken two jars of precious honey. The spilled honey had shards of glass through it. She had tried her best to collect the syrup in a bowl to feed back to the hives as the bee's honey production would begin to rapidly slow soon and she could not afford the waste. Perhaps sleep would let her forget about the day and its many failings, however, something told her that she would still wake tired with the memories of Samantha's weeping face burned rigid into her mind.

She began packing her things, carefully transporting the honey jars back into the wooden crate and rolling her lambskin pouch up, when a man came racing through the square red faced and huffing. He stopped as he made his way up to her and bent over hands on his knees trying to catch his breath.

"Miss Beeswood?" He asked between deep exhalations.

"Yes." Myrtle felt her whole-body groan inwardly, *who was dying this time?*

"I have an urgent message from Wattleshire."

Her heart fell into the pit of her stomach.

"I regret to inform you Miss." The man clenched a note in his hand, his knuckles were white. "Your mother has passed away."

A Royal Summons

"What?" Myrtle's mouth moved but she couldn't hear the words.

The man before her… the messenger, his free hand grasping his satchel continued.

"Your mother." he repeated, "She succumbed to illness. She passed away on Thursday morning."

There was no control as the edges of her mouth drooped, eyes unblinking, unseeing. The man became a smudge in front of her. Her legs became wobbling stilts.

"No." She mumbled, "N-No!"

The words came out as a howl. She felt the grit of loose dirt on cobblestone, the pain biting into her knees and sobbing shook her as she knelt upon the ground. A numbness enveloped her with its cold immobilising hands. The man's voice sounded incoherent above her as she rocked herself, back and forth, the coolness of the cobblestone radiating up through the ground. Tears ran, first warm and then dried salty against her cheeks and chin. She wasn't aware of anything other than the grief, its fists pounding on her chest. She had failed.

"Miss- I should get you home." The man placed a warm tender hand on her shoulder.

His words sounded like bubbles of air drifting up through the waters of a rapid. Small. Weak, amid the roar in her ears. The heat from his hand like a searing brand on a sheep. She recoiled trying to shrug him off.

I have failed.

"Miss, please I am just trying to keep you safe." He continued, "You're in shock- you see. I must take you home."

"No!" She screamed at him, mouth yawning wide with rage. *Failed.*

Something savage awoke in her and she clawed at his hand, weeping bitterly.

"Get your hands off me!!" *Failed. Like the quivering young girl holding a candle, in a dark room, beside the bed of her mother.*

"Please, calm yourself." His voice rose above the wailing.

She was still suddenly for a moment. Mumbling under her breath. *Words weren't enough then. Would they be enough now?*

"Two days…"

"Two days?" She asked, "She died two days ago?"

"Yes Miss, on Thursday."

"I can still save her."

The man was silent, but she didn't care. It didn't matter how crazy she sounded to a normal man. She was a Beekeeper, and Beekeepers were certainly not normal.

"I can do it."

Another hand was placed on her shoulder. Another man, another smudge through the blur of tears. She was shackled.

"We would like to take you home now Miss. To a nice warm house and get you some tea too." The man gently coaxed, "That'll help you feel better."

"I can't go home." Myrtle demanded, "I need to get to Wattleshire. I must go now."

"I don't think that's the best idea Miss." The man spoke, "Why don't you get a good sleep and leave bright and early tomorrow morning?"

"Every hour counts. I must go now."

The man sighed, a nervous bone rattling sigh. His lips made an almost inaudible 'tsk' sound.

"Miss I'm sorry but we must take you home tonight. You are hardly in a state for travel. Just a few minutes ago you tried to rip my arm off."

Myrtle turned to him with eyes like piercing daggers. Brushing away the tears with a tight fist, she locked eyes with him. Finally, seeing the man for what he was, a rather plump mailman, with a few days of stubble and yellowed teeth.

"I'll truly tear them off this time, if you don't let me go."

It was then that Finn appeared with other men, his father and Mr Jenson. They must have sent for the Strawbys.... How long had she been kneeling here on the ground? She could see in his eyes how pathetic she must have looked. As he came closer a look of bewilderment sparked in his freckled expression. He didn't know what to say, brows drawn together, mouth pursed.

"Look here, your friends have arrived to help you get home." The man said stooping to Myrtle, "They'll take good care of you."

"I can't go." She shook, her lips wobbling.

She turned to Finn, who still stood at a distance, clearly not knowing what to do. He held her gaze for a moment and then hung his head shuffling his feet nervously.

"F-Finn, don't let them take me back to the cottage." She mumbled, tears now freely flowing down her cheeks again, stinging, "I-I need to go home!"

Finn said nothing, though Myrtle waited expectantly, shaking, fists clenched against her chest. She let out a choked groan when she realised that he would not be defending her. The hard stone. She turned her glare to the stone beneath her. He would not protect her, he would let them force her home-.

"Myrtle."

She whipped her head up to see Finn speaking, meeting her gaze with a sudden composed courage.

"You need to come home. Tomorrow you can go back to Wattleshire."

Myrtle snivelled in reply, clenching and unclenching her fists, letting her fingernails bite into her palms. The other men turned to each other. *He has betrayed me.*

"She's in no state to return to the cottage alone," Mr Jenson muttered.

"Hmm." Mr Strawby nodded in agreement, "Myrtle can stay the night with us. We'll get her warmed up by the fire, with a nice bowl of stew."

Myrtle let herself go limp as the men hoisted her up to take her over to a carriage for the short ride down the lane to the Strawby's farm. She whimpered quietly, defeated. They didn't know what another night could mean. They didn't understand. There was a chance before, but that chance was continually dwindling. Time, she needed more time.

"Don't let them take me." She heaved through coughs and sniffs, "Please…. Please… you don't understand."

They sat her down in the back of the wagon on a wooden seat, Mr Jenson wrapped a thick blanket around her. Finn climbed the steps of the wagon to slip passed her and move to the front beside his father. As he passed her, Myrtle found a flare of anger ignite deep inside her belly.

"I won't forgive you for this." She whispered.

* * *
*

Swirls of interweaving orange, red, and deep blue. Ever changing, flicking like the tongues of a serpent. The colours bleeding into each other like dyes left to run, ruining the fabric. It popped and spat molten embers. The fire.

She stared into it until her eyes burned with the heat of the hearth. It had dried her tears. For now. They clung to her face as a stiff reminder that her nightmare was not over. And so, she stared into the flames, vacant and still. The Strawbys had given her a bowl of stew, which was left cold on the stool beside her.

"Oh, dear Myrtle, do eat up." Mrs Strawby's tone was firm.

Myrtle flicked her head around to see the woman, wiping her hands on her apron. Her hair was in a bun, which was presently attempting to escape its elastic confinements. When she caught Myrtle's gaze her features softened.

"I only mean...You must give yourself strength for tomorrow, child." She sighed, "You have a long journey ahead, and you can't make it without sustenance."

Myrtle turned away from her to fumble with the bowl of stew. The sight of it made her stomach churn, and then the smell lifted through the warm air and bile rose to her throat.

"I have half a mind to make Finn go with you… It's too long a journey for a girl to travel alone. Particularly, for…" She stopped, making a huff, "Well… never mind that now. You need to rest, we'll make plans for you tomorrow… that is, if you are still certain you have to leave right away."

Myrtle was silent. She let it settle around her, the absence of sound, punctuated only by the crackle of fire. The woman stayed there. Eventually she sat beside Myrtle on the ground.

"I'm so sorry child." The woman wrapped an arm around her shoulder, "What a sore blow you've been dealt."

"I can understand why you wouldn't feel like eating." Mrs Strawby gently rubbed her shoulder.

The woman's grey eyes were glistening, as she fumbled for more words, but Myrtle didn't need more words, she didn't want more words.

"Is…" The woman began, voice strained, "Is there a reason why you needed to leave so quickly?"

Myrtle sat the bowl on her lap, trailing the spoon through the broth. She couldn't eat. Not now. She would be sick.

"I understand you need your family, now more than ever-" The woman continued, seeing that Myrtle was not going to answer, "But, I sense that there is another reason for your urgency."

Myrtle shook her head. *I won't speak it.* She thought, *I can't speak it.* It threatened her, threatened to overwhelm her. The failure. The sting of tears came to the corners of her eyes, and then her lungs heaved. She buried her face in her blanketed knees, which she hugged tight. Mrs Strawby hugged her tighter.

The light had completely faded outside when she lifted her head once more. *Did I fall asleep?* She couldn't be sure, but the deep suffocating ache hadn't left her. Mrs Strawby was gone, and sounds came from the kitchen once more. Letting out a long shaky breath, she propped her chin on her knees. The front door squeaked open, and there was a low thump as it closed again. Light footsteps crept down the hallway and peaked into the room. Myrtle turned to see Finn, his eyes glinting in the light of the fire.

"I…ah." He stammered, "I brought Hodgepodge into the stables for you."

He must have ridden into town to grab Hodgepodge from the Jensons' paddock. Myrtle gave him a nod, then returned her chin to her lap. Finn's footsteps did not turn away. He stood motionless. *Am I such a spectacle?* And a spectacle she was, her eyes had become red sunken hollows, her curled hair was matted and stuck up at many different angles. She maintained the look of a shrivelled prune, shrunken into a huddled blanket, trying to make herself disappear. For if she could disappear, then so would the pain. The nightmare would be over.

"He's been wanting you." Finn shuffled his feet, "He looks like he needs a little company."

"I'm sure he'll survive." Her voice came out croaky and foreign. She coughed into the blanket.

Finn dipped his head and then turned on his heels and left. *If Hodgepodge wants anything it is probably just food.* But something pulled at her. Something beyond the thick weight of grief. What if Hodgepodge did want to see her? Maybe he was lonely, she hadn't found much time for him lately.

Something stirred her. She didn't have the willpower to leave the blankets and the fire's side. But almost as if on their own accord her limbs moved, and slipped out of the fort of wool fabric around her. She couldn't feel herself as she walked down the hall, her bare feet against the rough wooden floorboards… palm leaning against the wall. She reached the door and opened it.

"Myrtle?"

A rush of evening chill swept around her. She didn't shiver.

"Myrtle, where are you going?"

Her feet now on the stones and gravel, they were thousands of pointy pinpricks of sensation. She felt every tiny, gritted pebble and yet somehow… she couldn't feel it at all. Because everything felt dull. Small pains became less than an annoyance… numbed by the far greater pain of losing. *Failure.*

Mrs Strawby's face appeared, flustered, in the doorway behind her. She didn't turn to answer the woman. Instead, she made her way to the stables, it was a mere pinprick of light in the gloom. The shuffle of Mrs Strawby in her dress behind, told Myrtle that she had been followed. A lantern had been hung on one of the stable's corner roof eaves. It swung gently in the breeze, the metal making a quiet squeak.

As she approached, she could see the outline of fire, reflecting off its glass prison, quaking. A nicker sounded. She turned her head to see Hodgepodge, his shaggy head sticking out of his stall, ears pricked towards her. Mane tousled, she hadn't brushed it in weeks, leaves and twigs clung to it. His white splotches were muddied, as they always were. His auburn markings were growing darker, no longer were they a shimmer of dappled reds fading to an almost pink. Now they were growing into a deep red bay, as the weather turned.

"I won't leave." She addressed the woman, who had now reached her, and was stopping to catch her breath.

She could see the woman consider whether to believe her, face drawn in a weary, breathless expression. The woman nodded, but still stood motionless. Myrtle opened the gate on the stall and slipped inside.

A deep breath escaped her, it came from the very pit of her stomach, and she collapsed onto the pony's neck, letting her arms find his messy mane, and wrapping them around him. Sobs bubbled up, drawn out from her chest, cracking and breaking. She let her mouth yawn wide with it. Let her body rock and shake. And her voice wail. She did not try to control it. She *couldn't* control it. Grief spilled out from her like a dam wall bursting. Casting her face into her steed like a blanket, tears quickly wet his fur.

Hodgepodge stood, curiously still. He stopped chewing his hay. His ears listened intently to his Beekeeper. His breath came warm upon her back, she felt the soft velvet of his nose as he nuzzled her.

"She's gone, Podgy." Myrtle choked.

The pony's warm breath tickled her ear as he stretched around to her. She withdrew her face from his coat, to stare into his strange dark eyes. Oval pupils and a flecked brown iris reflected her broken figure in front of him.

"I can't bring her back."

"I know that I can't."

"Not now."

Another wave soared,
                    overshadowing
                          even the first one,
and she drowned in it.

"I've failed."

"I've failed Hodgepodge."

"I've failed."

That night Myrtle had cried until she couldn't cry anymore and then when she was finished, she curled up in the hay and fell asleep.

Her eyes fluttered as she stirred. Fingers brushed soft pillows and the duvet. They must have brought her inside. For a moment her heart was quieted, she smelled the frigid morning air. The clean feel of the bed and blankets. The fluffiness of the pillows. Everything was-. Wrong. It was all wrong. And the horror seeped in. The dread. It pulled the breath from her lungs once more and broke open her chest. *I don't want to cry again.* She groaned. Her eyes were wide open now and she heard whispers just outside her door.

"We can't wake her." Came Mrs Strawby's voice,

"Well, we must wake her soon, dear." Mr Strawby's voice was serious, "We can't keep him waiting forever, and the letter he has… it must be mighty important."

"But the poor girl John," Mrs Strawby's voice came worried, "She's had so much to deal with! Can't we just send him away? Couldn't he come again tomorrow?"

"Darling." Mr Strawby sighed, "Didn't you see his coat? The patch on his shoulder?"

"W-what do you mean?"

"He's been sent by the King, Martha! We can't just send him away."

"A-are you sure?" Her voice quivered, "No one's seen a King's man for over a century…"

"I'm as certain as I ought to be. Men don't wear that kind of uniform unless they have a good reason."

Then she heard a quiet wrap on the door. It was first meek and then firm and confident. The door was cracked open with a turn of the knob.

"Myrtle, are you awake dear?" Mrs Strawby's voice drifted through the crack.

"Yes."

"I'm sorry dear, but there is someone important here for you."

Myrtle let her eyes flick to the ceiling where swirls of oak wood panels created odd shapes with their irregularities. She knew she would have to bring herself to leave the bed, but she didn't want to. The thought of home made her stomach twinge. With a groan, she forced herself up and out of bed, stifling the tears that threatened. Breathing through the pain she pulled her petticoat over her underclothes and then slipped on her yellow dress, the sight of it made her stop. It reminded her of wattle blossoms, little cotton suns bobbing in the wind. It reminded her of home. It was wrong to wear, but she didn't have any other dress with her, and she had few dresses at the cottage. Then she paused to look in the mirror.

Oh, what a sight she was. Cheeks red and angry with a rash from tears, the rest of her skin remained pale and blotchy. Her hair looked as though she hadn't combed it in weeks. She felt the back of her head, disgusted to find it matted. *Did it matter?* She stared at herself. Getting lost in how much the reflection didn't feel as though it truly was her. She almost walked to the door to open it when an ounce of her dignity flickered to light within. So, she grabbed the pitcher of water beside her bed and filled the basin to splash her face. Then she grabbed the comb and tamed, somewhat, the bird's nest upon her head. She didn't look again in the mirror, she couldn't bear the thought of feeling disappointed, or of having some sense of needing to 'try harder'. She couldn't *try harder*. She wouldn't *try harder*. Not even for the King's man, if that indeed was what this man was.

She walked down the hallway and into the living room where the light filtered through the half-drawn curtains. Outside was a covering of mist, thick upon the fields, so thick that all you could see were a few apple trees just outside the window, their thin branches almost bare and what leaves that remained had faded to dandelion yellow. Her gaze fell on the man who had sent for her. He wore a blue coat with a crisp outline and golden buttons that glinted with embossed detail. There was also gold cord lining the edges of the coat and two gold chains that ran from his pocket to the gold tassel shoulder pads and on the pocket was a medal, striped with vibrant red and blue. He was sitting on a stool with some tea. At first, he seemed like a cold man, hardened by years of royal service. His bulky figure, strong hands and uniform, were far more regal than anything Myrtle was used to. It commanded even more presence than the attire worn to Romero's ball. But that was before her gaze came to rest on his face. He looked to be in his forties, wearing a light beard and full moustache. His eyes were unexpectedly kind. At the sight of her, the man set the tea aside and stood quickly holding out his cupped hand. Uncertain, she gave him her hand and he kissed it.

"Miss Beeswood."

He dipped his head, "It is an honour."

Myrtle was taken aback, and she was too tired to keep the shock from her face as she took a step back and frowned.

"And who may I ask am I making the acquaintance of?"

"I am General Arnold Nikoloski." He grunted.

Myrtle found herself unable to answer. So, he *was indeed* someone important.

"I have been sent by the King." General Nikoloski, he paused. "You have been summoned to the Northern Front."

Her body went limp. She felt herself, falling backwards and stumbled, catching herself just in time. There were shocked stares and exclamations from around the living room.

The General held out a letter, sealed with two seals one was the marbled blue and red of the King it depicted an ornate crown with a dazzling halo of light surrounding it. The second was a seal of swirled yellow and teal, it depicted a bee in flight, its wings spread wide. Myrtle again took a step back, her hand went to her mouth.

"N-no…" She mumbled, "How can this be…"

She couldn't bring herself to take hold of the letter, she couldn't bring herself to read the words from the King himself. She found herself almost turning…. Turning to race out of the door, tears pounding at her chest…. Wind whipping past her as she ran to the fence and took the post and wires in her hands, tripping as she scrambled over it and leaping through the grass until she was so very far away that she couldn't even see the house…

But she couldn't. Something stopped her this time from running away. Something rooted her feet to the ground, not like shackles, but almost like courage. She met the General's gentle brown eyes, shaking. He nodded to her and held the letter further aloft.

And she took it. In trembling hands.

"It's alright Miss. There is no need to worry."

She tore the flap, breaking the two seals and slipped out the letter. It was written on heavy thick parchment, with a precise fold in its middle and the print was first scarlet ink for the address and then in elegant dark teal was written:

Dear Myrtle Beeswood of Wattleshire,

Your reputation as a faithful healer with a compassionate heart has reached the King's ear. It is Requested by His Majesty that you present yourself for Service at the Royal Army at the Northern Border, in Koplin Plain. This order is effective immediately.

Face of Shadows

The aching stopped. Stilled suddenly by an awful thing, worse than grief's river. Myrtle's eyes flicked over the parchment once more, finger's straining and leaving a crease in the paper. Again, her eyes darted over the words.

'Present yourself for service'

She brought a cupped hand to her mouth. Shaking.

'At the Royal Army on the Northern Border, in Koplin Plain'

Her eyes couldn't be torn from the paper and yet she couldn't go on, she couldn't read the words again, for they were seared painfully in her mind, resounding inside her. Words, from the King himself. He wasn't only a legend. Not just rhymes in an old children's book or a faint whisper on the breeze, but real, tangible. Writing on a letter. A letter addressed to her. *Present yourself.*

"Oh dear, are you alright?"
"What does it say Myrtle?"

Her knees suddenly gave way, and she stumbled backwards catching herself on the door post. Her vision blurred against a hint of tears, obscuring the words of the letter. *No. No Not Now. It can't be. Not now.* And the King's words were as terrifying as they were real. It was unimaginable. She blinked.

Present.
Yourself.

The words leaped from the page. A command. From the King. The King of The Wild.

"And if I refuse?"

"If you refuse to go to the Northern Border?" The soldier clarified

"Yes." Her voice cracked.

The man hesitated before replying.

"You would be stripped of your title as Beekeeper and be unable to practise Beekeeping throughout the kingdom."

"And if I delay leaving?"

"I'm afraid the outcome will be the same, Miss Beeswood."

Suddenly she couldn't hold herself together any longer. The letter fell to the ground, and she did not want to see where it landed as she ran. Truly ran this time. She couldn't think as she raced down the hallway, as she unlatched the door and felt the sting of gravel under foot. She couldn't see as she ran, not caring where. Shapes blurred into shadows of green and brown. The soft light crunch of leaves and textured swirl of grass. The sun, its rays flickering through the mist. She felt the steel of a wire fence, and bent it with quivering hands stretched wide, scrambling through the gap into the field. Except, now that she had stopped, she could see that she wasn't in the field after all. She had ducked

279

through the fence between the Strawbys and their neighbour A fence line that began at the road. Did she dare go back? They would see her running. She wobbled forward and knelt on the ground, one more decision was too exhausting. Better to give up. Better to give up now.

I can't. I can't do it.

There she sat perched on the edge of tears, but somehow unable to cry. Staring at the dust, the leaves, the bark. If she didn't heed the King's call… It would mean the end. The end of Beekeeping. The end of the Beeswood line. A legacy put to death. But, losing… Losing the chance to try. The consequence was unimaginable. However, slim the chance was, she had to try to save her mother. However slim. She heaved. Letting silence seep in. Letting the absence resound within her. She was worn thin. It was hard to care, because she cared too much, so much it threatened to spill out from her. Again.

I can't do it anymore. I don't want to be a Beekeeper. Not if I have to fail, over and over again.

She waited. Waited for it to consume her. Waited for it to swallow her whole with its embrace. It would be just like at Ambling's End. Nearne Forest. It didn't frighten her anymore. The strange forest and the witch, *Melinda Cloverfoot.* The name of the elder Beekeeper came flooding back into her memory like a snap, but the realisation of the witch's identity meant nothing now. *If only I had stayed,* the chill air caught against Myrtle's cheek and made her shiver. *Then I wouldn't have had to endure this. None of it would have happened.* Wendermere would have continued on without her. Despair rattled inside her. Its jaws creaking open, sharp teeth waiting, ready to snap.

On the breeze came a scent. A sweet scent. Myrtle lifted her head. It was familiar. A scent, sweeter than honey. As she stared through the bushes around her, she became aware that she wasn't alone. Tiny ants ran in a line over the leaves. A large dead beetle had been cracked open on the ground and the ants were slowly chipping away at it. Harvesting it. Leaving nothing to waste.

The sweet stench rose through the air, filling her senses. The ants seemed to notice it too for their procession slowly grew to a stop, antennae waving in the air as they turned towards the source of the stench, which was wafting from over through the fields.

Branches clacked as a chill wind swirled through the air. Myrtle shivered. She glanced through the thick trees into the dark undergrowth of the forest. Wind came like sea spray. Shade in between the trees thickened. It became *blacker.* Suddenly, absent of the textured dirt, leaves and bark that littered the ground. It bent. *Shifted.*

She felt her breath coming quicker. Perhaps she would finally discover what it was. What the shadows truly were. Tears pricked in the corners of her eyes, tears of exhaustion, and of fear. She couldn't run. Her legs seemed paralysed. What did they want from her? She had nothing else to give. *There was nothing.*

They flickered through the trees, shapes of darkness. merging shadows. Bleeding to deep black. Making dark outlines too long, too wide. There were many of them. Seeping through the trees. Blurring. Drawing nearer and nearer.

And before her eyes they transformed. Finally, seeing them for what they truly were. The shadows, the sweet scent. They shifted into writhing creatures. They were monsters, made of sprouting vines, continually growing from the ground as they leered closer. Red thorns glistening. Trumpet flowers blooming, their heads drooping, withered with decay. Horns. Black horns twisted from their heads. They didn't have eyes or any detailed features, but only the vague shape of man, an impression.

She opened her mouth to scream. She couldn't. The ants on the ground scattered and ran. She needed to move. But she couldn't. The disjointed snapping of branches filled her ears, the wind whipping her curls back from her head. The shadowy figures loomed nearer. Inching closer, vines snaking across the ground, worming through the undergrowth. They moved bark and leaf litter as they crawled, wavering over the ground. One reached its arm, vines twirling outward. Trying, trying to take her.

For a terrible moment, she looked up. Gazing into the face of shadow. Stilled in awful wonder. Drowning in the darkness, as it sapped away at her. Jaws snapping. Despair knocking at her heart with a heavy fist.

Give up. Give in.

The howling deep yawned wide before her. Resounding. It was bottomless. Unchartable. It blinded her. An unfathomable nothingness. Filling her senses until she choked on it. It was loud and yet noiseless. Cosmic ebony blinked its eyes open and showed her its secret. Echoing strangely. It pulled at her, until she was being stripped. Stripped away. Nothing. It was nothing. And it wanted her to be nothing with it. Wanted her for its own.

Wanted her life, because it could not live in the dark in the nothingness with nothing. It was absence itself. *The absence of everything.*

Something.
　There was something.
　　It stirred her sleeping soul.

Awake.

Something flittered past her ear. It was the unmistakable buzz of a bee, its tiny wings whipping back and forth, suspending it in the air. It appeared in front of her, golden stripes glinting in a stray ray of sun.

"Myrtle!"

And it disappeared. The vines, the shadows. Gone.

"Myrtle!"

It was Finn's voice. Desperate and much louder than he usually made it. She turned to see him ducking through the trees, pushing back branches. When he saw her, he visibly weakened, letting his hands fall to his knees, panting.

"Myrtle." He breathed, jogging over to her.

"I can't do it." She whispered, "I don't want to be a Beekeeper anymore."

He paused, letting out a long breath. Then he crouched beside her. She looked out over the field before her, away from the forest with those awful creatures. The mist had vanished, burnishing the fields with sunlight, the grass shone like newly washed linen, and underneath was the vivid green of new shoots. Life. The neighbour's house in the distance was partially obscured by the tall grass. A plume of silky grey smoke rose into the forget-me-not sky from a chimney. The bee drifted to land in her hair, its sticky feet crawling.

"I couldn't save her." she murmured. *And I can't save them.*

A breeze, very unlike the strange cold gusts from before, brought momentary animation to her hair. It was warm, playful. The wind tickled her cheeks, making her tears run askew dripping down to her chin. She could feel Finn's gaze turn to her, her cheeks burned with the humiliation of it all.

"Do you get to decide if you save them or not? Surely not. I thought your honey was similar to the medicine of a doctor, only stronger or does it not have limits?"

His words fell like lime juice into paper cuts. It stung. She felt herself begin to sob all the more. How could he even begin to assume the duties of a Beekeeper? How could he know the burden a Beekeeper bore?

"You don't understand." She shook, "It is my responsibility. They are all my responsibility! And if I couldn't save her, then I can't save them!"

She swiped a fist across her face, smearing the tears, the salt prickling her skin and eyes. His gaze was on her again, for a moment before he looked out over the swaying field. The grass undulating in the breeze like tiny ripples on a lake, glinting as they bent and caught the light at a different angle.

"That's why I stayed so long at Ambling's End. That's why I never thought that Melinda was a witch." Myrtle sniffed, "I didn't have any responsibility there. There were so many things to do, but never the responsibility to do them."

"Were you happy?" Finn's eyes met her, a deep hazel reflection.

"I thought I was happy. She needed me… somehow, she still needed me."

Finn nodded silently, the breeze catching his short curls and setting them bouncing. He leaned back on the palms of his hands.

"But in the end, she had sapped all of the life out of me. I was nothing but skin and bones. It was a lie, some kind of magic." She murmured, "And then, my bees died, the Fodderhill's baby boy… who knows how many other countless people had to suffer… all because of me. I chose to stay, Melinda wasn't forcing me."

"And perhaps then? If you did have a part to play? If you did choose to believe this, lie?" Finn's gaze met her's, "What can be done now? You can't just give up."

"It is my fault. It is all my fault." Sobs shook her, she couldn't stifle them, she felt as though a hammer was cracking her open, spilling her insides out for him to see, and for the world to see.

"I couldn't save them. I can't save her. It's too late… I'm too late."

"It isn't your fault. Her death isn't your fault."

She felt Finn's hand grip her shoulder, the warmth of his hand for a moment made her sobbing cease. But then it continued, waves upon waves of pain, radiating through her. He shuffled closer and wrapped his arm around her and there they stayed.

*   *   *
*

It felt like an age before she gained the strength to lift her head again. Finn's face was silhouetted against a darkening sky. His features framed in the gloom, his eyes following the horizon. He hadn't tried to move her or push her to go back to the house. But he had stayed there. It must have been hours. She could feel her stomach gnawing at her, but the thought of food made it churn. Her eyes were dried, but only because she had no tears left.

"Why?" She whispered, "Why are you still here?"

He turned to her, freckled face like the dappling of sun rays through trees, except in reverse.

"Because I want to be your friend Myrtle, if you'll let me and sometimes that's what friends do." He then paused for a moment, pursing his lips before adding, "And that's all Samantha wants too. She just wants to be your friend."

Myrtle let her gaze fall once again on that distant field, now beginning to glow like copper flames, gleaming and twinkling with the wind.

"I don't deserve to have friends."

"And who does? Who deserves their friends?" Finn let a smile sneak onto his face.

Myrtle couldn't answer. She didn't know how to answer anymore. Her body ached, every breath felt laboured.

"Will you let me take you inside? Mother will be sick with worry, and what would be even worse is you catching a chill."

She let out a deep rattling sigh, but then motioned to stand, her body quivering with the effort. Finn moved to help her and took her hand. They made their way back through the underbrush, ducking under the fence and back to the front door where a lantern had already been lit. Mrs

Strawby opened the door, eyes glistening with tears and enveloped Myrtle in a hug that she had not been expecting. She wasn't angry, she seemed to know somehow that Finn had found her. She gave him a nod and briefly clasped his arm smiling. Then, without missing a beat, Mrs Strawby rushed to the kitchen to procure a steaming bowl of stew and a mug of tea.

Myrtle was thankful that the tea at least went down easily, warming her aching chest. She was even more thankful to have found that the general had left, and the Strawbys said nothing more on the matter. They warmed her bed with a water bottle and decorated the nightstands with bunches of lavender. The scent wafted throughout the whole room, and of course it brought with it a few stray bees, lazily drifting through the air. The Strawbys had left the window open, perhaps they knew that she would find comfort in them. As the sun was going down, she doubted that they would stay long, but something stirred in her, something more than the deep ache of fear. One hummed through the air, softly landing on a stalk of lavender, its antennae waving, swirled tongue sticking out, sensing where the sweet pollen lay.

A memory stirred in her. The scent of lavender in another garden. Stalks shaking as a rather boisterous young girl, blond curls bouncing whizzed through them, practically flattening the bush. Behind her trailed a white sheet, flapping in the wake of her wind when she ran. She felt like a bird, catching the wind beneath her wings and setting them sailing.

"Look, look I can fly!" She chortled.

And the bees saw her. They saw her try to fly and they laughed, just as her mother did, from the wooden bench that she sat in while labelling jars of honey. The bees surrounded her in a humming crown of interest, excited by the pots of honey. All of a sudden, one of the bees departed from the woman, its striped body buzzing through the air. It collided with the girl, alighting on her nose. She stopped suddenly, the sheet falling to the ground behind her. The girl's heart began to pound as she braced for that unmistakable sting, opening her mouth to cry out for her mother…

But it never came. The bee stayed there, antennae bouncing in the air. Large reflective eyes caught her own eyes in what could only be described by the girl as a tickle. And she laughed.

"Mama! Look at this bee! Mama, I have a bee!"

The mother turned to her daughter, hurrying to see what delighted her so. She leant down, her hair like the grass as it turns golden in autumn, fell like a curtain over her face before she swept it back to examine the girl and her bee.

And there they were, a curious pair. A young brown eyed girl and her little striped bee.

"Can I have the bee mama?"

And the mother beamed with pride, "My dear, they are already yours."

*   *   *
*

As the memory faded the ache returned, but this time, it was familiar. Not the alien ache of fear, but the familiar ache of the woman with straw-coloured hair. And Myrtle began to cry. But this time, it was not for herself, but for her mother. Her mother who she had lost. Her mother, who she would not see in this lifetime again.

A Season to Turn

Myrtle awoke to the smell of pancakes and maple syrup. The now familiar ache still pounded softly in her chest, but today, it was a little easier to breathe. Myrtle's room was still and quiet. The bees had long since flown back to the hive, and she had a peculiar feeling that she wouldn't see them for much longer. Winter's footsteps were coming steadily closer. The frigid air stung her nose and lungs. She lay in bed longer than she wanted to, but she couldn't care enough to push herself to get up. So, she lay staring blankly at the ceiling, the wooden panels with dark knots and swirls, until a vivid image stirred within, of her mother, straw coloured hair flowing down her shoulders as she bent to stir a bowl of honey. Her grey eyes shining with compassion. Myrtle would never see those grey eyes again. Never see her soft hair shining. She had hoped that she wouldn't cry today, she didn't have any tears left to give and yet still they came. Not silently, but not hysterically cither. They were sobs that rose from somewhere far inside of her, deeper somehow than the pain of the last few days. Her chest became heavy with the weight of it all once more. It bore down, like stone grinding against stone, pushing harder. But this time she cracked. All the way through, and it spilled out of her hissing. Only this time she could breathe.

Mrs Strawby rapped softly at the door.

"You can come in." Myrtle called through sobs.

"My dear child," Mrs Strawby's face appeared in the doorway, her brow drawn into a concerned expression, and accompanying her was a tray of pancakes, "I hoped this might be a nicer way for you to start the day, but I can see that it's already begun awfully."

Somehow Myrtle managed a weak smile as she wiped her nose with a handkerchief, it felt unfamiliar, and it didn't last long. The muscles on the corners of her mouth seemed to have all but given up.

"Thank you." She murmured.

Mrs Strawby set the tray down on her lap, and tottered down the hallway again, coming back with a large and steaming teapot. She poured out the tea into a delicate cup, one that Myrtle had not seen used before. It had a detailed pink rose blossoming on its side. It must be for special occasions, Myrtle realised, or perhaps for 'unusual circumstances'.

"Now, is there anything else I can get for you? Do you need another handkerchief?"

"Yes please, mine is all but used up."

"Alright then." And she wandered off to go and find one.

The smell of the pancakes made her stomach rumble, but when she turned her gaze to the neatly stacked cakes, dripping with syrup, it was accompanied by a little nausea that still remained. Maybe trying the tea first would help - She hoped it would, she felt empty and was very aware of the lack of food that she had eaten - Mrs Strawby returned with the Handkerchief, a plain cream one. Then she left Myrtle to eat, after drawing back the curtains. The world outside was grey, the sky heavy with rain. Apple trees stood like skeletons framing her view. Most of the deciduous trees had shed their yellowed gowns and lay bare. But many of the trees in Wendermere were evergreens and kept their green leaves all through winter. There were pockets of green forest that could be seen on the edges of the paddocks and farmlands, throughout winter.

The tea was floral scented, a hint of rose and the bright purple of dried cornflowers floated on top. It instantly filled her chest with warmth, chasing away the chill of an almost-winter morning. She managed to finish the pancakes, although it took her three times as long as it should have, and she almost gave up halfway through.

Finally, she emerged from the bedroom clothed in the yellow dress, which Mrs Strawby had washed and hung for her. She even combed her hair, though she couldn't possibly remove all of the knots and ended up giving in to a messy braid. Once she came to the kitchen, she thanked Mrs Strawby and mentioned that she would take a walk in the garden. Myrtle knew that she owed it to Mrs Strawby to be forthright for all the worry she had caused the woman yesterday. Then she set herself down outside on a bench overlooking the floral portion of the garden, except, all of the flowers were long since gone, all save for the fragrant lavender.

No one had mentioned the King's summons. It was almost as though it were a dream. Yet another nightmare, in a layered fabric of horrible dreams. But the fear came creeping back as she had known it would. She couldn't hide from it forever. The choice was clear: give up Beekeeping and return home to Wattleshire, perhaps in time for the funeral.

Or travel to the Northern Front to serve the King without a chance to truly say goodbye in person. And if Myrtle were to go to the Northern Front, there was no guarantee when she would return. It could be months, years and there was even the possibility that she would never return. She didn't know how dangerous the war was, all she knew was that the war had been going on for an awfully long time. She would be leaving Wendermere and the surrounding towns without a Beekeeper for the entire time she was away. However, if she did not go then she would leave Wendermere without a Beekeeper possibly forever. It was hopeless.

Myrtle swiped her eyes with the clean handkerchief, it came back damp. She wanted to run, but what would running do? What had running accomplished before? A momentary respite from her pain perhaps, but it was so fleeting.

She sat on the cold bench for quite some time, wrapped tightly in a woollen blanket. Watching as the bushes trembled with the wind, the smell of wood burning filling her lungs with a familiar comfort. More memories floated into her mind, memories that she would rather have set aside so that she could make the decision that she needed to make unfettered from grief. But it oozed through her body like honey, being spilled into a top drawer, slowly trickling its way down through to even the bottom drawers, finding every crevice, crack and hole and filling it with sticky syrup. It stained everything. She knew nothing would be left untouched by the time it was done with her, if it would ever be done with her.

She didn't want to be reminded of her mother making hot lemon and honey tea, while a blizzard raged outside. The drink was sweet and sour, and though not a Beekeeper's remedy, her mother would always remind them of its special properties, claiming that the drink would not only comfort them, but help the snow settle outside. Nor did she want to be reminded of her mother kissing the foreheads of each of Myrtle's siblings, the warmth of her lips briefly brushing back her hair before sending them to bed. She didn't bother wiping them away this time, but let the tears flow freely once more down her face. The gentle sway of the garden with the breeze for a moment almost seemed to hold her and sweep her up in their dance. The dried leaves tinkled like the pitter patter of rain. She didn't want to join in, but the rhythm quieted her aching heart.

Finn appeared walking down the distant driveway. He must've been coming in from town, but he wasn't riding his pony so perhaps he had hitched a ride with someone. As he appeared through the trees it became apparent that he was not alone. The figure of Samantha Pineswood darted out from behind him. Her shorter legs found it harder to keep up. The sight of the girl made her cheeks burn. She had to keep herself from tumbling off the bench and crawling away somewhere to hide. Could she bear to see Samantha's face? The cracks in her chest widened a fraction more. She shook her head. *How could I? How can I? Why has he brought her here?*

But they had already seen her and were making their way over. Myrtle threw her gaze down to the blanket, its tiny fibres poking up as though struck by lightning. She ran a finger over them, watching the fibres bend and straighten.

"Myrtle-."

It was a choked cry from Samantha.

"Myrtle-! I'm…. I'm so sorry."

And Samantha threw her arms around Myrtle. Encapsulating her in a hug that cocooned the blanket around her. Tight and safe.

"My dear friend-!" Samantha sobbed, and she had real tears in her eyes. In fact, she had already been crying, they stained her delicate porcelain cheeks, blotchy and red.

Myrtle forgot herself, when she saw those brilliant blue eyes glimmering. She too began to cry again.

"What are you sorry for? I'm the one who should be apologising." Myrtle's words were caught between sobs.

Samantha flopped down on the bench beside her. Both girls gleaming with tears caught in the half-light of the grey sky.

"I was the one who antagonised you so-... I-I pushed you." Samantha sniffled, "And then… and then… Oh Myrtle. I cannot bear to think what suffering you have endured!"

Their embrace lasted until the two girls could finally console each other and stifle their sobs. Finn stood at a distance surveying the fields over the other side of the property while leaning on an apple tree.

"Well," Samantha wiped her nose with a handkerchief, "I guess we've both done some stupid things these past few weeks."

Myrtle nodded in agreement.

"And I have by far done the most stupid."

"Ha-" Samantha let out a smile, "I wouldn't be so sure as to go boasting about it."

Myrtle cracked a thin smile back, it faded quickly.

"Should we call Finn over? I do believe that he's been pretending to ignore us this whole time." Samantha gestured over to the apple tree, where Finn's brown vest could be seen poking between the 'v' of the tree.

"Of course." Myrtle murmured, and so they called to Finn, and he came to join them both beside the wooden bench. He was, of course, a little awkward standing there beside them, hands tucked behind his back, shuffling his feet in the sunburnt grass.

"Now, it would be very proper of you to refuse the subject." Samantha began, "But, I have heard that a general came bearing the King's summons?"

"Yes." Myrtle breathed.

"Well, I'll be-" Samantha's face suddenly turned blush red all over, her blue eyes becoming furious pricks of light and eyebrows crunching into a slant that could topple kingdoms, "How dare they! Sending a girl out into a war?! I've never heard of such a preposterous request! They're supposed to fight to protect us! And-.... and the timing! *Well*, they *could not* have picked a worse time!" She paused only to gather her rage before going on, "How could they?! Mongrels all of them! How many full-fledged Beekeepers to choose from and yet they choose to upend the *already tragic* life of a young girl! Oh- Myrtle, I assure you when I see that general I'll give him a piece of my mind-."

"The general was only relaying orders." Finn interrupted, "Orders from the King."

"A King who summons young girls into service for his army isn't a King in *my* opinion." Samantha glowered, "And doesn't he know what good you've done here? That we won't have a Beekeeper without you?"

"Samantha, he's the King. The summons wasn't threatening anyone, he was only stating the law." Finn interjected.

"Yeah, the law he made!" Samantha turned away from Finn, eyes burning an innocent lavender bush out of existence.

"And terrible as the circumstances are, the King must have a good reason for summoning Myrtle. He wouldn't do it just because he *could* do it. Perhaps Myrtle is different from other Beekeepers he could call upon." The effort of speaking in such confronting terms seemed to tax Finn, but still he turned to Myrtle, "T-That being said. No one will condemn you for refusing the summons Myrtle. Given the circumstances… I-I wish…" He shook his head, "It just isn't fair."

There was a long silence. The breeze tickling each of their foreheads brushing hair back and forth. It was cold and had the murmuring of snow in its breath. The sky remained murky, a marbled grey white.

"I have to go."

The words tumbled out of Myrtle's mouth before she had time to catch them and drag them back into the pit of her stomach where they belonged. But with them came an unexpected sense of peace. It was the truth. Both Finn and Samantha hesitated to speak, Finn out of a wisdom well beyond his years and Samantha from a somewhat controlled temperament even though she wanted to say a great deal of things. Eventually the fire subsided in Samantha's eyes, it was replaced by the glistening of new tears as she nodded in agreement.

"I know that there's nothing I can say to make you stay." She wiped her eyes, "But, oh-! How I wish you could."

"I would give anything to stay, anything except my title as Beekeeper." Myrtle sighed, and then a sob rose in her throat, "I won't even be able to attend my mother's funeral, will I? D-Did the general say when he was leaving?"

"He's leaving tomorrow, early in the morning." Finn said hesitantly.

"Oh Myrtle, how can this be!" Samantha wept in disbelief, "Can we petition the King for a delayed placement?"

Myrtle shook her head firmly, shaking tears onto the blanket, "The order was an immediate summon. If I stay, I risk forfeiting my title."

There was another long silence punctuated by sniffling, now curiously, from all three. Finn's normally stiff composure was breaking. His hazel eyes became half-moons of glinting light.

"If only there was a way that I could come with you." Finn's voice was almost cracking.

"Don't be silly. You're too young to enlist in the war, and I couldn't bear the thought of either of you putting yourself in harm's way on account of me." Myrtle said firmly, "No, I will have to do this alone."

"No, not alone." Samantha replied hastily, a splash of passion in her gaze once more, "I am sick of you doing everything alone."

Finn nodded in agreement, his fists clenching and unclenching, he lifted his gaze, a tear trailing down his cheek as he met Myrtle's eyes.

"You have to let us do something." Samantha went on, "We… We'll send letters! As many as we can. All the time so that you know you aren't alone."

"And if you don't come back soon." There was an intensity to Finn's voice, "I will go find you and bring you back."

She knew he meant it. He had not given up on searching for her when she was lost in the witch's web of Nearne Forest, even when everyone else had, even when his parents had forbidden him from continuing the search in the forest.

"Well, I guess that's that." Myrtle gave another weak smile, "And for all that it's worth Finn, I forgive you for making me stay before returning to Wattleshire."

"She had been dead for two days." Her eyes smarted again as she went on, "It would've been at least another four before I returned to Wattleshire, that's counting the shortcuts and Wendermere's fastest horse. Under ordinary circumstances it would've taken me a full week. I-I… I don't believe I could've saved her."

"I thought it wasn't you who did the saving." Samantha had a mischievous look upon her face, it faded a moment later.

Myrtle was taken aback by her friend's reply. Samantha had a frustratingly good memory, especially when you didn't want her too.

"I suppose that's right." Myrtle conceded, "However, I can't help but take some of the blame.'"

"But if it really is the bee's magic healing people… then do they ever choose *not* to heal someone?"

"Well." Myrtle started, "It's a bit more complicated than that. I don't truly understand it myself. But what I felt too embarrassed to explain down by the creek that day, was that… I am not sure it is really bees or their honey that do the healing."

"I believe that the King… The King of the Wild, bestows this magic upon the bees in the first place." Myrtle shook her head as if to clear it, "Something about being captured in Nearne Forest made me almost forget about that. But… well you see it's in the Beekeeper's creed. *A Beekeeper's Duties are to help others, above and before ourselves. Never accept money, but only what the poor can give. A Beekeeper's duties are sacred and what is lacking will be given unto us. Our power does not come from within us, we will not flatter ourselves with such thoughts lest they be our end. Our power is lent and borrowed from the Wild King.*"

Something stirred within her. Memories of tea-stained pages, rosemary and lavender. All at once, she was reminded of the unassuming book that she had found in the witch's cottage. The extra lines from the creed. Ancient, older than the hills themselves. The words bubbled up within her.

"*We shall not come to the end of ourselves, for he is our end, and he is infinite. For our lives, we live for him. And his call, and command is sacred above all.*"

Once she had finished reciting the words she blushed a little as her friends listened in earnest.

"That must be hard to follow." Samantha finally spoke.

"Not really. It becomes a way of life." Myrtle explained, "All Beekeepers have to adhere to the creed, and apprentices learn early. If this kind of sacrifice isn't for them, then they can choose another profession before taking the vows. But I must confess that I am still trying to figure out the last few lines. I only found them in the witch's cottage."

"That's why I have to go. *For when we hear his call, we shall answer it. For our lives, we live for him.*" Myrtle added as it too dawned on her, "If I didn't go, I would be breaking the creed."

"Why would you have found the Beekeeper's creed in the witch's cottage?" Samantha asked.

"Because the witch used to be a Beekeeper, and not just any Beekeeper. The witch was in fact Melinda Cloverfoot, Pinesdale's previous Beekeeper." Myrtle answered, bringing to light the recent memories which resurfaced yesterday.

The whole party lay silent as the weight of Myrtle's words set in. Samantha looked aghast, but Finn seemed less surprised.

"Are you meaning to say that Daffodil's mentor was in fact a witch?" Samantha asked.

"I'm unsure exactly when Melinda became a witch, but she was at least at one time also Daffodil's mentor." Myrtle replied.

"What happens when a Beekeeper breaks the creed?" Finn asked.

"I'm not really sure." Myrtle frowned, "I suppose the King would revoke their title."

"Perhaps Melinda broke the creed then?" Samantha thought aloud.

"Daffodil broke the creed." It was Finn who spoke, his gaze was fierce, brows knit into a frown.

"She took money for her healings." Finn muttered, "At first it was only food, a meal or some bread. But then she started taking money, copper coins. Then silver. Her prices became more and more unaffordable, and the poor suffered."

Myrtle's stomach churned at such a grievous sin. But she nodded, she had suspected that Daffodil was charging money for her healing. Still, the thought that one of her own kind would commit such dreadful atrocities was beyond her.

Both Melinda and Daffodil, at least at one point or another, had fallen, betraying their creeds. At least one of them had fallen so far, she had become the very opposite of a Beekeeper.

"Daffodil and Melinda must have both broken their vows." Myrtle suddenly was aware of the gravity of a town such as Wendermere having not one, but two Beekeepers who had forsaken their vows, "And been cursed for it."

The King

It was the end of a journey and the beginning of a new season. The sky was a bleak white sheet, a blank canvas. Tiny flakes danced through the still air, but they dissolved quickly when they hit the ground. The North was different from what Myrtle had expected. Gravel gave way to soft clay and then sand. It was muddy and the strong Clydesdale, a shaggy mare called Lilly, couldn't help but stumble at intervals. The countryside had slowly transformed over the last four weeks from dense forest and rippling, gold pastures, to scraggly hills and plains, sparsely decorated by foliage. The remaining trees were mere shadows of the grand oaks in Wendermere. They were hunched over, their swirled trunks gnarled with deep grooves.

Bushes stood, battered particularly on the branches that faced to the east. It was as if they were frozen in motion, a gale-force wind making them lurch to the side. But the air was still. Not even a whisper of breeze could be felt. Myrtle's bees were all huddled inside their hives, ready for the coldest of days. Before the colder weather came, she had opened up the hives and called forth the queens, Lavender and Petunia. Both were healthy, their striped bodies were glossy and strong wings buzzing. After murmuring a blessing over the queens and their kingdoms she had shut up the hives, and only a small opening remained. It was customary for Beekeepers to move their swarms into more permanent hives through the autumn and winter, the extra comfort of familiar territory kept the bees from wasting much needed energy on scouting. However, it was an impossible standard now. She was lucky, her bees had done very well over autumn, the hives had been overflowing. Jars she had collected from the height of their production gleamed in the boxes behind them. The wooden crates held stacks upon stacks of the honey sealed in jars. So many that they had to continually readjust them to make sure that none would break if they hit a bump in the road.

The weeks of travel had brought life more and more to a standstill. Travel suggested direction, adventure and progress. For Myrtle it had been enduring weeks huddled in a wagon. Pushing guilt and anxiety aside when it reared its ugly head had been all but impossible with nothing to do but think. She had however been pleasantly surprised by how little fear had visited her. When it had come, she had cried herself to sleep, but awoke in the morning with a certain kind of lightness that surprised her. Most of the time it was grief that came knocking on the door. Its head wasn't ugly or reared. It stared at her from the stormy-grey eyes of her mother. Waiting until she answered the door and let it in. But once she had let it in, it wanted to sit and drink tea with her all day. And before she knew it… it had become a part of her. When they drove through a town and passed a lovely garden, she couldn't help but notice how her mother would never see it. Or when they had stopped for fresh baked rosemary bread, how her mother would never again taste fresh bread - she had always delighted in freshly baked goods -it was odd, really. In Wendermere when she had taken a bite of fresh bread or seen a lush garden the thought of her mother had rarely, if ever, appeared in her mind. But now she saw her mother in *everything*. It stained the world around her, dyeing the world a shade darker, like the colour of clouds about to rain and the words *never again* lingered always on her tongue.

General Nikoloski wasn't one for conversation and much of the ride had been spent in silence. The thought of conversation had exhausted Myrtle, and she had been content to let the hours slip by quietly. He had occasionally surprised her in other ways. When she had cried, he covered her with a blanket and made her some hot tea. When they entered a town with a festival. Myrtle had not moved from the cart, and they hadn't the time to join in with the festival, but the General had gone to buy supplies and had returned with a stunning opal brooch for her. He had even bought her a book, one about old Fairy Tales called, '*River's End*', a graceful stream was embossed on its front. She had been grateful for something to read on the long journey and had ended up memorising each tale along the way.

They had engaged in short conversations as her strength returned such as:

'That town we last went past, Spine Pier.' Myrtle would offer.

In reply there was a grunt from the general.

'It was a pleasant town, but how do you suppose that they are able to grow any produce in the soil? Isn't it far too shallow? Sandy?'

Another grunt and then a little pause of silence.

'Fresh produce comes in from across the sea.' The General finally would murmur, 'From Allendale.'

More important questions had bubbled up in Myrtle's mind, but she hadn't let them slip out, as she feared the answer. Instead, she danced around them like a butterfly fluttering from one flower to another without landing to suck out the nectar.

'So, this war-' she had begun, 'how long have you been a part of it?'

'25 years.'

'What a long time.'

Another characteristic grunt in reply.

'Is 25 years a long time to serve in a war?'

Another static silence, punctuated only by the squeaking of the wagon wheels and the heavy clop of hooves.

'Not for this war.'

Myrtle didn't let any more words escape her mouth, but she so desperately wanted to ask, what exactly this war was? What made it different? What made it last so many years longer than a normal war? And many more questions that were even more dangerous.

Well, there was no point in asking now. She would find out for herself soon enough. Over the last few hours, the surrounding environment had levelled out considerably. Only in the far, far distant horizon could mountains be seen, swathed in a vague purple-blue smog. And now, they could see something else in the distance. Stalk white against the orange-sand. They would be tents and blue fabric, fluttering in the sky, which must be flags.

"We're here." The General grunted.

The war camp loomed nearer and nearer until Myrtle could make out the large banners set flying in the sky. They were a deep blue, inlaid with golden thread depicting the King's emblem, a white stallion rearing and a knight in golden armour, a crown floated above their heads. As the wagon drew closer seven stars became visible, glinting from the fabric around the stallion, as though they were basking in the mighty stallion's glory. Inscriptions underneath this particular banner could be read, *'For the glory of our King'*. Many other banners flew dotting the bleak sky with sudden vibrant colour.

Large white tents stretched ahead of them and to both sides. Tiny dots littered the camp making it appear speckled from a distance. They were slowly brought into view, the dots growing in size to become humans, with clothes, faces, different mannerisms and voices. The chatter from the camp too, grew in volume. The whinnying of horses, low hush of conversation punctuated by people calling to one another, or even the shout of an order. She hadn't expected it to be so noisy.

They lurched to a stop at the entrance to the camp which was noted from two shorter banners, both with the King's emblems and inscriptions which read, *Rex Regum et Dominus Dominantium*.

"Welcome to the Northern Front." The General cracked a smile at Myrtle.

Finally, the journey was over.

She jumped off the wagon stumbling before being caught by the General who gave her an arm.

"I too get travel wobble." He grinned.

The last few days they had barely stopped, and she found her legs shaking as they supported her full weight for the first time in seven hours.

"Thank you." She murmured to him, "I'm just glad it's over."

They walked over to the front of the first tent, which was a place for people to be checked in before they could enter the camp. The only people allowed into the war camp were people with written summons from either the King, or the King's court.

"General Nikoloski, you have returned." The man smiled jovially.

"Yes, yes, it is good to be back, Rakavan!"

"We'll have to catch up over dinner, I need some news from the outside world. Sometimes I barely think it exists!"

"Of course, I'll be glad to entertain you." He thumped the man on his back.

She handed Rakavan her letter of summons and he stamped it with ink that said, *probatus*. She didn't know what that meant, but Rakavan let them go through. They got back in the wagon and entered the camp.

There were so many people. All different kinds of people, some of whom she had never seen before. Some with rounded features, and others with more angular features. Darker skinned, pale skinned and some that seemed like a mixture of both. Some wore leather armour, or plain shirts and pants, while others wore glinting armour that reflected the white of the sky so painfully it made her squint. She was surprised to see a few women who appeared to be tending to the sick. They weren't Beekeepers, but nurses. Through the crowd she caught sight of a dark-skinned woman with wavy black hair dabbing at the wound of a man as he grimaced.

They rolled to a stop outside a tent. There was a banner on its side. It depicted a golden bee, its wings drawn open in flight.

"Your tent Miss Beeswood." General Nikoloski motioned.

"Oh-." Myrtle exclaimed.

"I'm sure you'll find everything that you need inside. The King looks after his people." the General grunted, "However, If you do need anything else you can take it up with him yourself."

"T-The King-." Myrtle muttered, "T-Take it up with the King?"

"Yes. The King has requested your audience."

"Ask him directly?" Myrtle suddenly found herself weak.

"I am to escort you to his Highness later."

"Oh." Myrtle's heart thudded in her chest.

General Nikoloski helped her off the wagon, she fumbled to give him her hand. Her butter-yellow dress whooshed as she plopped to the ground once more. This time her feet sunk a little into a patch of sandy ground.

"S-Surely, I ought not to ask the King directly if I should need anything else?"

The General gave a characteristic pause before answering.

"Why not? He is the giver of all things." The General gave a little grunt, "When I've asked him for things I've almost always received them."

Myrtle was still reeling at the thought when he began to unpack her things. Her shaggy duffle bag and jars of honey stacked neatly in boxes, their amber syrup gleaming in the light.

Then the General left her to settle in and she brushed open the curtains of the tent to step inside. Blinking in amazement. Inside, truly was anything she could have wanted. The ground was lined with wooden planks to keep the sand out and an ornate blue, green and red rug was thrown over the top. In the middle was an iron box fireplace, a fire that had recently been lit was crackling. A chimney made sure that the smoke flowed out of the tent. Next to the fire was a plush red chaise lounge with a footrest, the likes of which she had seen only in Romero's mansion. In one corner was a large queen-sized bed, a fluffy duvet was set neatly folded on top. To the other side of the room was a bookcase, with many books already lining the shelf in multicoloured volumes. There was a rocking chair beside the bookcase, and an oil lamp on a stand which was already lit. However, it was the little details that really made Myrtle stifle an exclamation. It was for the dried roses that sat in a delicate china vase on the bed stand, and for the olive-green pillows embroidered with lavender, petunia and rose. It was as if whoever had prepared the room knew her personally.

She shuffled her large duffle bag into the room, feeling as though she need not decorate with any of her own things, not that she had brought much in the way of decorating anyway. She did however need to freshen up after the long trip. A basin of warm water had already been set for her on a dresser with a small oval mirror. When she made her way over to the dresser, she found a stack of neatly bound letters sitting on top, alongside the basin. They were all addressed to her. *They must be from Finn and Samantha,* Myrtle found herself smiling. Sadly, they were letters that she would have to read later.

It was the first time she had seen herself in quite some time and she was a little surprised. Her hair had become frizzy and unyielding. Her cheeks were flustered red by the cold, and under her eyes was a hint of purple. Of course, there was also more than a little dirt. After washing her face, she set to combing her hair and managed to tame it into a braid. In the dresser's drawers she found a deep blue ribbon, which she tied to the end of the braid. That would have to do, she sighed at her reflection. This was definitely not how she had ever imagined meeting the King. She opened a closet besides the dresser and found more surprises within. Dresses. Many dresses, of different fabrics and colours. She didn't have time to fawn over them, but she did give the gowns a smile. It wasn't often that she had new dresses and there were, oh- so many.

She picked out a vibrant blue one to go with the ribbon. The rim of the collar, sleeves and hem were decorated with thin lace and each collar embroidered with two sprigs of lavender. And what's more was that it fit her well, and after tying it up at the back, it looked as though it had been tailored specifically to her measurements.

Only moments after she had finished getting ready, there was a cough at the tent's curtain door.

"Miss Beeswood." Came the General's voice.

"Sorry, just one moment." Myrtle's trembling voice came.

"Whenever you're ready." He grunted.

She didn't know what she needed, but she felt that something was missing. Searching the room frantically she couldn't find anything that sparked interest to her worry, so she hurried to her bag and started sifting through it. *What am I looking for?* She asked herself. Her hand grasped the edge of something familiar and she brought it to the light. It was the opal brooch that the General had found for her in a little town called Ross. The brooch was a swirl of greens and silver. After clipping it on she went to slip back the curtain. The General too had cleaned up. His face was now clean shaven and there was a faint smell of perfume.

"Sorry to keep you waiting." She murmured with a slight quiver to her voice.

Her heart pounded in her chest, making her ears rumble with the sound. The General's eyes caught the brooch, and he cracked a smile as he took her arm to lead her to the King's tent.

They made their way through the crowd. Weaving in and out through groups of people. There was something different about the atmosphere of this place. Myrtle had expected the encampment to be filled with chaos, each moment another tragedy would be happening, but instead it was a community of people, much like a town or village. Each person was going about their lives, perhaps a little less separately than in a town, but their lives were still…moving. Nobody seemed to be holding their breath.

Flags hung far up in the air above them, they were still, as snowflakes slowly drifted towards them encasing the edges in fine dust. They passed many tents, some had the rustling of life living within and others had an open front where the heavy blow of hammer upon anvil could be heard, or the stretch of cloth ripping.

There it was.

Myrtle's heart dropped as she saw the grand tent appear before her. Unlike the other tents this one was painted a blue, like the colour of a deep crystal-clear lake on a hot summer's day. The tent's curtains were embroidered with a rearing stallion on its left and knight with its sword raised high in battle on its right. Seven golden stars twinkled between them, the central most star had both of its halves caught between the two sides of the fabric curtain. Other thin details encrusted every inch of the tent's fabric in glimmering gold. Banners on either side depicted rising eagles, soaring on wings which trailed the rich blue in glittering gold and copper detailing. Underneath both banners was written Regis Tabernaculi. Myrtle let out a deep shaking breath.

"This is the King's tent Miss Beeswood." General Nikoloski, turned to her. His eyes twinkled with something... Something Myrtle couldn't quite grasp.

Clearly, he could see the anxiety plainly in her eyes. Could see her form hunching and retreating within herself.

"Don't be afraid."

Myrtle let out another swallow breath, setting a curl which had fallen from her braid momentarily bouncing. He leant over and placed a calloused hand on her shoulder.

"Have no fear young lady." He smiled, "You serve the King now. And he is good."

She nodded. Without another moment's hesitation, he pulled back the brilliant tent curtain and she stepped into the King's tent.

*   *   *

*

Inside was bathed in the light of many candles. They flickered upon almost every upturned surface. The golden candelabras were caught in the flame's flare and set gleaming. Nothing. Nothing compared to the glow that erupted from the tent's heart. The dazzling sheen radiated in streaks of the white, the light refracting as it stretched further its edges dancing in tiny rainbows. The light grew in strength towards its centre where the rays shone brighter than if one were to stare at the sun in the heat of day.

Myrtle found herself stumbling and blinking, shielding her eyes from the throne where the light exploded in pure white. Her hands found the floor as she tripped.

"Beekeeper."

Myrtle stiffened at the voice rumbling from the throne. It was... familiar.

"Do not be afraid."

A sudden relief flooded her. Blessed peace unclasped her chest, pouring air into her lungs.

"You have heeded my call. You chose to follow my summons though it cost you."
"I am well pleased."

The voice was like the tinkling of a warm summer's breeze and the mighty gust of a storm all at the same time. Myrtle found her feet once more. She knew it now. She knew what the voice was. It had been the whisper in her heart, there with her as she worked to heal the sick, there with her when she was lost in the forest, there with her when the shadows stalked her...

"It was never the bees that spoke," She found herself murmuring, "T-The whisper." And she frowned, "You were the whisper?"

"Yes child. For bees cannot talk."

"Is it you then whom Beekeeper's borrow their power from?"

"Yes. It is I."

"You lend me power to heal the sick… Should I ask for it?"

"It is I, who cures the sick and who makes the honey heal."

Suddenly, Myrtle found rage seeping into her heart. It was dangerous. For she was in the presence of the Wild King. But she let the anger simmer, building block, upon block around her heart. It was a feeble attempt. For suddenly, the wall-toppled, crumbling as her true emotions seeped out. For who could deceive a King whose power seemed to grasp through the very fabrics of the world.

"Why?" Tears came to her eyes, she could not stop them. They tumbled down her cheeks making her lips tremble with sobs, "Why could I not heal my mother?"

"Why could I not save her?"

"It is not you who heals. It is not you who saves."

"I asked." The words spilled out of her as she shook with great sorrow, "I asked you."

"You asked, but she did not need saving. For she has already been saved."

"But she died!" Myrtle cried, "Why did you not heal her?"

The rumbling from the throne faded for a moment. Myrtle sensed that it wasn't hesitation, but rather a moment for her to collect herself. A moment to gather herself to be ready to listen again. She dried her eyes on a sleeve.

"Come nearer child."

She picked herself up and stepped hesitantly towards the throne, but the light still stung at her eyes, as she drew nearer. Then the voice came again.

"My ways are not for you to see.
Do you give the horse its strength?
Do you make it leap,
flying like an eagle or clothe its mane as with a flowing river?
Do you give the bees their quivering wings or show them how to store their sweet honey?
Do you craft for the plants flowers, adorning their heads in gowns more splendorous than queens?
Do you know how to tend the river and make its streams flow?
Do you cut it through the earth so that it will reach the thirsty?
Do you stretch out your hands to the air and command the clouds to come forth and soak the earth, to fill the rivers?

Do you provide for the wild mother bear and her cubs, or make for her a shelter in the mountains when the wind turns cold?

Do you see time like a string, knowing its beginning and its end?

Do you see the cosmos, like a pool, its waters deep and endless?

I knit the night sky together, formed each light in the darkness and gave it a place to hang in the sky, and all just so that creation would look at the night sky and see stars, too many to count, like threads from a tapestry, the beauty unfolding before them.

Just so that they would look up and see my glory

And know how much I love them."

The roar resounded. Deafening. It expanded before her, light like galaxies, a million stars. A mother covering her children, a father brandishing a sword against their enemies. The humble flight of a bee. The sweetness of honey. Rays streaming, brilliant fire. Burning. Brighter than the sun. Shaking the ground beneath Myrtle's feet.

"Can you love them as I do Myrtle?"

"No."

"My ways are not for you Beekeeper."

And the voice faded from the throne, as did the light. Until Myrtle could see the golden throne from which the light had sat on. A faint echoing remained.

My ways are not for you.

For I love them all.

With a love that is not broken or bent.

But perfect and true.

The End

A Letter from Finn

Dear Myrtle Beeswood,

I hope you have arrived at the Northern Front in good health. Both Samantha and I miss you dearly, along with the rest of Wendermere. Don't let yourself worry about us too much, I'm sure you have more than enough worries of your own. As for the town's news, Michael and Miss Merryweather are betrothed and it has been the talk of the town. They are to have a winter wedding, and I shall bear the rings. I am very glad that my brother is finally able to begin his own family. Now, I have many questions for you. I wonder what it is like in the war camps… Are knights truly as regal and brave as they appear in the pictures? Have you caught a glimpse of the King?

P.s. Hodgepodge is missing you dearly, he keeps looking at me with sad eyes… I can't help but feed him carrots because of it, and I am afraid he has gotten terribly fat. He can't stay here. He needs to be with you, and I am determined to find a way to bring him to you.

Finn Strawby

WENDERMERE PUDDING

By Ellesha Meurant and Elena Timms

Serves 6

Pudding Ingredients:

2 cups thickened cream

3/4 cup milk

1 tbsp vanilla paste

1/3 cup caster sugar

1/4 tsp salt

3 tbsp cold water

1 tbsp apple cider vinegar

4 gelatin sheets

Method for Pudding

Using spray oil, grease 6 small ramekins.

Heat the cream, milk and vanilla in a pot over medium heat, until steaming but not yet simmering. Remove from the heat and whisk in the sugar and salt. Meanwhile, mix the vinegar and water in a small bowl and add the gelatine leaves until they bloom (when they are very soft and slippery to touch ~ 5-10 minutes). Ensuring the cream mixture is still hot, add the wringed-out gelatine and whisk in. Discard the water mixture. Pour the cream mixture into the 6 ramekins and allow to cool for 20 minutes. Place them in the fridge for 4 hrs or preferably overnight.

To serve, dip each ramekin into hot water for up to 10 seconds and then flip onto a plate. Spoon over the top the raspberry sauce and sprinkle some candied almonds.

Candied Almonds

Ingredients:

1 egg white

1 tsp vanilla paste

2 cups almonds

2/3 cup caster sugar

2 tsps cinnamon

1/2 tsp salt

Method:

Preheat oven to 120C and line a baking tray with baking paper. In a mixing bowl, combine the egg white and vanilla. Whisk very quickly for about a minute or until nice and frothy. Add the almonds, sugar, cinnamon and salt. Fold into the egg mixture. Pour onto the lined baking tray and evenly space apart. Cook for 40 minutes, stirring halfway through. Allow to cool.

Raspberry Sauce

Ingredients:

12 tbsp sugar

.5 cups frozen raspberries

Method:

Cook down in a pot over medium heat for 10 minutes or until broken down. Regularly stir with a wooden spoon. Allow to cool.

Acknowledgements

Firstly, I want to thank our Heavenly father, without God I never would've had the motivation, creativity or will power to start let alone finish The King's Beekeeper. Much prayer and praise went into the writing of The King's Beekeeper, and I hope that this is reflected in its story.

Secondly, I wanted to thank my loving husband Mitchell Timms, for his support, advice and his hard work in editing The King's Beekeeper and doing so all while bedridden. Mitchell has helped me to achieve one of my longest, biggest dreams! I also want to give thanks to Eilidh Direen who has been a massive help in the publishing process and who devoted hours to formatting The King's Beekeeper. Much thanks to my biggest fans and closest friends Julia Walter and Ellesha Meurant whose encouragement spurned me on through the arduous process of editing for publication and many hours spent testing and making the Wendermere Pudding Recipe. Thank you so much to my family for all their financial support and excitement. And thanks to a tiny snag (a Dachshund named Chipolata) for slowly eroding my sanity but bringing a lot of joy along with it.

And a big thank you to all my financial supporters on kickstarter!

Ynez Howlett-Jansen, Amber Lohrbaecher, Julia Walter, Anon, Finn Clarke, Denise Walter, Ellie Zelniker, Ellesha Meurant, Fiona Lohrbaecher, Katherine Young, Anais, HAA, Katie Dean, Naomi Dickers, Debra Watkins, Rhys Gray, Melanie, Nick, Kayla & Family

(Mum and Dad) Snez and Darryl Cook and (Grandparents) Baba and Dedo - Fala mnogu Baba i Dedo.